The DESERT of DEATH

THE SKY ELDERS

The DESERT of DEATH

R.J. YOUNG

4 Horsemen
Publications, Inc.

Published By: 4 Horsemen Publications, Inc.

4 Horsemen Publications, Inc.
PO Box 417
Sylva, NC 28779
4horsemenpublications.com
info@4horsemenpublications.com

Cover & Typesetting by Autumn Skye
Edited by Jen Paquette

Library of Congress Control Number: 2024950761

Paperback ISBN-13: 979-8-8232-0755-3
Hardcover ISBN-13: 979-8-8232-0756-0
Audiobook ISBN-13: 979-8-8232-0758-4
Ebook ISBN-13: 979-8-8232-0757-7

DEDICATION

To my good buddy Ron. Thanks for always listening when I need to rant.

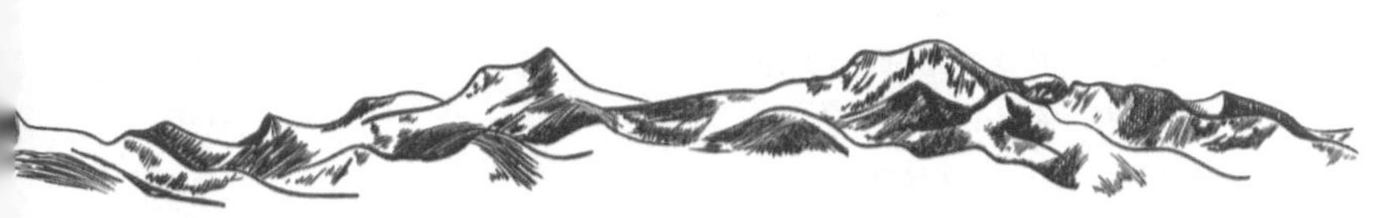

TABLE OF CONTENTS

HISTORICAL MAP REFERENCES

Anu-Naki Caves—The Fairy Caves in Glenwood Springs, CO

Big Sand—Basin Salt Flats in Death Valley, CA

Bitter Root Valley—The Verde Valley, Arizona

Blackening Bog—The La Brea Tar Pits, Los Angeles CA

Blue Patowa'Kacha—The Pacific Ocean

Canyon of Legend—Black Canyon, the site of Hoover Dam

Cave of Seven Thunders—Van Damme Sea Caves in Little River, CA

Crystal Cave of Spiders—Cave of the Winds in Colorado

Gitche Gumee—Lake Superior

Kolhu—Chaco Canyon, New Mexico

Kuwahi the Mystic Mountains—Clingman's Dome, TN

Land of Everlasting Summer—The 4 Corners region of CO, UT, AZ, NM

Manitou's Rise—Manitou Incline in Manitou Springs CO

Norumbega—The Great Lakes Region

Red Sky Forest—San Bernardino National Forest, CA

Shining Rock Mountains—The Rocky Mountains

Shipapa-Lina—Mesa Verde in Colorado

Shouting Mountains—The Coso Mountains Range of Eastern California

Ulah-Nane—North America

Valley of the Blue Mists:—Monument Valley, Utah

Wala-Wa—Concho, AZ near the St. John's River

Wet Beaver Creek—Wet Beaver Creek, AZ

PROLOGUE

1252 AD—The Red Debi-Quay Season
of the Great Turtle's Trek

"One must either move toward honor or away from it," Pahana said as he climbed on his imposing bison mount.

The people of the Itiwana tribe had gathered to offer their support and best wishes as their leader prepared to go on his hazardous quest. As Pahana sat high upon his new mount, which was named World Giant in homage to his lost previous bison, everyone in the village of Shipapa-Lina watched with mixed feelings as the young chieftain primed to begin his journey.

"My entire life, I've been taught to serve something greater than myself," Pahana said loudly.

"This is what I've fought and bled for. Honor and courage are the measure of a great leader. I can only aspire to have those qualities in half the proportion my father did. In his name, I must bring glory to my clan and my tribe."

Only hours earlier, Pahana had been officially anointed as the Kik-Mongwi of the tribe because his father Tawa had died during a dangerous mission to reclaim the golden arrowhead, which would be used to kill the demon Sanopi. Pahana was obliged to resume his father's journey, lest they earn the ire of the Na-Ash-Gi Spider Women. The Itiwana certainly did not need a new enemy, considering how many they faced currently.

His grandmother Atira, like many in the village, was torn on the idea of Pahana leaving the village. Tawa had been absent for several months, and his dead body was brought back by his family. Now their new leader was leaving them. Atira felt Pahana had left Shipapa-Lina too many times in recent months.

"The people feel insecure without a leader," Atira said. "We cannot always keep our vows, no matter how much our honor dictates we must. Let someone else go on this quest."

Pahana was latching his mystic spear Dragonfly to the side of his mount World Giant. "The people feel unsure because Tawa is gone. My presence will not change that. The only thing I can do to win their confidence is to do what even Tawa failed to do. I must prove myself a worthy successor if the Itiwana are to ever have faith in me. Just as my father won the faith of our tribe by finding the Tree of Life, I must also succeed in an impossible quest. Please don't argue further. It must be this way."

Atira frowned, disappointed. "And if you die, as Tawa did? How will that affect our people?"

"This will be only the first of many risks I must take," Pahana said. "A true leader must never cower from the weight of doing whatever needs to be done in order to protect his people, no matter how perilous. Courage is the spine of a great chieftain."

The frustrated Atira grabbed her grandson's hand. "This isn't about being a great chieftain. You're doing it because you think your father can see you."

Pahana raised his voice. "I *know* he can see me! And I will make him proud, just as I will make my people proud."

"At least take Faw-Faw with you," Atira suggested.

"The burden is mine alone, and so must be the risk," Pahana replied. "Now please, Grandmother, I implore you to delay me no longer."

His mother Pinga, the alabaster northern Goddess, stepped forward. "Yes, it's time to carry out the last unfulfilled obligation of my husband. Of your father Tawa. Bring glory to our clan."

Pahana nudged World Giant a few paces forward and addressed his people. "There are unimaginable forces at work around us. For good or ill, the Itiwana are trapped in an incomprehensible trial. We have been since the days of Morning Star, and recent events have only set our destiny ablaze with danger. We're tied to a perilous destiny. It's undeniable. Everyone here has witnessed the unfathomable—things unexplained and inconceivable to the mortal mind. Bizarre puzzles that can only be deciphered in our wildest dreams. We have responsibilities given to a chosen few. We have no recourse other than to ride the wind of events and do what honor demands of us. I go because the Gods need me to, because my father wanted me to, and because I must! Wish me well, and I will bring glory to you all. Farewell, my friends."

Pahana urged World Giant to canter out of the village. The people of Shipapa-Lina let out an emboldening chant to give their chieftain a loving show of support. The members of the Shakowin—Atira, T'Soona, and Pinga—were left responsible for the tribe. They watched Pahana trot away, feeling the burden of his departure. Pinga was particularly troubled because Pahana was taking the golden arrowhead with him. It had been reclaimed by Tawa, and Pinga had made a bargain with someone to use that arrowhead for a very personal task. She prayed Pahana would bring it back so she could utilize it for her purpose.

Pahana rode out of Shipapa-Lina armed with a mystic spear and arrowhead, determined to kill an unkillable demon to complete a family debt to the ancient Spider Women. *Nothing in my life makes sense at this point. I must reshape events to my will in order to bring peace to my people and prove myself to everyone.*

As Pahana left Shipapa-Lina behind, he spotted someone hiking in his direction, rushing to intercept him. It took a minute to realize that the approaching man was Hayoka. Pahana did not want to be delayed by talking to Hayoka now.

Jogging to get in front of the bison, Hayoka waved for Pahana to stop. Pahana considered going around him but reconsidered this. Hayoka had participated in the recent battle despite people's doubts about him, so Pahana halted his bison. "I'm in quite a hurry, Hayoka. Whatever you want to talk about, this is the worst possible moment for it."

"I apologize for the delay," Hayoka said, panting heavily. "I wished to offer my full-hearted sympathy for the loss of your father."

"Thank you," Pahana said. "His passing has left me with many obligations that I must attend to immediately. If you'll pardon me, I must fly."

"Perhaps I could come with you," Hayoka said. "I have much to discuss with you. Your father promised me something, and now that he has sadly left us, I had hopes that you could..."

"It will have to wait," Pahana said. "I have greater priorities. And as for you accompanying me, it is out of the question. I must do this alone. You must trust me that I will not forget about your request. It will be done, in time."

"You had faith in me when your people did not, so I must have faith in you," Hayoka said. "What can I do for you while you're gone?"

Before Tawa died, he told Pahana to be wary of Hayoka and not trust him. Many among the Itiwana had told him the same. Pahana decided to finally take their advice. Now that he was a leader of men, he could not let friendship interfere with his decisions. There were too many problems associated with Hayoka to accept him as a close friend. A chieftain must choose his allies more wisely.

"I think you might make a good roadman," Pahana said. "Speak to my mother about that."

Hayoka couldn't hide his disappointment. An Itiwana roadman spent most of his time outside the village as a messenger to other tribes in Ulah-Nane. He could tell that this was Pahana's way of getting him out of Shipapa-Lina. "Is that truly your wish for me?"

"I can speak to you no longer, Hayoka," Pahana said. "Become a roadman, or go back to your people in the north. Nothing else suits you for the moment. I must leave now. Goodbye."

"But..."

Pahana nudged World Giant into action and almost trampled over Hayoka, who had to leap to the side in order to avoid the hooves of the big bison. Hayoka watched unhappily as Pahana left him behind. *Every time I offer friendship to these people, I am rebuffed again and again. Why do I hesitate in joining their enemies who treat me much better? My mother would be happy to see me declare the Itiwana as my enemy.*

What should I do now? Naya-Nazgani wondered.

The great monster slayer ambled across the mesa near the Itiwana cornfields. He had come to the Land of Everlasting Summer to bring the message that Tawa was dying, and he stayed because of the attack on Shipapa-Lina by the fierce bear beasts. He loved a challenge, and he lived to kill monsters. Slaying strange beasts and ogres and hideous creatures was all he had left since his family was killed. He existed for revenge and nothing else. Because of this, he enjoyed these wild battles, like the one against the bear beasts. With the fight over, he had to decide on his next move.

He had spent centuries hunting, wandering, and killing monsters as revenge for his family. He didn't know anything else. It was a rootless existence with no ultimate goal other than more fighting. And for the longest time, he'd fought alone.

But he liked these Itiwana, and they were in the midst of a war that brought many dangerous creatures to their village on a regular basis. He had the notion that he could help these people and still fulfill his goal of slaying monsters. It would save on the endless traveling, and he would not have to fight alone. It had been a very long time since he had allies to guard his back in combat and felt it might make a welcome change to join the Itiwana in their cause.

Perhaps, just for a short time, Naya-Nazgani thought, *I can have brothers-in-arms.*

CHAPTER ONE

Hayoka could tell a magic wind from a natural wind by this point. He'd been acquainted with Dagwona for long enough to be able to differentiate between the two. As he was walking dejectedly across a field that had recently been rejuvenated by the power of Pahana's sacred spear Dragonfly, his attention was drawn to the sudden gusts of air.

The wind blew the leaves around, forming them into an arrow. She'd done this before to summon him when she needed him. *I believe the lady wants my attention.*

Hayoka followed the arrows. It had been five days since he saw Dagwona. They had made love during their previous encounter. Afterward, Hayoka spent two days hunting and fishing, followed by an additional two days of visiting the

Itiwana as Pahana was declared the new chieftain. He didn't get a chance to talk to the new Kik-Mongwi and left Shipapa-Lina to meditate in private while he waited for an opportunity to speak to his friend. He was on his way back to the tribe when he spotted Pahana riding out. Saddened by the result of that meeting, he was glad for the invitation to meet with his enigmatic, mystical lover.

He was led to a cave where the Snow Fox Spirit Agwara was waiting outside as if he knew exactly when Hayoka would be arriving. Despite Agwara's manipulative nature, Hayoka had come to like the trickster and even considered the fox a friend. Perhaps it was because Hayoka had so few people he could speak to openly and who treated him with a touch of respect, but regardless, he was glad to see Agwara.

"Arrived, you finally have," Agwara said. "Very tardy, you are."

"I wasn't aware I was due at your convenience," Hayoka replied.

"The convenience is not mine," Agwara said. "Dagwona's it is."

Hayoka was glad to hear that Dagwona was thinking of him. "Is she in need of me?"

"Your presence she desires," the fox spirit said. "Unaware you are of what you've wrought."

"What do you mean?"

"Quickly, you should come," Agwara demanded. "Miss this, you should not."

Agwara slipped into the cave known as Anu-Naki. Hayoka followed, puzzled about Agwara's cryptic comments. The cunning fox was always evasive and ambiguous, so Hayoka didn't expect straight answers. Rather than engage in a verbal struggle to decipher the facts, Hayoka decided to simply follow the fox to Dagwona and see for himself what was happening.

The Anu-Naki cave itself was inside a mountain, formed by the natural hot springs above, and was home to the Ant People. Running for miles within the mountain was a large plethora of stalactites jutting from the cave roof. The whistling wind often made people believe that fairies or kachina spirits lived within these mysterious caverns alongside the elusive Ant People.

Agwara had set up a line of torches along the side of the caves. Hayoka wasn't sure if they were for his benefit or for Dagwona. She was a sky spirit and not comfortable in the darkness of the expansive caves. *Why is she hiding down here? Is she still suffering from her old wound? The last time I saw her she seemed fully recovered and very ... energetic!*

After a lengthy walk through surprisingly beautiful tunnels, Hayoka saw Dagwona reclining on a pile of leaves, hay, grass, and wood chips. Her hands were on her belly—her very pregnant belly.

Hayoka stared with slack-jawed befuddlement. It had only been five days since he had seen her, yet she looked ready to give birth. *This can't be. Is this some cruel prank by Agwara?*

"Staring stunned?" Dagwona asked. "Hayoka hesitates? Surprisingly silent."

Hayoka kneeled in front of her. "Dagwona, I'm confused. When I left you..."

"Lustfully lovemaking," she said. "Enjoying extremely erotic evening."

"A wonderful night, indeed," Hayoka said. "But that was only days ago."

"Handsome Hayoka hastily hiked home," the witch Dagwona said with a touch of accusation. "Missed much."

"Clearly," Hayoka said, struggling to comprehend. "Can you explain to my simple mortal mind what has occurred during my absence?"

"Seed spread," Dagwona explained. "Fatherly fluid filled female. Manly mettle makes me multiply motherly. Children coming. Sons soon. Daughters due. Infants imminent."

Agwara interrupted. "Like a mortal woman, Dagwona is not. Birth is swift after conception comes. Nine risings of the sun it will take. Sunrises five have all passed since your seeds were planted. Imminent, the birth is. Only days remain."

Hayoka tenderly reached out to touch her stomach. "My children?"

"Hayoka's heirs," Dagwona said, taking his hand in hers and encouraging him to rub her belly gently. "Our offspring. Finally, family."

Hayoka felt a bond of love that he had never felt with any living being before. He kissed his lover's belly. "I needed some encouragement in my life. A ray of hope about the future. An inkling that happiness was possible. And here is a miracle greater than I expected. What a magical day. I had not considered being a father, but now I want it with all the longing in this lonely world."

Dagwona kissed Hayoka on his forehead. "Two together."

Agwara slipped quietly away, leaving the soon-to-be-parents alone, plotting how this could be used for his cause.

And now I fulfill my father's vow, Pahana thought as he reached the ominous, isolated Black Road.

After several days' travel, World Giant trotted down the Black Road, allowing Pahana to get his first good look at the tarry, sticky pits of viscous pitch known as the Blackening Bog. The oily pitch seeped up from the deep Earth. The remains of many trapped animal were inside. This black, gooey pit was the home of Sanopi, the demon of tar and mud.

Pahana didn't know why the Na-Ash-Jai Spider Women wanted Sanopi destroyed. He only knew that his father had taken a vow to slay the creature and bring its remains to the Na-Ash-Jai, and now that task had fallen to him. Tawa had been fatally wounded retrieving the only weapon that could kill the tar demon. Pahana could not let his father's death be futile. He had to succeed in preserving the family honor. Also, if he were to fail in killing Sanopi, surely the angry creature would kill him. *There will be no second chances in this matter. Sanopi dies now, or I do.*

As Pahana's mount neared the edge of the bog, he yanked the reigns to stop the bison. He didn't want this new mount to sink to an unpleasant death just as his previous bison named World Giant had lost its life. He unlatched the bow and arrow from the saddle. The arrow had the sacred golden arrowhead affixed to its end.

My father died for this, he thought, looking at its golden sheen.

"So, where is this demon?" he said to no one. "How do I invite his appearance?"

Pahana dismounted his bison and stepped carefully forward, half expecting to be attacked by the demon and also fearing that one misstep could cause him to sink into the bog. The silence, broken only by the wind, seemed portentous to the young chieftain. He'd rather see an army poised to attack than to wait for a hidden adversary to strike.

"Show yourself, Sanopi!" Pahana yelled. "I challenge you to face me!"

No answer met his challenge. Sanopi remained elusive. Pahana paced around the outside of the tar pit, impatiently awaiting his foe. The delay gave him time to think.

I'm about to enter a life-and-death battle with this creature, and I know nothing about it. I'm told it's a demon, but is it evil? I must slay this being—or be slain by it—and I have no malice toward it. It does not threaten my people, yet here I am to destroy it. It seems another pointless death. Yet I must fulfill my family's vow. It's distasteful, but a leader must do many unpleasant things. Doubts are the enemy of duty.

The minutes crawled by, and still there was no sign or sound of anyone or anything other than Pahana and World Giant. The chieftain called out another challenge to the unseen demon, only to be angered by further silence.

Losing his patience, he pulled Dragonfly from his saddle. "Perhaps a more assertive method of making my presence known is necessary."

Pahana carefully tiptoed as close as he dared to the bank of the tar pit. Raising his sacred spear over his head, clutched tightly in both hands, he tensed his firm muscles. "Let's learn whether our evasive opponent can ignore a gift of the Sky Elders."

He thrust the spear down into the tar bog. The Dragonfly sank halfway into the tar before hitting something solid. The power of the mystic spear caused the tar pit to bubble and gurgle and burp. A wake from the point of impact spread out across the tar pit.

"I suspect this will get a response, World Giant," Pahana said.

This latest attempt at forcing the appearance of his quarry was successful. Up from the viscous, tarry pitch rose a vaguely manlike form. The amorphous demon stood taller than Pahana. It was composed completely of bitumen but maintained its near-human form, despite the lack of a skeletal structure. The demon had no face or identifiable features. It reminded Pahana of a shadow with thickset bulk.

Sanopi's bizarre, otherworldly nature was chilling to the young chieftain. Perhaps it was the lack of a face that made it seem so foreign and incomprehensible, or maybe it was the fact it seemed part of the larger tar pit. Either way, his heartbeat increased in dread. Of the many strange things he'd seen, this demon of muddy tar was the most unnerving.

"Man comes," Sanopi said in a deep voice that was a gurgling vibrato. "Man hostile."

"My intentions are, indeed, hostile," Pahana said. "I challenge you to battle."

"Man challenges Sanopi?" the tar man asked. "Man enemy?"

"I must declare myself exactly that," Pahana said. "I have come to fight."

"Man threatens?" Sanopi asked with a tone of confusion. "Why fight Sanopi?"

Pahana was about to answer, but he found himself tongue-tied. What could he say? Why was he here to kill this creature? Because someone asked him to? What had this strange being done to deserve death? *I cannot falter. I am responsible for the Itiwana. I will do what I must.*

"I fight for honor," Pahana said. "I fight for Awona'Wilona. I fight for the future."

"Man is violent," the tar being said. "Danger to Sanopi. Hostile foe. Sanopi must kill!"

"I await your worst onslaught," Pahana said.

Pahana took the special arrow in hand. It was the shaft with the golden arrowhead affixed to its tip. He put the arrow in his bow and prepared to fire the lethal volley. But before he could let the weapon loose, something grabbed his foot.

A squid-like tendril of viscous pitch clasped his ankle and yanked him with tremendous force. Pahana was pulled off his feet, tumbling to the ground. To his alarm, he was being dragged into the lake of tar.

No! I mustn't die like this!

CHAPTER TWO

As Pahana was pulled by the unyielding power of the tendril, he felt his legs sinking into the tar. Looking around for some salvation, he saw Dragonfly sticking out of the pitch. *Thank Awona'Wilona!*

Dropping the bow and arrow, he grabbed the sacred spear with desperate strength. Pahana knew that nothing could dislodge the Dragonfly unless its owner wanted it dislodged. The spear held firmly, despite the formidable force dragging Pahana down. The young chieftain had the formidable strength of a man borne of parents who were more than human. His mother was a fallen deity and his father a Mastop-Kachina. Also, he drew energy from contact with the magical spear. Pahana's grip was extraordinary, although the power pulling him was even stronger.

Pahana did not know how long he could hang on, but help came in the form of World Giant. The mighty bison galloped to aid his master. Pahana saw an opportunity. Releasing the grip of his left hand, he grabbed his bow and held it up in front of World Giant's face.

"Pull!" he yelled, hoping that the animal would comprehend the command. World Giant had done some plowing and the word "pull" was familiar to it. After a moment's hesitation, the bison understood. It grabbed the bow in its teeth and began to back up, pulling Pahana with him.

Pahana felt for a moment that he would be torn in half but then found himself slowly being dragged to the safety of solid land. "Good boy," Pahana shouted.

He saw the rear-half of the arrow still sticking out of the pitch. Letting go of Dragonfly, he grabbed the arrow and yanked it out of the tar. The arrowhead was still intact. *The Elders are with me.*

Safe again on the sturdiness of land, he put his arrow into his bow once more and fired at Sanopi. His aim was flawless, and the golden arrowhead pierced the tar demon's form. The very moment the arrow penetrated it, Sanopi exploded like a geyser of mud. Its tarry remnants were launched into the air and in every other direction.

Tattered fragments of Sanopi landed on the banks of the tar pit, falling at Pahana's feet. The young chieftain looked down at the scattered remains of what had moments ago been Sanopi, and he felt sadness instead of triumph. *I can find no joy in this victory. That creature was not my enemy. But a chieftain does not have the luxury of pity. Duty is all that matters.*

He gathered the physical remains of the slain Sanopi and deposited them in a sack tied to his saddle. He then pulled an apple from a different sack and fed it to World Giant. "You're a fine and true mount. A worthy successor to Mountain Fury. We're going to have a fine companionship."

The golden arrow was lost in the depths of the tar pit. Pahana reclaimed Dragonfly and mounted his bison. "Let's be away from this place, my friend. I wish to see the last of this dismal pit. We have other matters to attend to. The Spider Women are waiting, and honor must be satisfied."

He nudged World Giant, and they headed onward to their next adventure.

On the ninth day, Dagwona's children were born. Hayoka watched as Dagwona lay screaming in labor pains as she delivered her portentous brood. Hayoka did his best to help with the delivery, although the natural process needed little assistance. In quick succession, the three offspring were born.

Hayoka's joy was lessened by the sight of the unnatural infants. These were not normal children. *I should have expected this*, he thought. *I have the Coyote spirit inside me, and Dagwona is an elemental witch. How could I not have anticipated that my offspring would be something other than human?*

He pushed his disgust of their appearance out of his mind and continued assisting with the birth. After the third baby saw light, Dagwona stopped screaming.

"Beautiful babies," Dagwona said wearily. "Witness wonders. Our offspring."

Hayoka lifted one of the babies and gave the other two to Dagwona, who cradled them. Hayoka studied the abnormal children, hiding the fact that he was repulsed by their appearance. He was embarrassed by his own reaction. *I am shameful. These are my children. Ugly or not, human or not, I am their father.*

The first-born of the children was a female with sickly yellow skin wrinkled like an old crone. Her hair was half black and half gray, and she had black lips and watery eyes. Hayoka held her, forcing himself to ignore her appearance.

"Sweet Skadega-Muth," Dagwona said, smiling.

"Ah, Skadega-Muth," Hayoka repeated. "Our little Skadega-Muth."

Dagwona gently squeezed one of her children. It was a male child with owl-like feathers covering its stocky body and a very sharp beak. Hayoka stared at the winged infant with both fascination and distaste. He reached down and touched the feathers, forcing himself to accept the wings and down as part of his family.

"Splendid Stikini," said the witch woman.

"Hello, Stikini," Hayoka said, still caressing that plumage.

Dagwona kissed the third child. This one was a six-legged feline with black fur. "Welcome, wonderful Wampus."

Hayoka pet the cat-like infant. "Welcome to our family, Wampus."

As the minutes went on, Hayoka quickly found himself warming to the bizarre appearance of his children. However they might appear, he was their father. He had a family: Skadega-Muth, Stikini, and Wampus. *I won't reject them for their appearance. People have unfairly rejected me because of what my father did, so I would be equally unfair to shun my own children because they don't look human. I'll care for them and learn to love them.*

Dagwona beamed proudly. "Beautiful brood."

"You're all beautiful," Hayoka said. "This is a moment to savor. The greatest moment."

It was the first happy day Hayoka had had in quite a long time.

"So, this is it, eh, World Giant," Pahana said.

The bison and its determined passenger arrived at the Crystal Cave of the Spider Women. Pahana had heard about this place since he was a child. He'd been told the story of how his father had come here so many summers ago on his quest to find the Tree of Life. It was then that he was compelled to promise a service to the spider sisters. They wanted the remains of Sanopi. Why, he didn't know. It had taken twenty years, but the debt had now been honored.

Dismounting from World Giant, Pahana took the sack containing the pieces of Sanopi from his saddle as well as the Dragonfly. He patted the big bison. "Graze here, large one. I hope to be back soon."

Stepping into the limestone arch of the cave-mouth, Pahana was trepidatious about meeting the legendary Spider Women. *What will they be like? And what will they do with the chunks of tar that used to be Sanopi?*

He walked through the darkness, feeling the wind blow through like a funnel. He spotted a glow in the deep innards of the cave. Pahana marched quickly onward until he reached the cavern he had envisioned so many times in his mind since he was a child. The shining, iridescent crystal cavern was more beautiful than he had expected. He could stare at those crystalline formations for a very long time. In the center of the cavern was a circular pit, too dark and deep to see the bottom.

And now to meet the daughters of the great Spider Mother, Pahana thought as he tapped the Dragonfly on the edge of the pit. After that, he leaned on the spear, waiting for the sisters to arrive.

His wait was not a long one. A soft skittering sound came from deep within the pit. It got steadily louder and louder, heralding the sisters' appearance. Pahana felt a chill of nervous expectation.

And then they rose, a trio of imposing figures. As Pahana had heard, the top half of their bodies were very humanlike, while their lower half was that of a spider. Spindly legs walked out of the dark pit. Despite being prepared, Pahana was fixated with amazement at the sight of them. All three stared at the new arrival.

The old crone Oona spoke, saying, "Mortal intruder. You dare invade our…"

"…sanctuary," Echigas, the middle sister, said. "Explain yourself or…"

"…face our fury!" said Abit, the youngest of the sisters.

Pahana focused himself, knowing he had to talk fast or die faster. "I am the son of Tawa, descendant of Morning Star. You once charged my father to do you a service. You recently reminded him of this. Do you recall?"

"Of course," Oona said. "We forget nothing. We…"

"…sent Tawa on an important quest," Echigas said. "But where…"

"…is Tawa?" Abit asked. "We summoned him, not his offspring."

Pahana spoke sadly. "My father died performing the debt of honor demanded of him. He fell in your service."

"We grieve for your father," Oona said. "We found Tawa…"

"...very honorable and brave," Echigas said. "But why have you come..."

"...here today?" Abit said. "What is your purpose here?"

Pahana upended the sack and emptied several pieces of stringy tar, which were once part of Sanopi. "I have completed my father's debt and slain the pitch demon as you requested. I bring you your prize. My family's duty to you is fulfilled."

"Excellent!" Oona said as the three sisters skittered toward the pieces of Sanopi. "At last we..."

"...can complete the web of fate," Echigas continued. "We will finally..."

"...know the future which has escaped our sight," Abit added. "The veil will be lifted."

Pahana, who had been prepared to leave these eerie women behind forever, was suddenly intrigued by the turn this conversation had taken. "You plan to observe the future?"

"All will be revealed," Oona replied. "We shall..."

"...spin a web," Echigas said. "One that pierces time itself. All we needed..."

"...was an aspect of Sanopi," Abit added. "Now that we have the final piece needed..."

"...nothing will be hidden from us!" Oona declared. "We will know everything."

Pahana desperately wanted this knowledge. If he could learn the future, he could protect his people from whatever peril was to come. "Will you do this now?"

"We will begin..." Oona said.

"...immediately," Echigas continued. "We shall not..."

"...waste another moment," Abit concluded.

"May I remain to watch?" Pahana asked politely.

"Do as you will," Oona replied. "We have..."

"...no objection," Echigas said. "As long as..."

"...you do not interrupt," Abit instructed.

"I wouldn't dream of it," Pahana said. "Thank you for your kind consent."

Without further hesitation, the three arachnid sisters began their work. Each one began producing glittering silk strands. They skittered up the walls and across the cave roof. The sisters commenced weaving a giant web.

I must know! Pahana thought.

CHAPTER THREE

I need a good kill, Naya-Nazgani thought as he sat on a moss-covered rock, sharpening his battleax on a whetstone.

Ever since the legendary monster slayer arrived at Shipapa-Lina to deliver a message from the dying Tawa, he had delayed his departure. Naya-Nazgani was unsure of his next step. He had only planned to stay for the night, just to rest and then move along. However, the attack of the monstrous bears gave him a motivation to fight alongside the Itiwana. He had enjoyed the fight. Killing monsters was what he had lived for over the centuries. It was all he had lived for.

He wasn't sure why he'd chosen to linger so long in the Land of Everlasting Summer. His normal tendency was to keep moving. He never stayed very long in one place. His was a nomadic existence. Yet, every time he planned to leave this village, he put off his departure.

Was it because Atira had asked him to stay, and he felt a sympathetic connection to her since he had failed to deliver her son's message to her in time? Or was it perhaps because the prospect of further monster attacks on Shipapa-Lina meant that he didn't need to wander in order to find creatures to kill...? They would come to him. Or possibly it was because he had become weary of his rootless, friendless existence. The offer to remain with the Itiwana meant that he no longer had to be alone. He had fellow warriors at his side, and he had friends he could speak to between battles.

Whatever the reason, he was a willing guest of the Itiwana, and the slayer felt he needed something familiar to make himself feel normal and focused. He needed to do what he did best. Naya-Nazgani needed to kill some monsters. He had not had a good kill in days, and he was getting antsy. *There must be something nearby that I can slay.*

Naya-Nazgani wasn't familiar with the Land of Everlasting Summer and didn't know where the local monsters lurked. He usually got information about which monsters where hostile and needed to be killed in the form of visions from the Uwanami Spirits who had once befriended him. He hadn't heard from those voices recently, and so now needed a guide, or he'd have to hunt by himself in this strange terrain and hope he stumbled across a hostile beast.

As he rose, ax in hand, he debated in which direction he would search. Looking around, he spotted a small figure meditating cross-legged. Bizarrely, this petite form was floating like a wisp of smoke above the ground. Naya-Nazgani recognized young Kia, sister of Pahana. Despite only having seen fifteen summers, Kia had become a frighteningly powerful shaman. Naya-Nazgani had marveled at the way she had dispensed of the hoard of bear beasts. *It's rare in my long life that I'm taken aback, but the power of this child is staggering.*

The monster hunter walked around her, giving her a wide birth while curiously examining her. It was difficult to believe that this small girl contained such immense mystical energy. He wondered what she was capable of. *I'd best not disturb her. Who knows how a child with such incredible power will react to being startled?*

He softly passed her, watching her warily. He saw her eyes open, and she fixed her piercing gaze on the monster slayer. "Are you leaving us?" she asked.

Naya-Nazgani paused, not wanting to offend a powerful shaman who happened to be a relative of the tribal chieftain. "For a short time. I want to hunt."

"Want?" she asked. "Or do you *need* to hunt?"

He raised his eyebrows, impressed that such a young girl would make such an insightful observation. "Does it matter which?"

"I know the answer," she said. "I was wondering if you did."

Can she see into my thoughts? he wondered. *Or is she playing games, making herself seem wiser and more powerful than she is?*

"Why can't both be true?" he suggested.

"Yes, that's the answer," she replied.

I'm not interested in playing this little game, he thought. "There are monsters impatient to be slain. I must be on my way."

"Would you like to kill Agwara?" she asked.

Naya-Nazgani had heard about Agwara, whose reputation had spread all across Ulah-Nane. The snow fox spirit was renowned as one of the most cunning and manipulative of the winter spirits. Agwara didn't often kill people with his own paws but was responsible for so much death and destruction by his machinations. The critter was one of the deadliest inhuman creatures in the mortal realm.

"I would like that above all things," Naya-Nazgani replied.

"I feel him," the young girl said. "I sense him. The fox is not far away."

"Where?"

Kia smiled sweetly. "I'll lead you to him."

Naya-Nazgani waved a hand to dismiss the idea. "Thank you, but I prefer to hunt alone."

"You should know that your quarry is not alone," Kia replied. "There is another."

"Who?"

She closed her eyes for a few more moments and then shook her head. "I can't be certain. It's someone powerful. I sense elemental magic, but I can't accurately determine the identity of his ally. But you may need help."

Naya-Nazgani debated this offer. Normally, when he went into battle, he had the advantage of intelligence given him by the Uwanami Spirits. He did not like the idea of charging into battle against unknown opponents with insufficient knowledge. Kia might have some valuable information for him. *Perhaps the child could be a beneficial ally.*

"Very well, my young friend," he said. "Lead our way. Let's see monster blood flow."

CHAPTER FOUR

The three spider sisters had mostly completed their huge web. The web of fate. It was an intricately complex lattice, ornamented with vague outlines of unidentifiable forms. The silvery silk fibers glimmered in the glow of the cave crystals, but the center was pure ebony, made from the remains of Sanopi. The sisters worked with a deeply concentrated fixation on their ominous auger weave.

Pahana watched in nervous fascination as the silken framework grew. He tried to determine what the strange images in the web represented but could not decipher the shapes. *What new threats to my people will this glittering matrix reveal? I'm both captivated and timorous at what I'm going to learn when their work is done.*

Finally, the sisters stopped their web-spinning and skittered to the cave floor. They took several minutes to look over the black-and-silver web, becoming dourer as they studied their beautiful yet foreboding creation.

Pahana was desperately anxious to learn what the enigmatic sisters saw in that silken mesh but was reluctant to disturb them when they were deep in contemplation and obviously perturbed by what they saw. *It's not wise to anger Spider Women.*

The three sisters continued to study the web pensively until they finally broke their silence with words Pahana did not want to hear.

"Tragic is this revelation," Echigas said. "The three omens of doom..."

"...have come to pass," Abit added. "The fall of the world tree..."

"...is inevitable," stated Oona. "The war will be lost."

"Our revered Spider Mother will..." Echigas began.

"...be heartbroken that her favored mortals will fall," Abit said. "Winter will soon..."

"...cover the world!" Oona exclaimed.

Pahana could no longer stand silent. What he was hearing was terrifying, and he needed to know everything. "What do you see?" he shouted with atypical emotion.

The sisters ignored him at first. He repeated the question, and finally, Echigas turned her head, acknowledging him. "We grieve for..."

"...your people," Abit said. "You do not..."

"...deserve your fate," Oona told him.

"I implore you to tell me what you saw!" he loudly cried. "I must know!"

"If you wish to know, we will comply," Echigas said. "But..."

"...know that this ill news cannot be changed," Abit said. "You must..."

"...accept what you hear as your unavoidable destiny," Oona proclaimed.

"Tell me!" he said, filled with a profound dread.

Echigas pointed to the web. "We see the three omens that..."

"...foretell the return of Malsumis," Abit said. "And begin the..."

"...unstoppable tide of tragic events," Oona stated, gesturing dramatically.

"What are these omens?" he asked.

"The death of the greatest hero is the first," Echigas said. "Secondly..."

"...three inhuman children have been born," Abit said. "They will bring destruction. And third..."

"...an unholy bargain has been made," Oona claimed, "leading to the Winter Elders gaining a tool that will free Malsumis."

Pahana felt a wave of panic at hearing he was too late to stop these omens he had long dreaded. He had been raised to fear the culmination of these predictions. He tried to decipher these cryptic clues. He assumed the death of the greatest hero must obviously refer to his father

Tawa, but the other two baffled him. He calmed himself, hoping to gain more information.

"Can you tell me nothing more?" Pahana pleaded. "Is there no bit of hope or useful intelligence that you can tell me? I need some encouragement. A ray of hope about the future. An inkling. How can I save my people?"

"You cannot," Echigas told him. "When the final battle of this war comes..."

"...and the enemies converge on Shipapa-Lina, it will not be you who leads the defense of the Itiwana," Abit said. "In the final days..."

"...it will be a different descendant of Morning Star who stands against the servants of the Winter Elders," Oona informed him.

"Is there nothing I can do?" Pahana asked.

"No," Echigas said. "The Tree of Life, Yaxche, will die. Soon after..."

"...your mighty bison will begin to die," Abit said. "And then..."

"...the long winter will begin," Oona said. "The final battle will be tragic for your people."

Pahana took a few steps back and then paced the cave, tormented by the knowledge of his fate. *Are my people really doomed? Will I fail in the duty my father entrusted to me?* Burning with emotions, he couldn't restrain himself. "No! I will not accept this! It is my home they threaten, and I defy fate! I swear to do whatever needs to be done, commit whatever act of brutality possible and more! I will use the fire of life Awona'Wilona gave me to vanquish all our enemies decisively.

This will not be the end! It is the beginning of our finest epoch of glory!"

His emotions a tumult of anger, fear, and determination, he disrespectfully turned his back on the spider sisters, striding out of the crystal cave. He glanced contemptuously at the web, determined to disprove the portents of doom displayed within by any means necessary.

Pinga walked through the village looking for her daughter Kia but could not find her. They had been reunited after Kia had returned from their sister-community, Kolhu, having spent two years therein being trained by Molowia as a shaman. Kia returned to help defend Shipapa-Lina against the stiff-legged bear beasts. Her power, along with the arrival of Naya-Nazgani, turned the tide and saved the village. Afterward, Pinga finally got to spend some time with her daughter. She was amazed by the way the young girl's power had grown exponentially. At the age of only fifteen summers, her abilities were astonishing. Even the ageless ex-Goddess Pinga had never seen her like.

After Molowia had told her that Kia was becoming too problematic with her fast-increasing powers, Pinga had been trying her best to be a positive influence on her daughter, being a stable rock of honor and integrity while not discouraging her amazing growth. Pinga knew quite a lot about power, having once been a Sky Elder herself. She felt certain she could lead her formidable daughter to glory.

She had planned to have a motherly conversation with Kia this afternoon, but the youngster was nowhere to be found. Pinga often worried about what Kia might get up to unsupervised. No one so young could adequately control such power without guidance. And the one person Kia was likely to obey was her mother. *Where is that girl?*

After asking around and learning that no one had seen her daughter, Pinga walked to the buffalo pens and the aqueduct. Still, Kia was nowhere to be seen. As she stopped near the Deep Well, she paused to wet her dry lips. While she was doing so, she spotted the exceptionally large scorpion that inched its way toward her. She was accustomed to such creatures since coming to the Land of Everlasting Summer, although this one was disconcertingly oversized. She kept a wary eye on the arachnid as it neared her. She didn't expect it to speak.

"Click, click. She once stood a Goddess. Click. Now she stands a liar. Click," the scorpion said.

Pinga wasn't startled or frightened by the talking critter. This was not an unusual sight to her. She had walked among the Gods once, and talking scorpions were the least extraordinary thing she had seen. "Are you a messenger?" she asked.

"Click, click. I come as one," the scorpion said. "Click. I come with borrowed words. Click."

"Words from whom?" she asked. "This One had called to the Sky Elders for assistance, and they refused her. She does not feel inclined to listen if you speak for them."

"Click, click. I remind you of a debt. Click," he said. "I remind you Malsumis is owed something. Click."

If Pinga were not already an albino, she would have turned pale. When she made the bargain with Malsumis for the sake of saving Tawa, she had not been naïve to the danger she was courting by making a deal with the enemy. Malsumis wanted the golden arrowhead. It seemed like a small sacrifice, considering what she stood to regain. Pinga would do anything to have Tawa back, but she could not help worrying about what would happen when the deal was done.

"This One has not forgotten," Pinga said. "She keeps her vows. This One wants Tawa back."

"Click, click. He waits for satisfaction," the scorpion informed her. "Click. He waits impatiently. Click."

"This One is unsure of how to give satisfaction to your master," she said. "We received a message from Pahana through Black Crow. The arrowhead has been lost to us."

"Click, click. Explain how this occurred. Click," the creature inquired. "Malsumis deserves an explanation. Click."

"The arrowhead was used to slay Sanopi," she replied. "It sank in the Blackening Bog. Pahana saw no reason to retrieve it. He didn't search the tar pit for it. It is lost somewhere deep in that vast pool of pitch."

The scorpion began to fidget, apparently excited. "Click, click. But it was used? Click. Pahana used it? Click?"

Pinga didn't understand his reaction. "He did so. He no longer has it."

"Click, click. This news is welcome. Click. Thank you for the news. Click."

Abruptly, the scorpion scampered away with alacrity. Pinga didn't grasp why the little creature seemed so pleased with the news about Pahana having lost the arrowhead, but she knew it wasn't going to benefit the Itiwana. However, she was willing to risk the repercussions if it would bring her husband back.

As she walked back to her chamber in the cliff dwellings, she wondered how Tawa would respond if this did succeed in bringing him back. *Will he resent me for risking the tribe and betraying the cause of Awona'Wilona, even if I am doing it for his sake? Will he hate me for it?*

This One must risk it, she thought. *She must have Tawa back.*

"I now understand what my father once told me about the onus of great men," Pahana said aloud to World Giant as they made their way back to Shipapa-Lina. "Responsibility can crush even a good man. As a callow youth, I often prayed for a challenge to prove my mettle. Now I find that our most deeply coveted desires are sometimes not to be touched."

Deeply anguished by the awful burden, he used his natural ability to create a ball of ice, which he threw at a nearby rock, shouting at the heavens with frustrated rage. He slumped dejectedly as the mighty World Giant brought him home.

Pahana was so distracted, he didn't notice the small flying creature until it glided into his direct view. He jerked upright and grabbed Dragonfly off the tether on his saddle. "It would satisfy me endlessly if you were here for a fight. Never have I been in more of a killing vein!"

The creature called Piasa was a small, dragon-like avian with a large mouth. It fluttered its bat wings, hovering in front of World Giant. Green orbs stared at the ivory-skinned chieftain. Pahana raised his spear. "Come closer, tiny one, and you'll end up skewered on my spear."

When Piasa spoke, it wasn't the fact that it could speak which made Pahana incredulous. It was the specific words he heard that shocked him.

"My joy is as great as my surprise. My heart will be full when it stops beating," Piasa said.

Pahana lowered his spear, startled by the words. They were words his father had spoken to him on Tawa's deathbed. Pahana would never forget those words. Piasa went on to parrot more of the things Tawa had said in those final moments of life. Pahana's mind was brought back to that day when he, Pinga, and Calian watched

Tawa die. The emotions hit him like a lightning strike, reliving that devastating hour.

"What are you, creature?" Pahana asked. "What magic allowed you to know those words?"

Piasa next said, "In empathy, I feel for your family. In patience, I say that I will be here when you need to return—to help you when you need it."

"That was what the Earth Mother Eithinoa said to me after my father left this world," Pahana said. "Did she send you?"

Piasa floated higher in the air and began to slowly drift away from Pahana and World Giant. "Does she want me to come with you? I owe her a debt for the way she helped my father. Am I meant to follow you?"

"In warning, I say you will," Piasa said, repeating something else the Earth Mother had said.

"Very well. I'll come with you," Pahana said. "I might as well settle all my debts today. Onward, World Giant. Let's anticipate danger but hope for a happy journey. I expect we'll be disappointed. It's been that type of day."

CHAPTER FIVE

The Black Road was even more silently foreboding now that Sanopi was dead. Not even the wind or bird sounds intruded on the quietude. Without the supernatural sense of danger, the Blackening Bog was like a ghostly, soundless limbo.

Lucifee the Wildcat sat near the edge of the bog, staring over its ebony surface, as if he were waiting for Sanopi to rise again. The feline spirit was expressionless and unblinking as it waited with the patience of a natural hunter.

Finally, something stirred. A small slosh of pitch was more noticeable in the noiselessness. Up from the tar came the scorpion, covered in muck. It shook itself and rubbed the pitch from its many legs. Folded in its lethal tail, the scorpion had the golden arrowhead secured. Covered in the black goo, its shape gave away what the arachnid had retrieved.

The scorpion skittered toward the wildcat. "Click, click. I have found it. Click. What's lost is now recovered. Click."

Lucifee tilted his head to examine the prize. "AAA-Roooow!"

"Click, click. It is indeed the arrowhead," the scorpion said. "Click. It's the arrowhead needed to free Malsumis. Click."

"Maal-suuuu-missss!" Lucifee repeated. "Freeee-dom!"

"Click, click. We could not touch it before. Click," the scorpion told him. "Not before an honorable, courageous Mastop-Kachina such as Pahana has touched it first. Click."

"Paaaa-haaa-naaa," the wildcat repeated. "Uuuused aaaa-roooow."

The scorpion continued his explanation. "Click, click. The spell to protect the arrow was placed by the slain Pautiwa. Click. The spell to protect the arrow was broken by foolish Pahana. Click."

Lucifee sniffed at the arrowhead with the curiosity of a cat. Whatever he smelled did not impress him. He backed away as if he didn't totally trust the little arachnid. Their only bond was a loyalty to Malsumis.

"Click, click. I need you to carry me once more. Click. I need to be carried on the wings of the wind. Click."

The wildcat shook its head. "Noooo."

The scorpion had had a difficult time convincing Lucifee to allow the arachnid to ride on its back once. No one trusted a scorpion, and it was foolish to allow one to get too close. Letting one ride on his back was risky for the wildcat once. Doing it twice was certainly tempting fate.

"Click, click. It is for Malsumis. Click," the scorpion said. "Mighty Malsumis will be grateful when he rules again. Click."

It didn't take long for the wily scorpion to persuade the wildcat that it was imperative to their cause that he be carried swiftly to his destination. Slowly and warily, Lucifee crouched, allowing the scorpion to scamper onto his furry back.

"Click, click. You must hurry. Click," the scorpion ordered. "Hurry to Agwara. Click."

"Aaaaa-gwaaaa-raaaa!" the wildcat said as it broke into a run.

The scorpion stood proudly on the cat's back, tightly holding the precious weapon. "Click, click. An ancient avowal by Manitou predicted that the arrow would be used to slay a Sky Elder before he can be free. Click. Only Agwara can lead us to the one who must be slain. Click."

"Deeee-strooooy!" Lucifee shouted. "Kiiiill!"

The hooves of World Giant clacked along the rock-strewn path, leading up the slope of Kuwahi Mountain. Pahana no longer needed to follow Piasa because he recognized the region from his previous visit, which was very memorable since that was the day his father died. He looked around at the distractingly beautiful panorama of the Mystic Moon Mountains. He knew Kuwahi was the home of the great White Bear. He hoped he wouldn't meet the bear because his family's encounters with bears had not been pleasant in the past.

Waiting at the top of the path was the towering figure of Gah-Oh, the horned giant. The goliath peered down at him, brandishing his intimidating club. Pahana wondered if the behemoth was here to welcome him or if he was going to be forced into another pointless fight. "I hope this club-wielding colossus isn't looking for a fight, World Giant. I can't speak for you, but I'm tired."

"Yon milky white visitor returns to this sacred place," the gargantuan man said. "Grand Gah-Oh greets you. The majestic Earth Mother, Eithinoa, awaits thy honored presence."

"Thank you," the relieved Pahana said. "I am keen to hear the reason I have been summoned to this place which holds so many disagreeable remembrances."

The colossal Gah-Oh gestured toward the grass house. "Yon esteemed mortal may enter the sacred home of the great Earth Mother."

Pahana dismounted World Giant, patting the animal. "Graze, large one."

"Mighty Gah-Oh shall provide water for thy loyal mount," the immense titan said.

"Very greatly appreciated," Pahana said as he walked toward the divine grass house.

Pahana felt pangs of melancholy at returning to the spot where his father had died. Entering the grass house, he relived the emotion of that terrible moment. *You were the greatest of us, Father.*

Inside, he saw the Earth Mother kneeling with her hands spread out to her sides, palms up. She was looking at the roof, eyelids half-closed, while steamy mist floated from her hands. Pahana watched closely, curious and intrigued by the sight of this divine, serene, brown-skinned holy woman.

Eithinoa turned, having either sensed or heard the arrival of the Itiwana chieftain. "In hospitality, I welcome you. In courtesy, I invite you to be seated."

"Thank you," he said, sitting on a carved log lined with hay and grass.

Eithinoa turned slightly to directly face him. "In empathy, I pray your mourning has been endurable."

Pahana glanced at the spot where his father had died. "Some pains have no cure. They must be endured. Life consists of endless struggle, and while we live, we must continually find reasons to keep struggling or else we offer our throats to the fangs of the wolf."

"In sadness, I must agree with you," she said. "In sympathy, I wish to help you in your time of crisis."

"That's most kind," Pahana said. "I can use allies at such a moment at this. I'm burdened with the need to change what is unchangeable and to defy the plan of beings far greater than myself. The Sky Elders have their plan. They have a plan for everything and everyone. Whether we want to call it a force of destiny or the sublime inspiration of ancient minds we can never know or understand does not matter. Terrible fate is hatching like a butterfly from a cocoon, and we Itiwana are inescapably intertwined with it. I want to free them from this. I would pray, but sadly, the very beings I would be praying to are the source of our distress. To be honest, I don't think highly of the Sky Elders at this moment."

"In commiseration, I understand your feelings," Eithinoa said. "In caution, I advise you to follow your instincts and do what you judge to be right. In concern, I agree action must be taken to protect your people."

"Forgive my suspicion, but I have learned to be cautious," he said. "I must ask why we of the Itiwana deserve such an ally? Why are you helping me?"

She gently touched his knee. "In regret, I failed to save your noble father. In obligation, I feel the need to make amends. In truth, I find you interesting. In perception, I detect you are a bright star of potential. In fear, I wish to avoid an endless winter. In logic, I must unite with Pahana and his Itiwana."

Pahana looked at his hand as he abstractedly formed a snowball in his pale hand. "Why do answers seem so much like questions these days? I remember when the truth I saw and heard did not require faith to believe. I am not now certain of anything. I have nothing more than a feeling. An image that evaporates whenever I try to touch it. I can only take a risk and trust my instincts and accept you on your word. We shall work together."

Eithinoa bowed slightly. "In reassurance, I swear my loyalty upon the green spirit of the world. In wisdom, I say we shall be a magnificent team!"

The chieftain watched as the snowball melted in his hand. "The world as I knew it melts away. As much as I might wish it otherwise, change is upon us, and nothing will stop it. But that doesn't mean we can't win. I swear on my father, I will do what needs to be done."

CHAPTER SIX

In the Anu-Naki caves, the sounds of children echoed joyously. Hayoka held two of his newborns. Cradled in his arms were the wrinkled skeletal baby Skadega-Muth and the winged, feathery Stikini. Multi-legged Wampus Cat struggled to crawl along the cave floor. Hayoka beamed happily, enjoying being a father.

"Well done, Wampus," he said to the cat as it slowly crawled. "You're doing fine. You are my child. My sweet, little child."

Aside from his mother, the Painted Woman, Hayoka had never loved anyone before. He hadn't expected to ever have the blessing of a family. Now, having suddenly become a father, his whole attitude changed. He was overcome with love—love for his offspring and love for Dagwona, who had given him these children. His intense feelings for this new family dwarfed his tenuous friendship with Pahana.

Dagwona napped nearby. He had come to find the familiar sound of her breathing comforting. Her features were so soft and gentle when she was sleeping, unlike the sternness of her countenance when she was plotting. He wondered if she was dreaming of him or the children. *I cherish her with all the longing in this lonely world.*

He was still reluctant to raise these wonderful blessings as weapons and warriors as Dagwona intended. She wished them to be her agents of vengeance against the Itiwana, but Hayoka had a different vision for them. "We'll walk far away from this madness. All of us. Your mother as well. I'm past caring about the vendettas of others. We shall find a place where the war of Sky Elders will not follow us. I'll convince your mother somehow. This family will not fight endlessly until we come to our own end. We'll be happy somewhere."

The ever-so-slight sound of long nails taping softly but quickly across the cave floor caught his attention. Although the newcomer tried to conceal himself in shadow, as was his habit, white fur stood out in the darkness. "Hello, Agwara."

The snow fox spirit stepped into the light from the fire, smiling with those frighteningly sharp teeth. "Charming, this is. A doting father, you are. Tender, this moment is."

"If you've come for any reason related to the Itiwana or the God war, I insist you turn around," Hayoka said softly, as not to wake Dagwona. "I want no part of any conflict at this moment. I want nothing else now except to be with my family."

Agwara sat on the cave floor, looking down at the Wampus Cat. "No plans have I. Just a friendly visit, this is. The babies, I wish to see. Delightful, they are."

Hayoka could never fully trust him, but despite the fox's frequent manipulations, he liked Agwara. The cunning critter had become the witty, charismatic friend whom Hayoka enjoyed conversing with. He found Agwara's visits refreshing.

"Whatever your reasons, you're welcome here," Hayoka said, cuddling his babies. "Look at my precious children. Nothing that either Malsumis or Awona'Wilona could deliver will ever match these small miracles."

"Blessed, you are," Agwara said with no hint of sarcasm in his often-taunting voice. "A magical moment, childbirth is."

"It is indeed," a female voice interrupted. Dagwona had been awoken by the sharp voice of Agwara. "Birthing becomes blessing. Cherish children."

"I apologize for waking you," Hayoka said. "We have a guest."

"Agwara arrives," she said. "Welcome, wanderer."

The snow fox nodded slightly in a respectful bow. "Pleasant to see you, it is. Happy, you look. Becomes you, motherhood does."

"Beautiful brood," the witch said. "Lasting legacy. Future fighters."

Hayoka was about to argue with her regarding this plan, adamantly against the idea. He never got the chance.

Agwara jerked his head toward the cave entrance. His nose twitched, sniffing the scent of danger. "Alert, we must be! Arriving, danger is! Approaching are enemies!"

"Who?" Hayoka asked, worriedly.

Dagwona sat up, suddenly on guard. "Is it Itiwana intruders?"

Agwara sneered toward the cave entrance. "The Itiwana, it is. Coming, the young shaman is. Her scent, I recognize."

"Kia!" Hayoka cried, tightening his grip on the children. "She's powerful! Dangerous!"

"Alone, she is not. An ally, she has," Agwara warned.

Dagwona jumped to her feet. "Infants imperiled! Fight foes!"

Hayoka looked around desperately. "Where is my spear?"

Dagwona held up a hand, signaling for him to stop. "Stay safe. Conceal children! Protect precious progeny!"

"But I..." he began.

"Avoid argument," she insisted. "Female fights for family. Dagwona defends daughter. Saves sons. I incapacitate Itiwana invaders!"

"Alone?" he asked.

Agwara arched his back in an aggressive pose. "Alone, she won't be. Alongside her, I will fight.

My enemy, the Itiwana are. Willingly, do I battle these attackers."

Hayoka dithered uncertainly. "I should be with you."

"No, not now!" Dagwona said. "Newborns needy. Oversee our offspring. Whirlwind witch will win war with wicked worms!"

"At your side, I shall be," Agwara said. "Fall, these foes will."

Dagwona marched to the cavemouth with Agwara close behind her. All the tormented Hayoka could do was scoop up his children and retreat to the shadows near his spear. "I'll keep you safe, my little ones. Let's put faith in your mother to win this battle."

He needed to know what was happening outside and so, kneeled in the darkness, leaning his head into a stream of light so he could get a look at the event outside the cave. He could see Dagwona and Agwara walking together, boldly advancing to head off the aggressors. Watching his Dagwona's determined stride, he felt he had never loved her more than this moment.

Two people came into view, tiny in the distance at first but slowly coming nearer and nearer. One was a large, sturdy man with an ax. Hayoka recognized the muscular form of Naya-Nazgani from the battle against the stiff-legged, man-eating bears in Shipapa-Lina. Next to him was a slender female floating atop a miniature gray cloud. Hayoka knew this attacker as well. He had seen Pahana's sister in that same battle and worried about the incredible power she had displayed. *Be careful, my love. Those two are dangerous.*

Dagwona pointed, gesturing for the two newcomers to depart. "Away and avoid aggressive action. Coming closer causes conflict."

"The Witch of the Whirlwinds?" Kia asked. "I thought you were dead. Pahana impaled you."

Dagwona sneered at the memory. "Whirlwind witch withstood wound. Hatred healed her."

"Then I will have to rectify my brother's error," the young girl said. "You menaced my people for so many years. You can't be allowed to threaten us again. I'm quite anxious to test my power against yours."

Naya-Nazgani pointed at Agwara. "And I would savor adding this sly snow creature to my list of slayings."

Agwara offered a mocking grin. "Disappointed, you will be. Tried to slay me, many have. Still here, I am. Still here will I be tomorrow."

"I do treasure a challenge," Naya-Nazgani replied. "Shall we begin?"

"Come if you dare," Agwara said. "Ready to repel, we are."

Dagwona raised her hands threateningly. "Advance and accept annihilation. Perish painfully. We will win!"

Naya-Nazgani smirked and charged at the snow fox, who began to bounce around in an evasive maneuver. Hayoka watched as Dagwona and young Kia gestured dramatically, clearly summoning their eldritch powers. While two of these combatants would fight it out with flesh and blood, the other two would use more divine, uncanny gifts.

A swift and powerful swing of Naya-Nazgani's ax was wasted as Agwara dodged with embarrassing ease. Naya-Nazgani was taken aback, rarely having seen any living thing move as swiftly as the snow fox spirit had just done. The fox circled him like a buzzing insect, taunting the warrior.

"Slow, you are," Agwara said. "Like a man underwater, you move."

Being an experienced warrior, the monster hunter quickly calculated that a change in strategy was necessary. Hayoka could tell that the ax-wielding warrior was reevaluating his tactics.

Naya-Nazgani slowly stalked Agwara, forcing the snow fox to keep moving. Periodically, he would take a wild swing, inducing the fox to leap away for safety. Hayoka could see what the new strategy was. *He's trying to tire Agwara out. If he keeps my friend moving, eventually Agwara will exhaust his energy and slow down. Once he does, Agwara is dead.*

As that slow struggle proceeded, the women were beginning their own battle. Dagwona pointed at Kia, electrical energy crackling across her hand. The young girl lifted her own hands, palms facing her enemy.

"Kill Kia!" Dagwona yelled as lightning spit from her boney fingers.

The electric bolt was reflected away as if it had bounced off an invisible wall. "I must disappoint you."

As the witch spread her arms, the wind kicked up, quickly increasing to dangerous levels. Everything not rooted to the ground was blown around. Sticks, dirt, and small rocks were scooped up and thrown at the young shaman girl. Even Agwara and Naya-Nazgani were threatened by the howling winds. Agwara was nearly carried off by a surprise gust. Stocky Naya-Nazgani managed to keep his footing and tried to use the changing conditions to his advantage. The lighter, smaller Agwara now needed to use his sharp claws to clutch the ground to prevent himself from being tossed around by the gusts. This slowed the fox down. Naya-Nazgani tried taking advantage of this, advancing on his furry foe.

Hayoka worried that Dagwona's attack was endangering their ally. *If Agwara falls, Dagwona will be alone in this battle. I fear she's using a flawed battle tactic.*

Dagwona was focused on her attack, which did not seem to be having the desired effect. Young Kia seemed to be protected from every bit of dangerous debris. Even the wind itself refused to touch the Itiwana shaman. Kia's hair was not being blown in the breeze. Looking at her, he might assume she was sitting comfortably in meditative calm, enjoying some peaceful field. Hayoka didn't understand the power this girl possessed, but clearly her magics were formidable.

He had seen this child perform miracles. What she had done against the stiff-legged bears was both amazing and frightening. Now, her defenses seemed unbreachable.

Dagwona's expression demonstrated her frustration as her usually devastating attacks were turned away with infuriating ease. The witch angrily emitted further lightning attacks, all of which failed to injure the young girl. "Cursed child!" Dagwona cried, enraged.

While Dagwona screamed in rage, Kia began her counterattack. The girl muttered a silent chant while spreading her fingers and wriggling her pinkies like two worms. Moments later, the ground beneath Dagwona transformed into something akin to quicksand. Dagwona's expression showed that she was startled as her feet sank into the slush. Before Dagwona could react and use the winds to levitate herself, thick roots burst out of the ground, quickly wrapping themselves around the legs and waist of the Witch of the Whirlwind. Dagwona cried out in alarm and used her bolts of power to cut through the roots, but more and more popped up from the ground and entangled her, squeezing tightly. She continued to sink into the muck.

Hayoka wanted to help the mother of his children, but he couldn't leave those children unguarded. He looked around to see if Agwara was able to assist her but saw Naya-Nazgani throwing his ax at the fox, who was still clutching at the ground and distracted by Dagwona's situation.

The ax spun handle-over-top until the sharp edge hit the fox's exposed side, cutting Agwara open. The snow fox shrieked as the blade cut him wide.

Hayoka gasped, not only because his friend had been fatally wounded but because his precious Dagwona was now alone on the battlefield. *Curse these Itiwana!* Not knowing what else to do, he looked upward and prayed to the Sky Elder who Kia served. "Please, mighty Awona'Wilona. Spare Dagwona and the children. After all I've done... If you want someone to suffer, take me. We both know I deserve it. Selfish and weak. I have failed so many people. And I have killed. I'm not asking for your forgiveness. But spare my beloved and her innocent children. Punish me instead. I beg you!"

Outside the cave, Kia was on the verge of victory. After minutes of desperate struggling, Dagwona's arms were pinned to her side by two particularly thick and heavy roots. Unable to lift her hands, she could no longer destroy the rhizomes that were encircling her. The roots began to cocoon her, dragging her down into the mire. As she screamed in rage and fear, Kia unleashed another method of attack. From out of the ground came an army of ants. Large ants and small ones. Red ants and black ants. Countless thousands of ants swarmed up the roots and then across the body of Dagwona. In less than a minute, the Witch of the Whirlwind was completely covered by a living mass of tiny creatures that proceeded to eat her alive. Dagwona screeched in torturous torment and terror as she vanished into the muck.

NO! Hayoka thought in horror, having to contain himself from screaming, lest he alert the attackers to the presence of himself and the children. He had a choice. He could rush to her aid and possibly be killed himself, leaving the children alone and undefended. His other option was to hide in cowardly fashion and let his wife die in order to give the children their best chance to survive. The beleaguered Hayoka had to force himself to stay concealed in the shadows while his beloved Dagwona was being horribly killed.

Meanwhile, the wounded Agwara stared helplessly as Naya-Nazgani stood over him, raising his ax with lethal intentions. For once, Agwara didn't have a clever quip ready. His voice was weak and frightened.

"Surrender, I do," Agwara said. "Not necessary is my death. Defeated, I am. Mercy, I ask."

Naya-Nazgani didn't react in any way. He didn't change his expression or hesitate for a moment. All he said was, "Don't shame the word mercy by suggesting it should be applied to monsters such as you."

He brought the ax down, separating Agwara's head from his furry body. Hayoka saw the blood splatter from the decapitated fox who had been his close friend. The merciless way Naya-Nazgani slew the fox spirit proved that he would not hesitate to kill the three children. And the brutality of what Kia had done to Dagwona left no hope of compassion for her offspring.

Wampus Cat made a slight sound, and Hayoka's heartbeat surged. He did his best to soothe and quiet his child, praying to Malsumis that the agents of Awona'Wilona did not discover his presence.

"A worthwhile day's work, I think," Naya-Nazgani said, watching Agwara's blood seep into the grass and dirt. "We should leave this cur here as a warning to others."

Kia agreed. "At the very least, he'll make a meal for some hungry animals. As for Dagwona, she got the burial she didn't deserve. I think we're done here."

"Heartily agreed," Naya-Nazgani said. "I could use a good meal."

"Then let's return to Shipapa-Lina and tell the others of our triumph," she said. "Pahana will be so embarrassed that I killed that vile witch when he apparently failed. I'll embarrass him, I predict."

The big monster hunter laughed. "Naughty girl. Still, just as long as the cursed witch is dead, everyone will celebrate. Two foes have been eliminated today. Now let's go get that meal."

Kia floated at his side, and they trekked casually back to Shipapa-Lina, both maddeningly smug in their triumph. Hayoka was appalled by their cavalier cruelty and mocking of his dearest Dagwona. Filled with hatred, he waited until they were gone and gently set his children down on the soft bed that Dagwona had been using only minutes ago. He rushed out, hanging on to a desperate hope that she was somehow still alive but knowing in his mind that this was not the case.

He frantically dug at the spot where his beloved had vanished into the earth. His fingers bled as he scooped the dirt from the ground, tossing it wildly aside. He touched something hard and realized it was the top of Dagwona's skull. With a bilious recoil, he resumed his digging until he partly uncovered the body.

Hayoka shivered at the sight of his beloved Dagwona. The part of her skin that hadn't been eaten away had turned blue from lack of air. Her eyes stared blankly, unseeing. Blood and dirt were in her mouth. Her death had been horrific.

Cradling her devastated body, Hayoka cried for the first time since he was a child. The absolute devastation he felt was unlike any despair he'd suffered before. He sat with her corpse for a long time, sobbing in anguish, until he heard the cries of his children. He forced himself to let her go, and he reentered the cave and attended to the infants. He set them down to sleep and exited the Anu-Naki cave with the intention of reburying the body. He didn't want his children to see what was left of their mother.

After he covered the hole and buried Dagwona, he created a marker out of sticks and stones to commemorate her grave. He continued to stare at the marker with a cold, emotionless expression for an hour. The sun began to fade, and Hayoka sat in the growing darkness, just as his soul was growing darker.

CHAPTER SEVEN

Lucifee the Wildcat had used its sense of smell and tracking skills to locate Agwara. As they neared the Anu-Naki caves, the wildcat announced that the snow fox was close. "AAA-Gwaa-raa. Neeeear."

The scorpion, still sitting on the wildcat's back, was pleased. "Click, click. That is good to hear. Click. No further need for you. Click."

The scorpion jabbed it's lethal poison tail into the wildcat's back. The cat shrieked at the sting of the jab and reared up, bucking the scorpion from its back. The angry wildcat tried to claw at the scorpion, but the little arachnid skittered across the grass too quickly. It took only a few seconds for the wildcat to succumb to the deadly poison. Lucifee collapsed to the grass, it's lifeforce fading rapidly.

The dying wildcat looked at the scorpion. "Whhhhhy?"

"Click, click. I am a scorpion. Click. It's what I do. Click."

Lucifee died and the scorpion immediately forgot about his latest victim. The arachnid, still clutching the arrowhead, crawled rapidly to the cave. The creature was mostly concealed in the thick grass as he approached the Anu-Naki cave. The scorpion first spotted the human kneeling in front of a small monument that smelled of death. The scorpion didn't care about that, but the arachnid did react to the sight of a decapitated Agwara. The little creature had come a long way to get the information Agwara possessed, only to find the snow fox spirit dead.

The scorpion scurried to the human. Hayoka hadn't noticed the creature and was startled by the voice that broke the long silence.

"Click, click. What has occurred? Click," it said. "Explain this disaster. Click"

Hayoka looked blankly at the scorpion, still shocked and numb by what had occurred. Hayoka said nothing to the scorpion. Hayoka was not in the mood to speak at the moment.

"Click, click. How did Agwara die?" the scorpion asked. "Click. His knowledge is needed. Click."

Hayoka closed his eyes and gently fingered the dirt that covered the body of his former lover. "Agwara can't speak to you just now. None of us are talking now. This is not a good place for conversation. All you'll find here is prey. That's what we are. Just prey. Aren't we all?"

The scorpion wasn't satisfied with that answer. "Click, click. I need an explanation. Click. Malsumis will not be pleased. Click."

Opening his eyes, Hayoka glared glassy eyed at the arachnid. "Well then, Malsumis will just have to learn to accept it. Tell him you got here too late. Now leave me alone."

"Click, click, I must know! Click!" the scorpion said. "This is of vital importance. Click."

The scorpion continued to explain his need for Agwara. Long ago, the arrowhead was discovered in a volcano by the legendary Morning Star, who used it to slay his nemesis, Shakok. After that, Agwara stole it, along with the sacred tomahawk. However, the mighty Sky Elder Manitou retrieved the arrowhead, while his fellow elder Pautiwa put an enchantment on it, ensuring that no Winter Elder could use it. Only the touch of a Mastop-Kachina could break the spell. Manitou and Pautiwa hid the arrowhead in a secret place, guarded by Nanook, the bear God.

Only Kokopelli, who is favored by great Manitou, knew a vital secret: that the golden arrowhead is the key to freeing Malsumis. However, Kokopelli was manipulated by the lovely Sedna, the Winter Goddess of the Frozen Seas. She seduced Kokopelli into admitting that the death of a certain Sky Elder would free Malsumis, but she didn't find out the name of the elder who must die. She did, however, learn that the golden arrowhead could destroy the unnamed elder. If the Winter Elders learn which Summer Elder must die, they will use the arrowhead to eliminate the unidentified elder, thus freeing Malsumis.

The Winter Elders became confident that the hypnotic power of the Kachina Asgaya, known as the Red Woman, could compel Kokopelli to tell the name of the intended victim. But Kokopelli was somehow hidden from the enemy, perhaps due to the magic of his flute. And only one living being knew where he was: Agwara. The sly snow fox claimed that he had once come across the solitary Kokopelli, quite by accident. Kokopelli used the power of his magic flute to cause Agwara to forget where Kokopelli was. Recently, the scorpion had come up with a way to restore Agwara's memory using the blood of Nanook. When Tawa obligingly killed Nanook, he inadvertently removed the defender of the arrowhead and provided the essential blood to cure Agwara's memory block.

The scorpion had planned to bring Agwara to a location where he had stored the blood of Nanook. Once Agwara recalled the God's name, they would select a sacrificial warrior, who would likely die in the act, to fire the arrow.

Now, however, the death of Agwara had ruined the plan to free Malsumis. There was no way to know which Summer Elder needed to die. They only had one arrowhead and, therefore, had only one chance at success. The scorpion was deeply disappointed by this turn of events.

Hayoka listened to this in silence. Just as the saddened scorpion turned to walk away, Hayoka finally reacted. "I know the name!"

He continued as the scorpion stopped. "I know it. I do. Dagwona was able to cure his memory loss. He told us the name, as an alternative should something happen to him. He was preparing to find you and other servants of Malsumis to claim the arrowhead and kill...a certain Elder."

"Click, click. Who? Click. What is the name? Click?"

"First, we make an arrangement," Hayoka said. "I want something from you."

The scorpion didn't know if Hayoka was telling the truth. It might be a ploy to gain favor with Malsumis, but the scorpion was desperate. He had failed his master Malsumis, and if this human could possibly help him, the scorpion had to put his doubts aside and take the chance. "Click, click. What do you want? Click. Speak your terms. Click."

"I want revenge!" Hayoka said with icy hate. "Those are my terms, and I will not change my mind. The Itiwana must die! To the last man, woman, and child. Dagwona intended to raise our children as weapons against the Itiwana and I was reluctant. I was a fool, and she was correct. I will raise my children to know nothing but hatred! I will teach them how to use their natural abilities in the most lethal ways! I will teach them to fight and to kill! And what I am unable to teach them myself, I will find a proper mentor to instruct them. When they are grown, they will lead the ultimate battle and be the weapons that will finally destroy the cursed Itiwana!"

"Click, click. I find your goals laudable. Click," the scorpion said. "What do you need from me? Click."

"You will help me protect and defend my children until they are ready to do what must be done!" Hayoka insisted. "You will help me hide them, and also assist me in forming a powerful army that will one day follow my children into battle. The Itiwana have many enemies, and we will gather them. When my children reach adulthood, they will spearhead the final war!"

"Click, click. Must we wait so many years? Click," the scorpion asked. "Malsumis awaits. Click."

"I'm told that time means little to the Sky Elders," Hayoka said. "Lifetimes are like hours to them. What can seventeen or eighteen summers mean to beings such as they? It's a mere wink of their ancient eye."

The scorpion considered all this, disliking having the responsibility to decide how many years the Sky Elders must wait to free Malsumis. The arachnid was not even certain Hayoka had the information he claimed to have, but he saw no alternatives. He had promised the Winter Elders he would do this. He couldn't tell them he had failed. Even if Hayoka was lying, it gave the scorpion several seasons to come up with a new plan to free Malsumis, or at the very least, he could think of a way to blame someone else for this failure.

"Click, click. Very well, I agree. Click," the scorpion said. "I'll help you protect your off-spring. Click."

Hayoka rose to his full height and looked to the sky. He suddenly broke into a wrathful scream, loud enough that even the Gods would hear him. "Murder is now my heritage! That is the lesson I will pass on to my children! Something in this universe has chosen me and my family to do what no one else had the will and the cunning to do. The Itiwana will all die suffering! The days of their kind are ending. The future comes to drive out the withered remains of that detestable tribe! Some may call me evil, but I embrace every evil deed I ever did and only regret my kindness. I see the truth and I proceed with perfect certainty in every vengeful thought I have. My intellect is the seed which will bring down the Itiwana, as a storm sent from the skies downs a towering tree! All the coming chaos and violence will merge into a single moment of pure and beautiful death!"

Still in a jubilant and triumphant mood, Kia and Naya-Nazgani returned to the familiar green mesa of Shipapa-Lina. Young Kia considered this a successful test of her ever-growing power, and Naya-Nazgani was just satisfied with a well-earned kill.

Upon their return, they had intended to brag of their victory but found that their homecoming had been overshadowed by the return of more prominent leaders. Seeing Faw-Faw sitting protectively outside the Cliff Palace indicated that the Shakowin was probably meeting inside. As Kia led her muscular ally into the Cliff Palace, they found the Shakowin assembled to greet its chieftain and its long-absent advisor.

Not only had Pahana come back safely from his journey, but Manabazo had also returned. Only minutes before, he had swooped down from the realm beyond the clouds. He had left weeks ago to ask the Sky Elders for some information. Time, of course, was a different matter to the Gods. Pahana sat on the seat of chiefs, while Atira, T'Soona, and Pinga sat facing him. In the middle was a large eagle. The new arrivals knew it must be Manabazo when they heard it speak.

"And so, I returned on crested wing," Manabazo said. "Dire tidings I sadly bring."

"Say on," Pahana replied. "We need to hear every sad detail."

Atira saw the two new arrivals and gestured for them to be seated and be silent while Manabazo spoke. They sat and listened, to catch up on what they had missed.

Manabazo began his explanation. "Many things have I learned. The tide has unmercifully turned. Of many deadly matters, I bring you word. Three deadly omens have occurred."

"My brother Pogum spoke of three omens, long ago," Atira said. "Tawa had long attempted to learn what they were."

With a flutter of his wings, Manabazo displayed his agitation. "I have learned this secret too late. We cannot avoid this fate. The first omen is the death of a great leader and chief. His time on this world was much too brief."

"Tawa," Pinga said sadly.

Manabazo continued. "The second omen is a foolish bargain with our foes. The detail of this, only one among us knows."

Pinga rose to her feet. "You refer to This One. She admits her actions. This One made a promise to deliver a golden arrowhead to Malsumis if he could return Tawa to us. It seemed a small sacrifice if my husband can be with us again, when we need him most."

Pahana defended his mother. "I was there when she made that promise in the pain of my father's death. She had a weak moment."

"There is more," Pinga said. "This One had a visitor. A scorpion messenger came to me to fulfill my promise. I told the creature that Pahana used the arrow and lost it in the tar pits."

"I'm sorry to hear this news, about the weapon he chose to use," Manabazo said. "Pahana accidently broke an ancient spell. Now the Winter Elders can wield it as well. Listen to the third of the omens I uncovered. The arrowhead has now been discovered. This scorpion retrieved it from where it lay. They will use it to free Malsumis one day. This threat lurks like a serpent in the grass. These are the three omens that have come to pass."

"And so, the moment we have long feared is upon us," Atira said. "Malsumis will soon rise, and the war of Gods will fully begin. Will we survive being in between them?"

"They haven't released him yet, so we still have time," T'Soona said. "We often seem to come upon some luck at the last possible moment."

Several nervous voices overlapped with their various opinions. A din of noise filled the room until Pahana stood up and raised his hand for silence. "We've been on the edge of doom before. Perhaps we have never wavered so close to falling over the precipice as now, but as T'Soona said, we have always managed to perform a miracle when we needed to. We have allies, some of which you may not even be aware of. Hopefully, we can count on the assistance of Awona'Wilona and the Sky Elders. But even without them, we will overcome. I don't believe it's the destiny of the Itiwana to fade from this wayward world. Life has a foreboding melody. A rhythm of notes which become your existence once played in harmony with the Gods' plans. We will once again play our song of victory! Let demons come. We will be ready!"

CHAPTER EIGHT

Seasons came and then vanished into time. As Hayoka predicted, the Winter Sky Elders waited for his children to become ready for battle before they pressed him to reveal his secrets. The eighteen summers that passed were akin to eighteen hours for the ancient Sky Elders. For the humans involved, however, many changes occurred. Hayoka found places to hide his children and people to help teach them. Skadega-Muth, Stikini, and Wampus Cat found homes that enabled them to grow strong and deadly.

Skadega-Muth was brought to the Big Sand, where Hayoka found a remaining faction of Tunerak Destroyers who used to worship Dagwona and her disciple, the Salt Witch. They were glad to have the heir apparent to their former leader back. They agreed to hide her. Wampus Cat was taken to the Valley of the Blue Mists, where Hayoka renewed his alliance with the Keeper of sacred objects. Both the Breathing Shaman and the Keeper resented the Itiwana, still believing that Calian had attacked the Keeper. They promised to guard the Wampus Cat. As for Stikini, Hayoka brought her to Nunusa, the insect-queen Kachina from the Shining Rock Mountains. Nunusa hated the Itiwana for destroying the great Grasshopper who she had worshipped. Hayoka implored her to take in his infant child and teach Stikini to fly, promising that one day the owl-like being would help to destroy their enemies from Shipapa-Lina. Nunusa agreed to allow Stikini to remain with her insect swarm.

Satisfied that his children were in safe hands and would be readied for the day when they would avenge their mother, he sought out other allies. He trekked to the Bitter Root Valley in an attempt to attain the aid of the diminutive but savage Puk-Wudjies, who had long held vitriolic animosity toward the Itiwana. Although Hayoka had been among the Itiwana during their last encounter with the Puk-Wudjies, the little carnivores did not see his face or hear his name. They would have no way of knowing Hayoka had once helped Pahana escape their grasp. Now he planned to convince the ruling council to assist him in his plan. He was certain of his success. Hayoka had a gift for persuasion, and the Puk-Wudjies were so driven by emotion and hunger, he calculated he would have little difficulty in getting them to agree.

He planned to contact the Vykans at some point in the future. He would have a much more difficult time getting them to assist him, since his last encounter with them consisted of being captured by them and escaping by bashing a Vykan over the head with a rock. They had no reason to be friends with him, other than the fact that Hayoka's father Hobomok had once been their ally. *It isn't much, but it's something to build on. I'll need to think heavily before I approach them, but somehow, I'll get them to help me. I will one day unite all the Itiwana's foes together. And then, along with my children, we will trample and burn Shipapa-Lina and end the cursed legacy of the Itiwana, leaving nothing but the echo of their dying lamentations.*

CHAPTER NINE

Eighteen years later:

1270 AD—The Moon Debi-Quay Season
of the Great Turtle's Trek

Another battle had begun. Such conflicts seemed endless in recent days. Peace was a fading memory. All that the people of Shipapa-Lina had known for the past season had been relentless attacks, all led by a figure from their distant past.

As a defensive line of Itiwana Two-Horn Riders created a living wall in front of the cliff housing in Shipapa-Lina, the enemy launched their weapons. Over 200 bellicose Puk-Wudjies unleashed stone slings and wooden spears with stone tips at the Itiwana. However, Pahana had recently added a new innovation to his army of warriors. The Two-Horned Riders had begun carrying triangular wooden shields, which protected their bodies from face to waist. The thick shields were designed with a colorful turquoise and shell mosaic. The rocks were mostly deflected by the defensive object, although some of the spears imbedded themselves in the shields.

The Bow Sisterhood stood atop the cliffs. The women were ready to fire their arrows at the attackers when they got the signal. However, the voice of their War Chief shouted, "Hold! Wait until they get closer!"

To the forefront of the attacking force came eight savage Skinwalkers. The frightening animal-men were hybrids of wolves, cougars, and bears, mixed with mortal men, servants of the Tunerak Destroyers. They roared and snarled and raised their claws, indicating their eagerness to attack. Swirling overhead, like a vulture waiting for its prey to die, was Stikini. The Owl-Man circled above, ready to swoop down and tear an Itiwana warrior apart with its talons.

Riding to the forefront of the invaders was their leader, Hayoka. He rode upon a huge, seven-foot moose simply named Moozoonsi. He held a heavy staff ornamented with copper and silver. At the age of thirty-eight summers, he had prepared for many years to wage this war.

"Come out where I can see you!" Hayoka shouted. "Pahana! Calian! Come and beg for mercy. Hurry on. Come to me as fast as your hands and knees can carry you!"

Trotting forward on their buffalo mounts, Pahana the chieftain appeared, accompanied by his new War Chief Calian, who had recently replaced Aholi. The chieftain was now a man of thirty-eight summers, having been born the same week as Hayoka. Calian was several months younger but still as fit and well-muscled as ever. Side-by-side, they faced Hayoka and his mighty moose.

"Ah, there you are," Hayoka said. "I thought you would continue to hide behind your loyal servants, and I wouldn't get to see my old friends. Were you two sleeping?"

Calian's hatred had grown over the years. He scowled contemptuously. "The last time I slept, I had a nightmare. I dreamed you died, and it wasn't me who killed you. A horrible thought."

"I must say, I've missed these verbal duels, Calian," Hayoka said. "You have no wit, but I still find your hatred entertaining."

"Perhaps you'll find my challenge entertaining," Calian said. "We have an unfinished matter of honor. I would happily settle it now, between we two. Will you talk or bleed?"

Hayoka chuckled and waved his staff dismissively. "It's not honor I'm after. It's revenge. And not just against you. I have a larger agenda."

Calian was about to answer, but Pahana held up a hand to silence him. He nudged his mount, World Giant, to trot a few steps closer to his enemy.

"If you have something to say to me, Hayoka, say it now. You didn't come all this way to trade insults."

"Yes, let's be direct," Hayoka said, grinning. "Here is my message of peace. If your people surrender and swear unquestioning faith to our cause, they may survive. Perhaps."

Pahana crossed his arms. "This is your message of peace? A demand for our total and unconditional surrender?"

"Consider it an offer of alliance," Hayoka said. "With us on top and the Itiwana crawling on the bottom. It's the best and only offer you will get."

"Are you deluded or insane, Hayoka?" Pahana asked. "Even if I believed you capable of carrying out your threats, do you think me so foolish as to trust a man who would see his father's people destroyed?"

"Not necessarily destroyed," Hayoka corrected. "Just subjugated, under me. As for you two, both of you must die. You may die painlessly, Pahana, but Calian, not so! I would also see painful death befall your shamanic sister Kia and that barbaric monster hunter Naya-Nazgani. My wife's death will be avenged. These four deaths will abate my desire for blood today, but the rest of the Itiwana must yield completely to us. Nothing else will be acceptable."

Stepping out of the assembled Two-Horn Riders came Naya-Nazgani, holding his ax. Big Faw-Faw followed behind him, having developed a bond with the monster hunter. "If you want me, Hayoka, here I stand. Send your Skinwalkers. I've killed so many of them, I've lost count. I'd enjoy adding these victims to my many victories."

"Such daring words," Hayoka said. "And such stupidity. Let's see you make your words truth."

Hayoka gestured to the Skinwalkers, and they rushed forward, charging at Naya-Nazgani with bestial wrath. The monster slayer raised his ax and took a defensive stance. Pahana gestured for his warriors to hold their position and let Naya-Nazgani fight alone, but Faw-Faw impulsively rushed to assist his ally, waving the iron hammer he had long ago won from the Vykans.

Ax joined hammer and the two powerful warriors did battle with the eight Skinwalkers. Faw-Faw knocked several aside with mighty blows, while Naya-Nazgani cleaved them limb-from-torso. The animal-men managed to get close enough to scratch the duo with sharp claws, but the pain did nothing more than anger the two warriors. Despite the persistence of the Skinwalkers and their numerical advantage, the battle was one-sided. Heads were lopped off or smashed in. Seven of the Skinwalkers fell to the strength of the monster hunter and the tall Wood Man. The eighth fled in a moment of panic. The creature ran past Hayoka, who was angered by the retreat. He bashed the Skinwalker with his club and ordered his massive moose to stamp the scared monster to death.

Naya-Nazgani and Faw-Faw celebrated their victory as the Itiwana cheered. Only Pahana retained his chiefly calm. The chieftain noticed

Stikini diving toward them, talons at the ready. He used his icy powers to quickly create a frozen spear. He pulled back his arm to spear the Owl-Man, but Hayoka waved to indicate that his son should withdraw. The owl creature veered away, resuming its circular patrol.

It seemed Pahana was ready to throw the ice spear at Hayoka but instead threw it at the ground. He pointed at Hayoka. "Once again, you see that your allies are inadequate. That's been the story of your entire existence. You chose the wrong allies from the beginning. Didn't you realize that? There must have been a moment of clarity sometime during this hellacious fiasco when you understood that."

Hayoka glared with cold intensity. "I detest the pompousness of you and your band of maggots. You Itiwana killed my father and my wife and then tell me that my allies are evil. My allies may attack you relentlessly, but when I recall that the Itiwana brought all this upon themselves, my guilt flies away like a bird."

Calian put a hand on Pahana's shoulder. "We cannot reason with this venomous snake. He is a traitor, like his father before him, and will suffer the same fate."

Hayoka pointed his club at Calian. "You may call my father and I traitors, but I take pride in naming you and your kind as my enemy. Let this day be the one chance for your people, Pahana. If you won't surrender, I'll be back with all the enemies you and your father have made over so many years. The forces I will marshal against you will overwhelm any defense or any plan you may dream up. The Itiwana have no chance of surviving. As for you and Calian and Naya-Nazgani and Kia, I will see you all dead. This is not a promise... It's a prophecy of the future!"

"You've had your say," Pahana replied. "Now I will simply say this... We have no fear of what you will do to us, but you should cower at what we will do to you if you dare to ever return here. We have survived every threat the Enemy Way has sent against us, and you are nothing but the latest challenge for us to overcome. Go away and find something else to do with your life other than useless vengeance, or you will join your wife very soon."

"And it will be I who does the deed!" Calian cried hatefully. "It does not take a prophet to know that we two will clash at the end! You know what's going to happen, don't you? I will have your blood on my hands in the end! My hate will only die with you!"

"I've had more than enough of you for today!" Hayoka said. "I gave you a chance and you refused. When I return, blood will cover Shipapa-Lina like a raging river."

Giving the signal for his army to follow him, he ordered Moozoonsi to lead them from the Land of Everlasting Summer. The Itiwana watched as the enemies departed their village.

"That man is evil!" Calian hissed. "And not even the Sky Elders will stop me from killing him when I get the chance!"

"Don't focus on one man, Calian," Pahana warned. "Our peril grows like tall weeds all around us. We have too many enemies to concentrate on Hayoka. You and Naya-Nazgani need to be alert. I must send a message to Kia, as well. I hope Kolhu is safe."

"You will not enter!" Kia shouted in a voice that was both commanding and threatening. "None of you will set a foul foot on Kolhu!"

Kia stood alone on the far side of a stream, just outside Shipapa-Lina's sister city of Kolhu. Kia, now a woman of thirty-three, had been anointed as the new ruler of Kolhu when Molowia became ill. In her seventieth summer, her health was beginning to fail, and she turned her city over to the powerful young shaman who she had trained to be her successor. Kia was now the Cacique: the shaman chieftain of Kolhu. Over the years her power had become so astounding, Molowia knew Kia could defend her city better than anyone else.

Facing Kia on the other side of the stream was the Breathing Shaman from the Valley of the Blue Mists, sitting atop a bighorn sheep. She led an invasion force consisting of 100 stiff-legged bear beasts, the six-legged Wampus Cat, and Atahsaia, the cannibal demon. As tall as a giraffe, Atahsaia had prickly gray hair and thick skin. His hands were so gnarled that his knuckles appeared like thorns. He possessed immensely muscular arms covered in black and white scales and a scalp overlaid with porcupine quills. His mouth stretched from ear to ear, and he had a wrinkled, swollen red face, with bulging eyes that did not blink and yellow tusks that protruded past his lips. The beast howled in a fearsome manner.

The Breathing Shaman, now aged with gray hair, was holding her bone tube. She shouted to Kia, "You drove us from Shipapa-Lina many years ago. But you had the backing of the Itiwana warriors then. Kolhu has no army. You stand alone."

"Do you think so?" Kia replied. "I suggest you don't make assumptions. I'll give you a chance to depart alive and without any painful burns or injuries. I strongly advise you to take advantage of my generous proposal."

"You think too much of yourself!" the Breathing Shaman bellowed. "You cannot overpower us all. Not without allies."

"Then allow me to introduce you to my ally," Kia calmly said.

With a softly whispered chant and a wave of her hand, the stream that flowed between herself and her enemies began to bubble as if it were boiling. Water spurted upward, and then Wishpoosh appeared. The massive beaver guardian spirit was as tall as Atahsaia and was legendary for its strength and invulnerability. The Breathing

Shaman backed up several steps, intimidated by the giant creature.

The demon cannibal Atahsaia roared a challenge at Wishpoosh, who stepped out of the stream, using body language to accept the challenge. Atahsaia lunged forward, while Wishpoosh stood its ground.

The two beasts locked up in a brutal, ferocious battle. The Wampus Cat moved away from the conflict. Even the fearsome bear beasts backed away, allowing the huge monsters room to fight. They rolled around, gnawing and rending each other wildly. Wishpoosh used its spiked tail to batter the demon. After several minutes of combat, they both rolled into the stream and vanished under the surface.

The Breathing Shaman chose to take advantage of Wishpoosh's absence and ordered her forces to attack. "Now, my friends! This is our moment!"

Led by the Wampus Cat, the bear beasts marched to the edge of the stream. Kia, however, did not seem alarmed. With a withering sneer, she spread her arms and mouthed a quiet chant. Within moments, a misty vapor rose up from the water. It covered the far side of the stream like a cloud.

The Wampus Cat got to the edge of the waterway and tried to leap over the stream to avoid the water. It jumped and crossed half the distance until it reached the mist. The cat bounced off the cloud, as if it had hit a rock. The Wampus

Cat fell into the water. Recovering its senses, it swam back to dry land. The cat yowled at the bears, warning them to stop. The grizzly beasts halted, confused.

I won't let her defeat me again! The Breathing Shaman thought, furious. She put her hollow bone tube to her lips and blew into it. The tube released several fireballs that impacted against the fog but exploded without piercing the defense. The Breathing Shaman cursed under her breath.

At that moment, Wishpoosh reemerged from the water, waved its paws and tail to indicate it was still willing and able to fight. The Breathing Shaman didn't know how to breach this dual defense and was forced to reconsider her approach. She would rather withdraw on her own terms than allow herself to be outfought.

"We were sent here to give you a warning!" the Breathing Shaman said. "And while I would enjoy seeing you begging in utter defeat, I will delay your destruction for the moment."

"Liar!" Kia said. "You know you can't pass my defenses. All you can do is retreat in bitter failure."

The Breathing Shaman felt her rage growing but knew it was best to restrain her emotions. "We will settle our personal issues another time. I came here to give you a chance to surrender before the wrath of an army unlike anything you've ever imagined will converge on Shipapa-Lina and then to your precious Kolhu. You have no prayer, despite your power. The only hope of survival is compliance. Hayoka wants your head, and I would enjoy seeing that, also. Kolhu will become a colony of the Winter Elders, but at least your people will live. Think well on your answer, before..."

"Get out of the Land of Everlasting Summer, now!" Kia commanded. "Lest Wishpoosh lose his patience and does something uncivilized."

"Very well, we will bide our time," the Breathing Shaman said. "Enjoy this petty success in defending your home. Next time, you will see it fall before your own life is exterminated. Goodbye, Kia of Kolhu. Our next meeting will be more final!"

The Breathing Shaman blew a note on her bone tube, and her bighorn sheep rode away from the stream. The Wampus Cat trailed closely behind, and the bears ultimately followed as well. Atahsaia never reappeared.

Kia calmly watched them leave. Despite her confidence in her power, she wondered if the Breathing Shaman was not bluffing about the destructive army Hayoka had amassed. *Perhaps I need to investigate this further.*

CHAPTER TEN

It was getting harder every day for Atira to climb the ladder from her chamber in the cliff housing to the upper and lower levels. Having reached the age of seventy summers, she had attained the status of village elder, but she missed the days when she could easily scamper up and down the Shipapa-Lina ladders. She had become very slim, and her long hair was gray and thinning. Reaching the intended level, she stretched a bit before she walked to the Cliff Palace.

She glanced up at the cliff overhang and remembered the days of her youth, when she and her lost Yana-Luah oversaw Shipapa-Lina, back when they lived atop the mesa. She relived teary-eyed memories of those long-ago days, when she was young and beautiful. Yana-Luha and vile Hobomok used to fight over her in those days.

The cliff dwellings were built after Yana-Luha vanished from this world, under the leadership of her son Tawa. But now Tawa was dead. All she had left of her family line was her grandson Pahana, who now ruled Shipapa-Lina, and her granddaughter Kia who ruled Kolhu. She was proud of her grandchildren, and she wished Yana-Luha and Tawa could have seen their development into capable leaders.

She was concerned about Pahana, however. Although he had shown himself to be a capable combat leader and administrator, his solitary nature and frequent absences had created an emotional distance between him and the rest of the tribe. The Itiwana respected Pahana, but they didn't have the love and faith in him as they'd had in Tawa and Yana-Luha. That devotion could explain the difference between the way the tribe thrived under Tawa, despite the God war, and their current mood of agitated gloom.

She climbed the steps to the top of the Cliff Palace where the Shakowin often met. She puffed, getting her breath back when she entered the chamber of the ruling council. Inside, she saw Pahana seated on the chieftain's carved ornamental stool, in front of the firepit. The Dragonfly was laid on the ground at his side. Pahana never allowed it to be out of his arm's reach. He was staring at the smokey embers of a fire which had obviously burned out.

"Hello, Grandmother," he said quietly. "Is something wrong?"

"Perhaps," she said, sitting on the floor in her usual spot, to rest from her climb. "I was speaking to your mother. Pinga tells me you're planning to leave us. Again. I'm concerned about these repeated absences of yours. You're needed here while we are constantly under threat from Hayoka and his demonic allies. The people worry when their leader is not here."

"Enough, Grandmother," Pahana snapped. "You've been singing this same tired tune for so many years. Even before Tawa died, you were chiding me about leaving Shipapa-Lina whenever I saw fit to depart. You once threatened to have me removed from my rightful position as chieftain if I was away too often. Yet here we are, so many seasons later, and despite my comings and goings, the Itiwana are still strong."

"The Itiwana still survive," Atira said. "But are we as strong as we were? Our greatest warriors are feeling the bite of advancing age, and the younger ones lack inspiration because their leader seems to prefer unexplained visits to unknown places while they remain here, guarding our home without you."

Pahana narrowed his eyes as his gaze burned into his grandmother. "You disrespect me. Can't you comprehend that I have reasons for the things I do? Or do you imagine I'm simply fishing and cavorting when I leave the village?"

"It would comfort me to know your reasons," Atira said. "It would comfort the warriors as well. The success of a tribe is based on its loyalty to its leader, and nothing can replace that ... or him! We need you. And if you're not here, we deserve to know why. At least confide in me."

Pahana resumed staring at the smoking embers. "I ask for your trust. You'll know when I decide it's best to reveal my plans to everyone. In the meantime, I expect your support."

"You have my support in front of the tribe," she said. "In private, I confess my fears that this is unwise, and I pray to the Sky Elders that you are not making a mistake. I hope Awona'Wilona grants you wisdom."

"We can't pray for the Sky Elders to come to our aid because they are not listening," Pahana said, glancing down at his spear, as if its presence gave him comfort. "They don't care. For over 300 years we have prayed to beings who do not care whether we stand or fall. The Elders are not on anyone's side. They are concerned only about the Tree of Life, not us. They are a force of nature, beyond good and evil. Good and evil—we created those. Do you wish to break the endless cycle? The cycle of fighting? Death? Fear? Destruction? Survival? That's in our hands, and in our hands only. It requires that we live in hope, not fear. Trust in me and let me do what I need to do. That's all I ask of you."

Atira looked at the ground, conflicted. She watched as some ants marched by, carrying specks of food, doing their duty for their queen, oblivious to the worries of the humans that tower over them. Can they understand what a human does? Can a human understand a Sky Elder? She remembered when life seemed so much easier to comprehend.

"Perhaps I'm too old now," she said. "I can't see the future as well as I see the past. I still feel the old ways are the best. I've found solace in worshipping the Elders for so long. Old legends are like old friends. We keep our old feelings for them, and we're glad when they revisit us through the years."

"But even old friends can stay too long and exhaust their welcome," Pahana said. "We would all be better off if the Elders had never returned from the skies. But such is not the case, and such thoughts don't help. All we can do is survive. No, let me correct that. I am too proud to be satisfied with merely surviving a war. I must win!"

Atira edged herself closer and touched her grandson on the knee. "I often feel I am standing on the bank of a river, watching you swim against the current while gators attack! I wish you would let me help."

"Plans are already in motion," Pahana said. "I'll ask for your help when its necessary. In the meantime, just believe in me the way you believe in the Gods."

"Very well," Atira conceded. "When will you be leaving?"

"Today," Pahana said.

"For how long"

"As long as is necessary," Pahana replied. "I'll likely return before the full moon."

"And if we're attacked during that time?" she asked.

"Calian is a fine strategic leader," Pahana said. "He has Aholi to advise him. And of course, there's you and T'Soona and wise Manabazo and my mother. You'll maintain until I return."

Atira pushed herself to her feet and her knees creaked. "There's nothing more I can say. I wish you success on your enigmatic journey. Despite our disagreements, I love you very much. Be safe, and I hope to see you again soon."

"Goodbye, Grandmother. Don't despair. Our race is not yet run."

The troubled Atira left the Shakowin hall and slowly made her way back to her chambers, resenting the ladders that made her knees ache. Absent-mindedly, she walked back into her cliff hollow. Her longtime companion T'Soona was dozing on their bed of hay, feathers, and animal skins. He had been more than a friend for so long, and she cherished him, despite her unwillingness to ever commit to anyone else other than her lost Yana-Luha.

The amiable T'Soona was sixty-eight summers old but had a youthful face that belied his years. Atira often commented on how much younger he looked than she did. He awoke when she entered and smiled at her. He quickly realized, however, that her mood was not a bright one.

"You seem to be having a discontented day, my sweet," T'Soona said. "You wear your gloomy face. Sit and tell me your thoughts."

She was always impressed with how well T'Soona could read her moods. She sat with him in their bed. "Make me laugh, T'Soona. I would like to laugh again. There's less laughter in Shipapa-Lina these days. Make me smile, dearest T'Soona. You're the one who could always make me laugh."

He ran his hand through her hair. "I think you've given me a daunting task, my sweet," he said. "When you're in a forlorn vein, it's harder to find a laugh in you than it is to find a precious stone in the ground. What's troubling you?"

"I fear the storm that's coming," she said. "I can't escape the feeling that we're overmatched this time. So many enemies, and Hayoka is so full of hate. And those children of his frighten me. Manabazo once told us the omens of doom had appeared, and the Spider Women predict we will fall. I lack confidence, and the fact that Pahana is being so vague with his mysterious schemes does nothing to ease my mind. And it isn't only me. I feel it all over Shipapa-Lina. There's fear. Fear which grows as fast as Hayoka's vast army."

"Fear can be both our friend and our enemy," T'Soona said. "It can keep us alive."

"I suppose," she said. "But life was good before all the fear."

"There's no good or bad in life, sweet Atira," he said. "There's just life. It's how we react to it that makes us happy or fearful."

She managed a weak smile. "You have a unique courage that I have always admired."

"I'm a rock of courage ... sometimes," he said. "Other times I have rocks in my skull. But I refuse to live in fear of the son of Hobomok. I never liked the son, and I hated the father. Perhaps I'm stubborn or predictable, but I will laugh in the face of Hayoka, just as I did to Hobomok. If I die laughing, there are many worse ways to pass from this world, wouldn't you agree?"

"Dear, precious T'Soona. It's only you that keeps me sane. Thank you."

"You never need to thank me," he said. "You owe me nothing. I'm a part of you. I ever shall be."

Atira lay down at his side and took his hand. "Let's just lay here for a while, T'Soona. Just you and I alone. The world doesn't have to exist for the next few hours. Not if we choose to ignore it for a while."

"My feelings precisely," he said.

A companionable quiet and the reassuring feeling of another hand in hers allowed Atira to find some much needed peace and comfort.

CHAPTER ELEVEN

The people of Kolhu greeted their new leader Kia with enthusiastic gratitude for her protection. She returned from her battle with the Enemy Way's armies, exuding calm confidence. None of them had ever seen a shaman as powerful as Kia, and her presence gave them hope. She acknowledged them with a regal wave but said nothing.

She entered the Sun Dagger House, the largest structure of the city, where the rulers of Kolhu have long resided. She had come here as a child to master her natural-born mystic powers and eventually surpassed her teacher Molowia. Since Molowia had no children, she chose the granddaughter of her missing brother Yana-Luha as her successor.

Kia walked into the living chamber of her mentor Molowia, who had now seen more than seventy summers. The venerable Molowia had been ill for many months, suffering from a weak heart after years of stress. She lay in her bed of grass and animal furs, being attended to by the devoted Wuti. Young Wuti utterly worshipped Molowia and spent many hours at her bedside. Molowia, who was dozing, became alert when Kia entered.

"What happened?" Molowia asked in a strained voice. "Are the enemy...?"

"They have withdrawn," she said. "Don't fear, Cacique. How do you feel today?"

Molowia shook her head. "I'm not the Cacique of Kolhu any longer. You are."

"You'll always be my Cacique," Kia replied as she kneeled at Molowia's bedside. "Are you feeling stronger today?"

"No," Molowia replied. "I feel weaker every day. My time in this world is nearly done."

"Don't say that, holy one!" Wuti cried. "You won't die."

"You think too well of me," Molowia softly answered. "My magic can't defeat the scourge of age. It will soon be time for me to join Morning Star and my other ancestors. Don't fret, Wuti. I'm at peace with it. This world has no further use for me. Perhaps I'll find new purpose in the world beyond this one."

"Can I do anything for you?" Kia asked.

"Just take care of my people," Molowia said. "I'll rest better knowing Kolhu is well protected. I've devoted my entire life to safeguarding this place. I trust you to do the same."

"You know I will, Cacique," Kia said. "Be assured that Kolhu is defended."

Wuti wiped Molowia's brow. "You should sleep now, holy one."

Molowia nodded, rolled over, and closed her eyes. Kia rose and left the room. She walked to the Cacique's ruling chamber and lit a fire in a small kiva. She sat cross-legged and levitated off the ground.

Kia knew about the Breathing Shaman and the women of the Valley of the Blue Mists, having had experience with them when she was quite young. She had a personal vendetta against them and was prepared for the day she would do battle with them. She also had a familiarity with the stiff-legged bear beasts, having defeated them once in Shipapa-Lina. And Atahsaia the cannibal demon was no longer a threat, thanks to Wishpoosh. But she wanted to know more about the Wampus Cat. She had heard many whispered rumors about the frightening children of Hayoka. These three young creatures were the offspring of the Kachina witch Dagwona and Hayoka, who is possessed by the Coyote spirit. What kind of powers did this terrible trio have, and how well have they been trained to use their power aggressively? She needed to know.

Tossing some powder into the fire, she chanted with alternating volume and pitch. After several minutes, she was able to bypass the walls of the material world. Distance and physical barriers meant nothing to her now. She stretched her astral form beyond the Land of Everlasting Summer and across Ulah-Nane. Wherever the ruthless children of Hayoka were, Kia would find them.

Her all-seeing perception led her spirit-form to a terrible scene miles away. A Navajo hunting party had the misfortune of coming upon Hayoka's group, returning to the Bitter Root Valley. Stikini the Owl-Man was attacking.

The savage creature circled around the group, swirling like one of his mother's whirlwinds. He clawed, pecked, bit, and rammed the unsuspecting Navajo. The monster was relentless, and not one Navajo escaped its fury. Only one survived. Hayoka watched with fatherly pride as his child devastated a team of armed warriors. Even the Puk-Wudjies seemed intimidated by what they were seeing.

After slaughtering most of the group, Stikini was prepared to kill the final man, but Hayoka gestured for his son to stop. The flying creature reluctantly halted, clearly wanting to claim his last victim.

Atop his moose, Hayoka trotted to the wounded survivor. His shadow fell over the bloodied Navajo. Hayoka was all smiles as he looked down at the helpless hunter. The man looked up fearfully, afraid the massive moose would crush him.

"You seem a bit anxious," he said to the wounded man. "Afraid to die? Believe me, there are far worse things my son could inflict on you than death."

"Your...son?" the man said in a trembling voice.

Hayoka pointed to Stikini. "Yes, this is my boy. Can't you see the resemblance? He's still rather young, so he's overly gentle and good-natured, but he's learning to be more hard-hearted as he grows. I'm confident he'll make me proud in his future bloodletting. He clearly gets better each massacre. You've had the honor of witnessing his next stage of development. You're welcome."

The man was silent, perplexed and horrified. His blood flowed quicker as his heart pumped faster. Hayoka was not moved by the blood or the fear. His smug expression showed that he was satisfied with what he was seeing.

"I'm giving you another honor, little man," Hayoka said. "No need for gratitude. You may live to tell all Ulah-Nane what you saw here today. Let every living soul know about the power and ferocity of my three children. The children of Hayoka, who will avenge their mother. My offspring will destroy the Itiwana, and any other tribe who even thinks about helping them will suffer the same pitiful fate as your friends here. Make certain that every tribe knows this. Don't help Shipapa-Lina or Kolhu, lest they find themselves on the unpleasant end of our wrath."

Without another word, Hayoka and his mount trotted away, followed by his bird-like child. The slightly unnerved Puk-Wudjies followed behind, heading back to their valley. The wounded man was left alive to stagger back to his nearby village.

Kia lost contact with her mystic vision, having allowed her emotion to destroy her focus. Not only was she disgusted and appalled by the horrid violence she had witnessed, but Kia was also faced with her own complicity. It was her, along with Naya-Nazgani, who turned Hayoka onto his path of revenge.

It's too late for regrets, she thought. *What's occurred in the past is unalterable. I must focus on the future. For the present, I need to learn more about Hayoka's terrible brood. Where is the third child he spoke of? What is the other child capable of?*

Resuming her ritual, she sent her spirit-form far across the plains and hills of Ulah-Nane, homing in on an eerie, unsettling power far away. She found herself in the vast region known as the Big Sand. The ominous, arid landscape was mostly silent except for an occasional wind.

Kia spotted a small band of wanderers known as the Half Moon Walkers, who traveled to various locations searching for peyote. They had come to the desert hoping to find the substance, which they traded with local tribes who need the substance for vision-quest rituals. The men seemed in good spirits, having come across a certain type of cactus which was essential in their trade.

Kia spotted another figure emerging from a cloud of windblown desert sand. The sand didn't seem to bother this being at all. The newly arrived figure walked directly toward the Half Moon Walkers with a measured tread.

The stranger was a sickly, thin female, with wrinkled, yellow skin. She looked to be ancient but gave the impression of youthful power and vigor. Her hair, half black and half gray, blew across her skeletal face, black lips, greenish teeth, and watery silver eyes. The strange woman was adorned in the hide of a desert bighorn sheep. It adhered to her body due to the sticky silk of the tarantula.

The Half Moon Walkers didn't spot her until she was very close. The leader of the group, Blowsnake, stepped forward to address her, despite his apprehension of her appearance. "We greet you, woman of the desert. It's unusual to meet someone wandering these dunes. Can we be of assistance to you?"

The withered woman spoke with a voice that was both croaky and high-pitched at the same time. "What is birthed in my domain belongs to me and no one else."

"What do you mean?" Blowsnake asked. "No one can claim the Big Sand as their domain. We have collected and traded peyote for many seasons. We have no wish to argue, but we do not recognize your rulership here. Who are you, old woman?"

The woman walked closer to them with a menacing mien. "I am Skadega-Muth. This place is my realm, the Desert of Death, and everything here belongs to me. You do not have my permission to take the peyote, nor do you have permission to be in my realm. There is nothing here for you but death!"

"Do not threaten us, woman!" Blowsnake shouted. "We..."

"Die!" Skadega-Muth bellowed wrathfully. More than angry sound came from her mouth. A green cloud of dense, toxic fumes spit from her thin, ebony lips. The cloud spread in mere moments and quickly enveloped the Half Moon Walkers. They began coughing, gasping, and then choking. Their skin immediately became pale and developed red pustules. Their tongues turned black, and their hair suddenly fell out in clumps. They dropped to the ground, clearly suffering. Within a minute, their suffering had stopped, as had their hearts.

The astral form of Kia watched with horrified revulsion as these innocent men died a ghastly death. She wished she could have done something to save them. She knew she should have tried, but she had had no idea of the power Skadega-Muth possessed. By the time she realized the dark energy she was faced with, she had no time to think up a workable spell, especially given her distance from the scene. *Unspeakable!* she thought.

Looking down coldly at the numerous diseased corpses, Skadega-Muth was clearly admiring her efficiency. She stepped over the bodies with no visible remorse. She took a few steps but then stopped. To Kia's astonishment, Skadega-Muth turned her withered head and stared directly at Kia's astral form. Since her spiritual form was invisible, incorporeal, and silent, no one should have been able to perceive Kia's visitation.

"Now you see the power I possess," Skadega-Muth said. "I am hatred. I am fear. I am death and worse than death. Call me vengeance. Call me your future. I am as inevitable as your guilty conscience. Accept death and perish as you deserve. I will see the Itiwana die!"

Stunned and shaken by the intimidating woman's inexplicable ability to see her astral form, Kia couldn't think of anything to say in response. Kia's astral form vanished.

She returned to her own body, back in Kolhu. Kia sat with a slack jaw, unable to comprehend how anyone other than a Sky Elder could conceivably see the astral form of a shaman.

What sort of otherworldly nightmare did Hayoka and his vile bride give birth to?

CHAPTER TWELVE

"Fear is a wonderful tool, my boy," Hayoka said cheerfully, proud of his day's work. Still atop his large moose, he was riding back to the Valley of the Blue Mists. He had parted ways with the Puk-Wudjies, who marched back to the Bitter Root Valley. His son, Stikini the Owl-Man, soared freely over his head, circling as if he owned the skies. Hayoka spoke to Stikini, although the Owl-Man was so high up, it was doubtful he could hear a word his father was saying.

"A sufficient dose of fear can be as useful in war as 100 arrows," Hayoka explained. "You make me very proud. Events are unfolding in a propitious manner. Soon, the world shall do what we want, when we want, for our reasons. I've planned this out too perfectly for it to fail. And as long as I continue to withhold the information the Winter

96

Elders need, they'll continue to support our offensive. My mission is just, and my plan is perfect. Your mother will be avenged."

He looked up to enjoy the aerial exuberance of his winged child. He wished he could also have the freedom of flying. He was sure Stikini would be valuable in his revenge schemes.

"We should be back at the Valley of the Blue Mists fairly soon, son," Hayoka commented. "While it's auspicious that the shaman sisters allow us to reside with them in the House of Many Hands, we need to watch them closely. They're wary of you and your sibling. I think they might be fearful of you. The sisters have joined us due to their fiery desire for revenge against the wrong they perceive Calian has done to them. And by that, I mean what I effectively convinced them Calian has done. Still, it's advisable to keep our wits about us. Everyone is leery of you three. Your power is intimidating, especially that of Skadega-Muth. Your sister is quite formidable. Even I sometimes get a chill when I see what she is capable of. So wonderfully lethal. She and you and the Wampus Cat will cause chaos the likes of which the Itiwana have never imagined, even in their worst nightmare. I am quite eager to see it. In fact, I think I should let you children loose, just to see the destruction and instill more fear in Shipapa-Lina and Kolhu. Yes, I think that would be entertaining. Quite entertaining."

A light rain created muddy puddles in the Mystic Moon Mountains, which World Giant stomped through with his heavy tread. Pahana sat regally upon his mount, ignoring the wet weather. His busy brain was occupied with far more important matters than comfort, especially since his nature as the son of a former Winter Sky Elder meant that the cold did not affect him at all.

Pahana had ridden this path many times, despite the fact that his absences from Shipapa-Lina were a source of anger from his grandmother. She didn't know his plans; nor did she know many other things about Pahana's secret life away from the Itiwana.

Before he could see the grass hut of Eithinoa, he spotted the head of Gah-Oh the giant, ever on guard atop Kuwahi Mountain. The giant was unflaggingly loyal to the Earth Mother. He was a proven, unquestionable ally to their cause.

When he reached the top of the mountain, he got a better look at what Gah-Oh was doing and who he was accompanied by. The giant was in the process of training a young man in close quarters combat. Gah-Oh swung a tree carved into a twenty-foot tapered pole called a caber, while the young man held a staff and mimicked the giant's movements.

"August Gah-Oh commends thy continued improvement, young one," the colossus said. "Truly thou art blessed as much as thy majestic parents themselves."

Pahana came close enough to see the very familiar form of the youth Gah-Oh was training. At the age of seventeen summers, the young man had wavy, light brown hair, just like his mother's lustrous mane. His skin was tan and beige, with a solid, sinewy frame. The lad was uncommonly handsome, with a firm jaw and a winsome smile. His name was Gluskap.

Watching with satisfaction, Pahana saw how smooth and confident Gluskap was becoming with his combat moves. His physical conditioning was superb, and he was a highly intelligent young man.

Gluskap noticed the stoic man nearby, dismounting his bison. He immediately ceased his combat exercise and rushed to greet the new arrival. "Hello, Father."

"Hello, son," Pahana said. "You're learning well. I'm pleased with your progress."

"Your approval is something I prize most highly, Father," Gluskap said.

Holding his spear Dragonfly horizontally like a staff, Pahana took a defensive stance. "Attack me."

"As you wish," Gluskap replied, moving into an aggressive pose.

Utilizing his staff with deft skill, he began an attack upon his father. His staff moved with impressive speed. Pahana, a consummate veteran, was able to parry every blow, but just barely. Taking advantage of an opening, Pahana swung the blunt end of Dragonfly and made contact with Gluskap's shoulder, knocking the lad off balance. Pahana kicked out, smashing his foot against Gluskap's stomach, forcing him backwards. Gluskap stumbled back several feet before he regained stable footing.

"Nicely played, Father," Gluskap said.

Lowering the Dragonfly to indicate that the fight was over, Pahana tapped his own forehead. "You're quite good, but it will be some time before you can match what I have in this brain."

"I'm humbled," Gluskap said, rubbing his shoulder.

"Continue with Gah-Oh," Pahana said. "I'll be with your mother."

Entering the aromatic grass hut of the Earth Mother as if he were quite accustomed to entering there at will, Pahana tossed the Dragonfly to the ground. "I'm back."

The sacred Earth Mother was kneeling, holding a small bird with an injured wing. Focused with deep concentration, the divine woman managed to heal the bird's damaged wing. She tossed the feathered creature, who flew past Pahana and out of the hut. She smiled warmly at Pahana.

"In affection, I am blissful to see you," Eithinoa said. "In divulgence, I have missed you greatly."

She kissed Pahana with all the passion of an ancient Earth Goddess. "In melancholy, I say your visits are far too infrequent."

Pahana let his dispassionate stoicism slip as he beamed with deep fondness. "It's always a pleasure to return to you. Your voice lightens my soul. I see our son has been diligent in his training."

"In honesty, I say it is Gah-Oh who has been his constant mentor," Eithinoa replied. "In pride, I say Gluskap exceeds our loftiest expectancies."

"I've seen him," Pahana said. "He is doing very well. However, very well is not well enough. I think I may need to take over his training personally. Not to impugn Gah-Oh."

"In mirth, I confess I enjoy your hunt for perfection," Eithinoa said.

"I intend to personally make Gluskap better than perfect," Pahana stated.

Eithinoa looked excited. "In joy, I ask if you are planning to live here with us?"

Pahana resumed his stoic demeanor and shook his head. "I wish to take him back to Shipapa-Lina with me."

The serene face of Eithinoa became gloomy. She stepped back from Pahana, as if she suddenly felt she didn't want to touch him. "In joylessness, I find you have come to take my son away."

"Don't think of it that way," Pahana said. "Understand that our son has a great destiny. You once said so yourself. He is vital in matters larger than the three of us. Gluskap will be needed in the final battle of the war against the winter forces, and if he is to survive—if all of us are to survive—I must take him with me. There are so many things he'll need to know that he can't learn here."

A dejected Eithinoa paced the hut with her head down. "In cheerlessness, I had hoped this day wouldn't come. In reminder, I cannot leave the Mystic Moon Mountains. In truth, I will miss Gluskap greatly if he should leave here."

Pahana came closer, but she pulled away. "Don't be difficult, Eithinoa. I know you love him deeply and he gives you happiness in your isolated home here. But we have discussed this. The time must be now. He should learn from myself and Manabazo and Calian."

She spun to face him with resolve. "In consequence, I ask about what I am capable of teaching him. What of the storm dance?"

"Pinga can surely teach him that," Pahana argued.

"In forcefulness, I say that I have already taught this skill to him," Eithinoa loudly proclaimed.

"Have you, indeed?" Pahana asked, his interest peaked. "This I must witness."

The chieftain marched outside, followed by the sad-faced Eithinoa. "Gluskap, attend!" he ordered.

"Always at your command, Father," Gluskap said.

"The Storm Dance," Pahana said. "Show me."

Gluskap seemed surprised. "Mother told me to be cautious about using this power. She said..."

"Do it now!" Pahana commanded, leaving no room for argument.

Gluskap looked to his mother, who gave him a slight, reluctant nod. "If that's your wish, I obey," the young man said.

With some assistance from Gah-Oh, who knocked his caber against a tree to create a steady drumbeat, Gluskap began to dance in a circle with specific hand and foot movements. He chanted as he danced, focusing all his concentration on the sky.

Patiently, Pahana watched as the minutes passed. At first, nothing happened. He looked back at Eithinoa, who was seated cross-legged on the grass. "Is he doing this properly?"

"In counsel, I say you need to be patient," the Earth Goddess said.

Pahana accepted her advice and silently watched. It was several minutes later that he noticed the clouds rolling in and the wind increasing. "Ah, now it begins. Excellent."

The sky became oppressively dark as the wind roared with power. A clap of thunder was heard as a light rain began. The rain increased steadily over the following minutes, and flashes of thunder lit the dim sky.

Soon, a torrential downpour crated deep puddles and thunder echoed. Gluskap pointed at a rock, and seconds afterward, a bolt of lightning struck that very same rock, charring it severely. The bison, World Giant, was startled by the blast. Gluskap pointed again, and lightning struck the ground where he had indicated. Pahana watched with satisfaction, impressed at the show of power.

"That's enough!" Pahana yelled over the wind. "Stop the storm."

Eithinoa spoke loudly to be heard over the ambient noise. "In wisdom, I say that the storm will not stop until it has satisfied its primal wrath.

In caution, I say this is why I advise our son not to utilize this power unnecessarily."

"I see," the chieftain said. "Gluskap, do you have the power I inherited from my mother? Have you mastered the cold?"

Gluskap looked somewhat embarrassed. "I'm trying, Father."

Kneeling over a puddle being pelted with raindrops, he put a finger in. After a minute of concentration, part of the puddle froze. However, he couldn't freeze the whole puddle. "I'm sorry, that's the best I can manage."

"As I expected," Pahana said. "You have many lessons ahead of you. Let us three go into the hut and discuss matters. I apologize to you, Gah-Oh, for the discomfort this storm might cause you."

Gah-Oh looked up and let out a boisterous laugh. "Mountainous Gah-Oh fears no storm. Let the wonderous rain fall."

While Eithinoa and Gluskap went inside the grass hut, Pahana led World Giant underneath a tree. "Apologies, my friend. It was necessary. Stay here."

Inside the hut, Eithinoa was explaining to Gluskap that he needn't blame himself for any storm damage. "In maternal pride, I say you did as you were told and did it well."

Pahana interrupted her. "You've taught him well, dear Eithinoa. This is a strong storm. I commend you. Well done. Still, he must learn things you cannot help him with. He must come to Shipapa-Lina."

Gluskap became energized with eagerness. "Am I to accompany you to Shipapa-Lina?"

"That is what we're attempting to decide," Pahana explained.

"I have wanted to see your village for so long," Gluskap cried with enthusiasm.

Both Pahana and Eithinoa saw the excitement in their son's face when he talked of leaving the mountain.

"In realization, I see that I may have been selfish," the Earth Goddess said.

"What do you mean, Mother? You aren't selfish."

"In truth, I am," she responded. "In selfishness, I have thought only of how I cherish you and want you to stay here with me. In foolishness, I was not thinking of what is best for my child. In truth, you need to see the world outside the Mystic Moon Mountains."

Gluskap gestured with boyish energy. "Yes, I want to see everything. I..."

Stopping mid-sentence, Gluskap looked sadly at his mother. Pahana noticed his change of demeanor. "What's troubling you, son?" Pahana asked.

"Because Mother can't come with us," he said sadly. "Her physical form can't exist outside the Mystic Moon Mountains."

"This is an unfortunate truth," Pahana said. "This is why I live in two worlds: here and Shipapa-Lina. I love your mother, but I have a duty to my people as their chieftain. And as much as my heart longs to stay here with the two of you, I have a greater duty. And you do, as well."

"But I can't leave Mother alone," Gluskap protested.

Pahana was surprised when Eithinoa spoke up. "In acceptance, I say you must. In truthfulness, greatness grows inside you. In reassurance, I will not be alone here, as long as loyal Gah-Oh and the Sasquatches and my animal friends remain. In fact, I will be perfectly fine here. In realization, you must go!"

"But..." Gluskap began.

"In authority, I call on you to mind my words," she insisted. "In faith, you will dishonor me if you forsake your higher purpose for my benefit."

"Your mother is wise," Pahana said. "We will still visit her, just as I've always visited her."

Gluskap took his mother's hand tenderly. "Do you truly want me to go, Mother?"

"In obligation, I say what we want is unimportant," she said. "In truth, what we must do is now at hand. In bluntness, I say you must go, even if it makes you sad to leave."

"I will always honor your words, Mother," Gluskap said. "If you and Father advise me to go, then I will leave this place. But I will miss you."

"In motherly love, I say I will think of you constantly," Eithinoa said. "In tenderness, I say I love you, too. In pride, I predict you'll do great things."

Gluskap had a tear in his eye. Eithinoa wiped it away. "In remembrance, I recall you crying when the deer you called Little Horn died. In truth, I would not have you weep any less for me."

Pahana put a hand on Gluskap's shoulder. "Go now, Gluskap. Take whatever keepsakes you want and say your goodbyes to Gah-Oh. I will join you in short order."

Eithinoa nodded to indicate that the boy should obey his father. Gluskap kissed her on her forehead. "Goodbye, Mother."

Gluskap left, not wanting to cry in front of his father. Eithinoa could no longer restrain her tears and they flowed freely. Pahana hugged her.

"In anguish, I dared to have some happiness in my life," she said. "In sorrow, I now watch that happiness walk away."

"Don't grieve, sweet lady," he said. "We'll be back. Both of us. And one day, when we win this cursed war, I will return here permanently. And when I do, I pray you will still love me and accept me as your man. This place will be the peaceful home for the both of us. That is the dream I have."

Eithinoa sobbed. "In honesty, I wish for that above all things."

Pahana kissed her again. "I am tortured at the thought of parting from you, but I must."

Eithinoa sat down cross-legged and closed her eyes. "In grimness, I sit to meditate. In explanation, I will close my eyes so I do not see you leave. In bluntness, when I open them, please be gone."

Eithinoa closed her green eyes and Pahana took a moment to admire her. He quietly left the hut, wishing she could come with him.

Outside, Gluskap had made his goodbyes with the giant and Pahana led him to World Giant. They climbed on the big animal's back, and Pahana took his son away from the only home he had known for seventeen seasons, taking him to a much more dangerous place.

CHAPTER THIRTEEN

They'll need this when the next battle comes, Naya-Nazgani thought as he repaired the ladder.

The ladder system was valuable for the people of Shipapa-Lina to access the various levels of the cliff housing, especially during an attack. This particular ladder was broken during the recent scramble to get the non-combatants away from Hayoka and his Puk-Wudjies. Naya-Nazgani had settled in Shipapa-Lina years before and was now a valuable asset to the Itiwana.

As he mended the ladder, Faw-Faw sat nearby, studying a butterfly which had landed on his huge hand. Faw-Faw had barely changed over the years since he'd come to Shipapa-Lina. Like the trees he and his people, the Wood Men, worshipped, he seemed to be perennially strong and sturdy.

Faw-Faw had bonded with Naya-Nazgani over time. Perhaps the odd friendship was formed because the two powerful men didn't age the way others did, creating a kinship due to their mutual unchanging nature. Or perhaps it was because they were frequently used as the main muscle of the Two-Horn Riders and the pair often fought side-by-side against the Enemy Way.

After having been a lone wanderer for so long, Naya-Nazgani had gotten to like being part of a tribe. He had made several friends and found a sense of purpose, camaraderie, and family in the Land of Everlasting Summer. But he also had one special interest that kept him there above all other things. One intense notion filled his mind with the kind of thoughts he had not indulged since his wife died, all those seasons ago.

He gazed longingly upward at the Cliff Palace and saw Pinga making her way down. Her flawless, lustrous form seemed to almost drift down the upper ladder. She wore a two-piece, white rabbit fur garb, with her naval uncovered. Naya-Nazgani was fixated on her graceful movements and the way the breeze blew her snow-white tresses. She reached the level with the broken ladder and looked down, irked by the inconvenience.

"There was a time when This One would have floated like a feather on the wind to the ground below," Pinga said. "Sadly, she can no longer do so. Is there another way down?"

"Being of service is always an honor," Naya-Nazgani said. "Please permit me."

The tall monster hunter lifted his strapping arms. With a bemused grin, she crouched and Naya-Nazgani clutched Pinga around her slender waist with his sizable, calloused hands. He effortlessly lifted her off the upper level and placed her with delicate gentleness onto the grass. He had never touched her before and so savored the moment.

"This One thanks you for the transportation, good warrior," Pinga said with a coy titter. "If she should need lifting again, she will most surely avail herself of your muscle."

Naya-Nazgani bowed. "I'm your steadfast servant, good lady."

"This One is comforted to hear that," Pinga said with a genial grin. "Hello, Faw-Faw. It's good to see you."

Big Faw-Faw held out his hands with the butterfly, as if he were offering it as a gift or tribute to the stunning Goddess. She waved away the offering.

"Very kind, but she could not possibly accept," Pinga stated. "Your tiny friend seems happy to remain with you. She will leave you both to your work now. Pleasant morning, warriors."

As Pinga departed in her graceful, fluid fashion, Naya-Nazgani watched her admiringly. *She's majestic, beautiful, and as ageless as I myself am. Could there be a more perfect woman for me?*

Pinga seemed to be walking with purpose, but then she stopped and looked out in the distance. She seemed like she was expecting something or someone. Naya-Nazgani wondered if he should join her to ask if she needed some assistance. He felt it might be too forward but kept his eyes on her as he worked.

Then he saw who she was waiting for. The tiny silhouettes of two men on a buffalo came closer. Pinga had somehow sensed their approach and clearly wanted to be there to meet these people. Naya-Nazgani was able to identify the huge bison, World Giant, and the chalky white rider. Pahana had returned. *But who's that with him?*

While Pinga drifted forward to greet her son, another bison came from the north. It was Calian, who was on sentry duty atop his mount, Walking Storm. Naya-Nazgani debated inserting himself into the conversation but decided to let it stay within the family. "Come along, Faw-Faw. We're done here. Let's find some trouble to get into."

She loved that deathly smell. Skadega-Muth looked into the lethal green cloud she had spit from her chapped, pitch-black lips. As it dispersed, it revealed the remains of her newest victims. A pack of desert foxes and the group of long-toothed rats they had been chasing all got caught in the toxic mist. Only a minute ago, they had been alive. Now their emaciated, rotting husks were emitting a putrid smell in the air of the Desert of Death.

Skadega-Muth looked emotionlessly down at the decimated remains. Kicking some of them aside, she knelt in the center of the slain bodies. Touching the sand, she chanted under her foul breath. Even the sand seemed to lose its color and turn pale white underneath her.

From out of that very sand came a being that would chill the soul of most mortals. It rose like a tall tree, casting an ominous shadow over Skadega-Muth. This horrifying creature had the shaggy body of an ape and a human skull for a head. Its eyes were balls of blue fire. Crowning its skull were antlers covered with maggots. The air became cold.

"These sacrifices are for you, mighty Taxet," Skadega-Muth said with unemotional respect, and foggy breath came from her mouth due to the chilled air.

Taxet, the God of death, looked down at the sacrifices and spoke in a moaning, eerie echoing voice. "Glorious death. Beautiful death. Only death makes the great Taxet content. Only death matters. Life is an affront to the peace of death. There can never be sufficient death. More death is always desirable. Your offerings of death please me."

Taxet inhaled, and wraith-like forms were drawn out of the bodies of dead animals, as if the death God was sucking out their souls. He breathed them in. Taxet then snatched up the carrion with wrinkled, leathery fingers and shoved the physical remains down his throat. "Death is divine. Death is delicious. Nothing tastes better than death."

"Then may I have my next lesson?" Skadega-Muth asked.

The death God belched out an appreciative grunt of agreement. "You honor death, so death will honor you. Those who bring death are blessed. You are a student of death. Death has much to teach you."

"Thank you, mighty Taxet," Skadega-Muth said. "Whatever you teach me will be used to bring magnificent death to Ulah-Nane. I will offer you legions of sacrifices. The afterlife will soon overflow with the offerings I will provide. Hail death!"

The Shakowin had assembled once again in the ruling chamber of the Cliff Palace. Pinga stood near the newly installed Shakowin members, Calian and Aholi. Atira sat in the place of the tribal elder, and T'Soona was in attendance as the Medicine Man. Pahana was in the chieftain's seat, with the Dragonfly on one side and a white rabbit on his other. This harmless looking rabbit was Manabazo in one of his many animal forms.

Standing to the side, Gluskap watched and listened with extreme unease. He was the reason for this meeting and the source of the conflict. It was an awkward and uncomfortable introduction to a new culture.

Atira seemed to be the angriest of all. She spoke with a loud and disrespectful tone to the chieftain, knowing she could get away with it, being his grandmother. "This defies belief! You gather us to say that you've been leading a secret life all these seasons? That all your mysterious absences have been dalliances on a mountaintop and that you have a son. And you deliberately kept this from us."

"You sum it up rather succinctly," Pahana said. "But why so hostile? I'm introducing you to your great-grandson. Have you nothing welcoming to say?"

"You may be chieftain, but don't mock me!" she snapped back. "I'm still your grandmother, and I am also your advisor. You will listen to my words!"

"I'm listening to every word, Grandmother," Pahana said calmly. "Be assured that I value your opinion above all others."

"And yet you didn't trust me enough to tell me, or any of us, about your other life?" she asked.

"I am not obliged to tell you of my private and personal matters," Pahana insisted. "I am chieftain, the son of Tawa."

"And I am the mother of Tawa!" she yelled. "I raised him to be a great chieftain, and he hid nothing from me. He surely would not have lived a secret life, hidden from his people! Wouldn't you agree, Pinga?"

Pinga seemed reluctant to take sides in the argument, but she nodded in agreement with Atira. "Tawa had no secrets from This One. She shared full honesty and intimacy with him at all times."

"Of course, Mother," Pahana said. "He was your faithful husband, but I have no wife, faithful or otherwise. I therefore have no reason to discuss my intimacy with anyone."

"You never brought home a potential heir to the Kik-Mongwi before," T'Soona said. "That's something new."

Manabazo chimed in. "I must agree with the rest. Some honest disclosure would have been best."

Aholi raised his hand to get the group's attention. "Perhaps it is not my place to speak on this matter..."

"Say what you wish to say," Pahana told him. "I won't hold any malice toward you."

"Respectfully, Kik-Mongwi," Aholi said with proper deference, "the tribe will be...uncomfortable with this. This will stir the memory of how you once welcomed Hayoka in as a friend. The arrival of another stranger, particularly one who is in the position to become your successor, will not be received well."

"He's correct," Atira said. "It will be as difficult for the tribe to accept this as it is for those of us in this room. We need to step cautiously. I suggest you take your son back to his home in the Mystic Moon Mountains while we consider this unexpected situation and explain it to the tribe. He can return at a later time."

Gluskap fidgeted nervously, feeling responsible for this outpouring of anger against Pahana.

They all seemed united against him, except for the man called Calian, who remained silent.

Pahana looked over his Shakowin counsel. His face was an impassive, unreadable mask. The silence was uncomfortable while they awaited his response. Finally, Pahana addressed them.

"I respect your honesty and understand your concerns," he said. "Your advice is valuable to me. But I am chieftain, and it is I who makes the final decision. My decision was made long before my son took his first step. I believe he is the descendant of Morning Star who will lead our people in the final battle. He will remain here to be trained by myself, and I charge all of you with assisting in his education. That is my final word."

Atira rose angrily. "Then this meeting is over. Obviously, nothing we have to say matters."

After Atira left in a stormy rage, T'Soona followed. "I'm with her. I'm always with her."

Pinga spoke softly into her son's ear. "This One thinks we should speak of this alone."

Aholi tapped Calian on the shoulder. "Perhaps we should leave as well."

"Agreed," Calian said.

When they were gone, Pahana gestured toward his son. "Wait for me in the adjoining chamber, would you, Gluskap."

"Of course, Father" Gluskap said, bowing his head slightly and backing out of the chamber.

Manabazo hopped to the door. "I leave you now to talk to your mother. You have much to say to one another."

Once alone, Pahana leaned his chin on his fist. "What did you want to say, Mother?"

She folded her arms and walked in circles around his seat. "You tempt fate by acting alone. This One knows you are cunning, but not even you can outthink Malsumis and Hayoka and the entire Enemy Way on your own. She urges you to confide in us for the future."

"I will inform you all of my plans as we go," Pahana said. "You'll know when you need to know."

"This One is your mother," Pinga said. "Do you not trust her?"

Pahana stroked the Dragonfly with his finger. "It's not a matter of trust, Mother. It's an issue of judgment. You once made a foolish bargain with Malsumis. As for my grandmother, she disagrees with me too often, and I prefer to avoid the verbal battles. T'Soona and Aholi take nothing seriously. Manabazo vanishes from time-to-time when I need him. Calian worries too much about my safety. So, you see, it's not a matter of whom I trust. I have faith in all of you regarding your loyalty. But in judgment, you're all emotional. I can't allow sentiment or fear or other emotions to ruin my impeccably laid plans. That's why none of you will know what I need of you until it's too late for you to argue. And as for Gluskap, he is part of the prophecy and part of my plan. He will be valuable."

"Perhaps so," Pinga replied. "She will trust you. For now, This One would like to meet her grandson."

"Gluskap, come here!" Pahana yelled.

Young Gluskap dutifully responded to his father's summons. "I'm here."

Pahana gestured toward Pinga. "Gluskap, this is my mother. Your grandmother."

"I've heard so much about you," the young man said, with a deferential bow of his head.

"This One wishes she could say the same," Pinga replied. "Still, she welcomes you to Shipapa-Lina. You must forgive the Shakowin for their antagonism. It is a time of war, and we are all nervous and agitated. No doubt Pahana has told you of Hayoka and his incessant attacks upon us. We have become a cautious people. This is how we survive. This One apologizes to you."

Gluskap was relaxed by Pinga's soothing voice and kind words. "I didn't expect flowers and speeches. It's I who should apologize. I seem to have caused much upheaval among you."

"Ignore the Shakowin," Pahana said. "They'll obey my ruling. In time they'll see your qualities and accept you as my son and successor."

"Don't be presumptive, son," Pinga said. "This One reminds you that the Shakowin chooses the new Kik-Mongwi when the previous leader dies. It is not for you to proclaim Gluskap as your successor."

Pahana let a strange, knowing grin slip momentarily onto his face that quickly vanished. "My plan leaves nothing to chance, Mother. Trust me. Everything has been taken into account as I strategized for these many years. All will proceed as I need it to. In the meantime, I will begin to train Gluskap, and you must help me. He has considerable divine power which you can help him master. I've seen him do a storm dance, and it is spectacular."

"A storm dance is indeed a remarkable feat," she said. "You have a great power, Gluskap. But This One is not a teacher. Her abilities are natural and instinctive. Remember that she sent your sister to Molowia for training. There is little she can do for you."

"I remember everything," Pahana said. "I remember that it was you who began Kia's training with your words. Words of wisdom that only a Goddess could provide. I will impose on Kia to take up his training later. I told you; I have thought of everything."

"As you wish," Pinga said. "You are the chieftain, and This One trusts that your plan is as infallible as you claim. Let us begin, and may Awona'Wilona grant us success."

Pahana narrowed his eyes and held his hand over his chest. "Don't look to the Gods for success. Look to me!"

CHAPTER FOURTEEN

From the time Gluskap was introduced to the Itiwana, Aholi's prediction proved correct. There was doubt and division among the tribe members. Some worried about a stranger arriving to be inserted in the line of succession, because of the past situation with Hayoka and because they felt someone who wasn't born and raised in Shipapa-Lina should never be considered fit to wear the headdress of the Kik-Mongwi. Could an outsider have the deep devotion for Shipapa-Lina and its people that the chieftain should have?

Atira worried that this disruptive move by Pahana would erode confidence in the chieftain. His repetitive absences had already made people question him, and this was doing nothing to rebuild that trust. She felt this was the worst time for people to be having doubts. Her husband

Yana-Luha and her son Tawa commanded unquestioning faith among the Itiwana. Pahana could not make that claim. And what was she to make of this boy Gluskap? Suddenly she had a mostly grown great-grandson who she knew nothing about.

Pahana himself remained frequently cloistered in the Cliff Palace, either with Manabazo or by himself. He found time to train Gluskap in fighting and strategic thinking, as well as using his ice powers. When he was too busy, he charged his twin cousins Masewa and O'Yewa to pick up the slack in the combat training, and Pinga motivated Gluskap to feel his natural aptitudes.

Calian, as was his usual nature, kept a very close eye on Gluskap. Although his duties as the War Chief kept him occupied, he would not ignore any possible threat. He had been correct all those years ago about Hayoka, and even though this boy belonged to the bloodline of Morning Star, Calian would not let his guard down. He never did. That was what made him a great and loyal servant for the Itiwana people.

As for Gluskap himself, he worked constantly, desperate to prove himself to his father. When he was not undergoing multifarious training, he was familiarizing himself with the terrain of the Land of Everlasting Summer or learning how to ride a bison. He needed to choose his own bison mount. Advised by the twin brothers, he finally chose a strong, sturdy mount named Flying Courage. The animal was considerably smaller than World

Giant, but it had impressed everyone with speed and maneuverability that was impressive for a bison. Gluskap and his new mount were developing a natural rapport in a very short time. He seemed to learn everything very quickly, which pleased his father.

One afternoon, after overseeing Gluskap's lessons and inspecting the Two-Horn Riders, Pahana retreated to the Cliff Palace and secluded himself in the adobe chamber of the chieftain. He slumped wearily into his chair, finally allowing his body to show the tiredness that he hid from his people. He grasped the Dragonfly, which always seemed to give him a jolt of extra energy.

He closed his eyes for a moment, savoring the brief rest, when he was surprised by a sudden light and a sensation of energy that made the hairs on his arms stand at attention. After a moment of alarm, Pahana quickly realized what was happening and relaxed.

The astral form of his sister Kia materialized before him, looking equally noble and aloof as Pahana himself. Her vast powers still unnerved Pahana, even after all these years of witnessing her mystic miracles.

"I received your messenger crow," Kia said. "When I saw the twig it carried, I assumed you had something important to say, so I decided it would be more expedient to contact you this way rather than sending that poor, tired bird back to you."

"I should welcome you home, but you're not really here, are you?" Pahana said. "Such witchery makes the pleasantries difficult."

"We don't need such banalities between us, dear brother," Kia replied. "I'm glad you contacted me. I have some things to tell you, as well. But you can begin first. What troubles you?"

Pahana spent some considerable time filling Kia in on Gluskap, going all the way back to the day he was summoned to visit Eithinoa. He told the tale in as much detail as was necessary to give her the full picture. The image of Kia remained enigmatically silent, showing no reaction to this momentous news. Pahana could not determine what she was thinking. *She was always inscrutable.*

"And so, the facts are told," Pahana said. "Nothing is left to add. You've heard it all. I would know your mind on this."

The image of Kia seemed to blink away and flicker for a moment, as if she had momentarily lost her focus. Reestablishing her astral form, she glared at her brother and put her hands on her hips like a mother chiding a child. "You've been too clever for all our sakes. This complication is worrying."

"Explain your thoughts," Pahana responded.

"Your plots are dug deeper than tree roots, but you miss what's on the surface," Kia told him. "You worry about the prophecy that another descendant of Morning Star will lead the Itiwana in the final battle against the Enemy Way. Therefore, you created one. You now have a son who you think will be the one to lead in the final days. But you discount the inescapable fact that there is another direct blood descendant of Morning Star. You have dismissed the obvious answer. You have dismissed me! I am the descendant of Morning Star, and I am the one."

Pahana said nothing, meeting Kia's gaze. They looked into each other's eyes, and Kia was able to decipher his thoughts. Her eyes seemed to burn, as if lit up with fire.

"I see," she said. "You don't trust me to lead our armies."

"No, I don't," he said with blunt honesty. "You have unbelievable power, and you will surely be a vital part of our final offensive. But you have never led armies in battle. Your city of Kolhu does not even have a proper army. It's been left to you and mighty Wishpoosh to defend Kolhu. When the final battle comes, you'll no doubt focus your energies on protecting the defenseless people who rely on you. But it will be the formidable armies of Shipapa-Lina who lead the charge. It will be my people who stampede headlong into the storm of relentless battle, and they will need a skilled warrior at the forefront leading them. Someone they have faith in. Someone much like our father and our grandfather. Someone like me."

"But not like me?"

"No, not like you," he stated coldly. "You are not the one. The prophecy says we will fall in that battle. I believe that will happen if you are left to lead both Shipapa-Lina and Kolhu alone. But I plan to change fate. I have added an unexpected element. My son will bring us the victory that fate attempts to deny us."

Kia glowered at him silently for long time. When she finally spoke, her voice was saddened. "I've found the way your mind works. Your lack of faith in me is enormously painful, Pahana. Worse than a spear wound. But this goes beyond my feelings. You think you can outwit fate, and you hope to do it without consulting anyone. You want to change the future alone. I hope we'll all find you're truly as crafty as you think yourself to be. As for this son of yours, I hope he is as adept as you seem to think he is."

"You can help me with that," Pahana informed her. "He has learned the Storm Dance, but he has not mastered it. Perhaps you can help him with that."

Kia raised an eyebrow. "The Storm Dance, you say? I would see that for myself. I intend to see what this boy is capable of before I put my fate in his hands."

"Wisely said, sister," Pahana said. "I intend to test him further. I am contemplating arduous ordeals that will permit the lad to demonstrate his optimum qualities."

"I believe I have the answer to that," she said. "That's what I originally wanted to talk to you about."

"Say on."

"I've had disturbing visions," Kia told him. "About the bestial children of Hayoka. Two of the young monstrosities are causing havoc and destruction. I've visualized them slaughtering many innocent random people. And their attacks are coming closer to the Land of Everlasting Summer. Soon these two will target the outer farms, killing the planters and cultivators who reside outside Shipapa-Lina and Kolhu."

"And the third?"

Kia hesitated, and Pahana saw apprehension in her face. She looked away, folding her hands together. "The third child concerns me. I've never seen anything like her. My visions give me chills. The powers she possesses are ... unsettling."

"Where is she?"

"Still in the Big Sand," Kia said. "But she won't stay there."

Pahana clutched Dragonfly and nodded. "Then she's not an immediate problem. You can tell me about her later. In the present, we need to address the other two creatures who sprang from Hayoka's traitorous loins. This will be a clear test for Gluskap's ability. Thank you for the information, Kia. Your aid is invaluable. I'll handle things from here."

"Be careful, Pahana," she said. "For all your cleverness, you are dealing with unfathomable forces. Don't become overly confident."

"Lacking confidence is a weakness I refuse to succumb to," he said.

"Now above all times... Don't bungle this!" Kia said as her image vanished.

Pahana stood up, holding Dragonfly tightly as he looked around the ruling chamber where his father used to lead the Itiwana. "Other people can afford to make mistakes. Chieftains cannot."

He marched out to find Gluskap.

The group of specially chosen Itiwana warriors had assembled near the Speaking Mound. Pahana stood imperiously upon the mound, while the men he'd summoned sat astride their bison mounts, except for one of them.

"What I ask of you is dangerous but necessary," Pahana said. "The enemy is monstrous and merciless. No normal man could defeat these demons. But you are the finest and most trusted of my warriors. I have faith in you."

Calian, who sat near Naya-Nazgani and Faw-Faw, bowed respectfully. "I would as soon hear that from you than from Awona'Wilona himself."

"You will lead one party, good Calian," Pahana said. "You will seek the Wampus Cat. Loyal Faw-Faw and Naya-Nazgani will accompany you."

Naya-Nazgani was astride his own mount, War Runner. Faw-Faw stood at his side. "We'll obey that order with unequivocal delight, won't we, Faw-Faw?"

The big Wood Man understood enough to agree, despite the word 'unequivocal' being far beyond his comprehension. "Gug."

"And me?" asked Gluskap, sitting atop Flying Courage. The twin brothers flanked him. "I'm afire to prove my mettle."

"You'll have your chance this day," his father said. "You will lead a party consisting of yourself, Masewa, and O'Yewa. They will observe you and advise you. Your goal will be to hunt Stikini. Don't delude yourself that this will be an unproblematic task. If you have a careless moment, you won't come back with a beating heart in your chest."

"And I would deserve it," Gluskap said. "But I promise you this... When I die, it won't be from carelessness."

"I'll hold you to that because our family always keeps its vows," Pahana said. "As for the dark spawn of Hayoka, I'd prefer them brought to me alive, but regardless, their threat must be eliminated. Do whatever you need to do in order to bring them to heel. The rules of battle are not for the likes of them."

"I'll be efficient," Gluskap replied.

"Then no more talk," Pahana commanded. "My sister has sensed that the Wampus Cat is near the site of Wala-Wa and Stikini is near the Shining Rock Mountains. Go bring glory to Shipapa-Lina."

Calian pointed north. "Ride!" he said, and nudged his bison into motion, followed by four other mounts and the long strides of a Wood Man.

CHAPTER FIFTEEN

This is the moment! Gluskap thought as they rode toward the Shining Rock Mountains. *I'll make my father proud.*

The twin brothers followed closely atop Lightning Charger and Thunder Rumbler. During the trip, Masewa had made no secret of the fact that he didn't enjoy being placed in a subservient role to young Gluskap. He was never the type to be gentle about people's feelings.

"Are we to wander aimlessly until the moon rises, boy?" Masewa asked. "Is your hope that Stikini will perish of old age while we amble?"

"It doesn't help to club the boy with your abuses," O'Yewa said. "Try a more heartening stance."

As they argued, Gluskap looked up and saw a flock of birds. He could tell the difference between birds that were flying to a destination and those that were flying in a panic to escape a predator. His mother had taught him the distinction. These birds were scared.

"That way," Gluskap said, pointing.

"How do you know?" Masewa asked. "Or are you simply guessing in hopes of convincing us you have some insight?"

The smiling Gluskap ordered Flying Courage to canter onwards. "That's for you to determine. Come along. Don't dawdle."

Masewa scowled and looked irritably at O'Yewa, who simply shrugged. They followed Gluskap toward the mountain and up the slope. Seeing more animals fleeing in the other direction, Gluskap knew they were getting close.

Finally, they came across a terrible sight. They saw the man-like owl eating the entrails of a bloodied, dismembered, disemboweled group of Kolhu who were returning from bartering with the Hopi and other tribes. They roamed into the wrong place at the worst time.

"Ghastly!" O'Yewa cried, appalled.

"Those people will be avenged!" Masewa shouted in fury.

Stikini, blood dripping from its beak, locked its large eyes on the three newcomers. It made an angry squealing sound and leaped into the air, flapping its wide wings. Soaring up to the sky, it circled the three Itiwana and their animals.

Masewa swiftly put an arrow in his bow and targeted Stikini. "Die for what you've done!"

Stikini easily evaded the shaft, and with a menacing caw, the beast swooped at Masewa, talons poised to rend the Itiwana warrior into pieces. O'Yewa lobbed a spear at the owl beast, but it swatted the weapon away with its wing, continuing toward Masewa and Thunder Rumbler.

As Lightning Charger bucked aggressively, its horns giving Stikini pause, Gluskap utilized his natural-born ice powers. Holding out his hands, he blinded the owl with a spray of ice crystals. Stikini flapped its wings, disoriented, while Gluskap leaped toward the creature.

He leaped so high, he landed on Stikini's back. The owl reacted wildly, rising upward and doing loops in the air to dislodge its unwanted passenger. Hanging on desperately, Gluskap used his cold powers to cover Stikini with ice. The owl didn't like the feeling, jerking around in panic and flying higher as the frosty coating covered its body. O'Yewa and Masewa could only watch, impressed by the boy's courage.

When its wings became too icy, Stikini could no longer maintain its flight. It began to plummet from a great height, along with Gluskap. As the ground came closer, the son of Hayoka managed to slow his descent by using the same levitation talent that his mother had frequently employed. Stikini fell faster than Gluskap, and the creature hit the ground first, crashing hard with a squeal.

O'Yewa compelled his mount Lightning Charger to break the boy's fall. Gluskap, dropping with diminished velocity, landed on the bison's lower back, just behind O'Yewa. He bounced and fell to the grass. Fortunately, his birthright of blood, which was a combination of Mastop-Kachina, Winter Elder, and earthly divinity, provided him with an abnormal level of endurance. He shook off the impact and forced himself to his feet.

Stikini was also hurting from the fall and trying to recover enough to continue the attack. It started to weakly flap its frozen wings but was unable to fly. Before it could restore its ability to take flight, O'Yewa caused Lighting Charger to trample over the owl with all its massive weight. Those weighty hooves trod upon Stikini's injured body several times. One of his wings was ripped off.

"Vengeance for the innocent!" O'Yewa said on the third pass.

For a few seconds, Stikini did not move, but then it began to roll around frenziedly, wailing in anguish. Blood mixed with the ice in its plumage.

Masewa was not satisfied with the injury. "O'Yewa, give me your spear. I'll finish this demon here."

"No!" Gluskap cried. "My father wants him alive. You heard him."

"He's right, Masewa," commented his twin. "Let the monster live."

Masewa sneered down at the mauled Owl-Man. "The luck of the wicked. You'll live to tell your father not to send children to do his fighting for him."

"He and his father will regret their choices," O'Yewa said. "And you, Gluskap. What an inspiring feat. I apologize on behalf of myself and my brother. You're rather remarkable."

"I must admit, you have courage," Masewa said. "Thank you."

"We're kin, aren't we?" Gluskap said. "And aside from that, it was my duty. The Enemy Way cannot thrive without followers. Now it has one less soldier."

Wala-Wa was a sacred site. It had once been the earthly home of the Sky Elders, back when it was overseen by great Pautiwa, who also planted the Tree of Life. Manabazo had been born in this valley before the elders left and flooded it, creating a lake. Manabazo gave directions to the hunting party on how to find the sacred spot.

Calian and Naya-Nazgani reached the lake, riding atop Walking Storm and War Runner. Faw-Faw ran briskly at their side, carrying his big metal hammer as if it were weightless. Faw-Faw had devotedly watched over Calian since birth, in honor of his father Pogum. Now that he had become so closely allied with Naya-Nazgani, he was the most reliable, trustworthy partner for the two men.

Naya-Nazgani had lived so long for the thrill of killing monsters that he relished the opportunity to do what he did best. He had a tendency to get bored in the village if there was no action. As extra incentive, he hoped that capturing or killing the Wampus Cat would impress Pinga. *I can't get her snow-white magnificence out of my thoughts.*

Calian spotted some tracks near the water's edge. Leaping down from Walking Storm, he examined them closer. "It's some type of big cat. Unlike any kind I've ever seen. And it seems to have six legs. These tracks are new. No more than an hour."

"Then whatever made those tracks is still close," Naya-Nazgani said.

"Depending on how fast it's moving," Calian replied. "It doesn't seem to be running. More of a steady stride. If we're winged, we should overtake it within the hour."

"Then let's not waste a moment," Naya-Nazgani said. "I'm anxious to meet this six-legged savage. Aren't you, Faw-Faw?"

"Gug."

Naya-Nazgani chuckled. "No one says Gug the way he does."

Calian hopped back onto Walking Storm. "Let's get at it. The son first, and the father later. Hayoka's whole family will join him in the punishment we will inflict."

"It's clear that you truly hate Hayoka," Naya-Nazgani said. "Good, honest hatred."

"I'll not deny it," Calian said. "For one such as he, hatred is the only sensible sentiment. Now let's ride."

They rode briskly, with Faw-Faw trailing behind, closely skirting the shore of the lake, and then moving further south. They followed the paw tracks until they came across a blood trail leading in the same direction.

"It's near now," Naya-Nazgani said. "That blood is fresh. Stay alert."

Within minutes, they found the remains of a pair of Itiwana planters from the outer farms who apparently decided to ignore the warnings about staying within the perimeter of the sentries. They were possibly hunting or foraging or some other innocent activity. Regardless of their reason, both of them had been ripped to shreds. The look of horror on their faces was grisly.

"This beast is truly a monster!" Calian said. "Possibly even more evil than its father."

Naya-Nazgani sniffed the air. "The smell of death is fresh. This happened only minutes ago."

Faw-Faw approached the two mangled bodies, dragging his big hammer behind him, taking a moment to comprehend what he was seeing. A tear ran down his hairy face.

"Faw-Faw, be careful!" Calian yelled. "Stay close to us!"

And then the Wampus Cat appeared, seemingly out of nowhere. Perhaps it was concealed behind a shrub or a rock. However it managed to hide itself, the Wampus Cat sprang into view with astonishing quickness. The ferocious six-legged cat came down on Faw-Faw's back, latching its many razor-sharp claws into the Wood Man. It bit

Faw-Faw on the shoulder. The big man howled in pain and tried to strike the cat with his hammer but couldn't quite reach.

Calian fired an arrow at the cat, but since Faw-Faw was thrashing and staggering around, the arrow missed its mark. As Calian raised his spear and rode toward the cat, Naya-Nazgani yanked his ax from the bindings where it was latched to his bison. "Time for pain!"

Calian rushed to the struggling Faw-Faw and lunged his spear at the Wampus Cat, who leaped off Faw-Faw's back, landing on all six of his padded feet. The cat crouched, preparing to spring at Calian, when Naya-Nazgani charged the creature, swinging his ax. The Wampus Cat leaped further away, creating some distance between itself and the trio of warriors.

"Check on Faw-Faw," Naya-Nazgani yelled. "Leave this beast to me. Killing monsters is my gift and my pleasure."

Although Calian knew his first duty was to capture the Wampus Cat, his heart went out to Faw-Faw who had been his friend and protector since birth. "Be calm, Faw-Faw. I'll tend to you. You've defended me so many times, I won't let you fall here."

Naya-Nazgani carefully approached the Wampus Cat. He'd fought too many monsters to be overconfident. The cat circled him menacingly, wary of his big ax and looking for an opening. It snarled and hissed, trying unsuccessfully to scare the monster slayer, who was unfazed. He saw the Wampus Cat as a great challenge.

Calian grabbed the cold weather garment he had tucked into the saddle of his bison and used it to clean up the blood from Faw-Faw's wounds. He remembered T'Soona once telling him about putting pressure on a wound. He then broke off his bow string to help make a tourniquet for the shoulder wound. "You'll be fine, my friend. When we get back to Shipapa-Lina, we'll have a great meal together."

Since Naya-Nazgani couldn't catch the Wampus Cat, he tried a more psychological tactic. "Keep running. You're a coward, just like your pathetic father. And I was one of the heroes who killed your mother. And do you want to know something? I enjoyed it. That's right, I laughed as she was buried alive! And I'll do the same to your craven, weak, pitiful father. And there's nothing you can do about it, because you're as weak as your mother!"

The Wampus Cat roared so loudly, it echoed for miles. Filled with crazed fury, the Wampus Cat launched itself wildly at the monster slayer. Slavering with savagery, claws and fangs poised to destroy Naya-Nazgani, the Wampus Cat was blinded by rage.

With a single slash of his ax, Naya-Nazgani chopped off the beast's two front legs. The cat's howl of anger turned to one of pain as it crashed to the ground, blood spurting from where its legs had been.

"Good work," Calian said, helping Faw-Faw to his feet. Faw-Faw saw the cat on the ground and pushed his way passed Calian. The Wood Man began to stomp the Wampus Cat's head into the ground with a huge heel. Blood and teeth spit out of the cat's mouth.

"Calm yourself!" Calian cried, trying to pull Faw-Faw away from his victim. "Pahana wants him alive! Back away! We must do as the chieftain says."

He finally managed to pacify the gigantic Wood Man, who gritted his teeth while being yanked away.

Naya-Nazgani stood over the injured cat, tightly gripping his ax. "I am so tempted to see your head separated from your furry body, so be thankful that Pahana has another plan for you."

"I suppose we'll have to keep this monster alive," Calian said. "At least until we can get it back to Shipapa-Lina. After that, maybe we'll have the honor of killing it anyway."

Naya-Nazgani grinned. "You're just saying that to cheer me up."

CHAPTER SIXTEEN

"**D**eath!" Pahana proclaimed.

The Itiwana chieftain stood on the speaking mound underneath the Cliff Palace, wearing the traditional feathered headdress of the tribe's leader. The Shakowin stood behind him, all looking very stern and grim. Even Kia had made the trip from Kolhu to be part of this summit. She stood beside her brother, showing her equal authority. The entire Itiwana tribe had been summoned for this unusual gathering.

In front of the speaking mound was a wooden cage containing two prisoners. The Wampus Cat and Stikini sat weakly inside their makeshift prison. Both were injured, although Pahana told T'Soona to do enough of a patch-up job to keep them alive. Wampus Cat was suffering from missing two of his legs and Stikini from the loss of its wing.

Pinga, standing behind her son, felt a swell of pity for these two injured creatures. Despite their horrid deeds, seeing those wounds made her heart go out to them. *This One wishes such violence was not necessary. These two beings were raised to hate. They are victims as much as they are killers. But the Itiwana must be united in this.*

"The Shakowin and myself are in complete agreement," Pahana announced. "These malefactors deserve a punishment of death."

The tribe reacted to the proclamation with mostly supportive cheers and chants, although a few among them were less enthusiastic, sharing Pinga's sympathy regarding wounded prisoners. As for the two captives, they sat silently, seemingly resigned to their fate.

"However," Pahana continued, "we may be lenient if we can make better use of these prisoners. Since the real enemy is their father, we can use them to get to him. My sister will explain. Say on, Kia."

"Thank you, Pahana," she said. "I have the means to get a message to their father, Hayoka. We will offer him an exchange. If he has any fatherly feelings for his children, he'll exchange himself for them."

"Hayoka has been the real threat," Pahana said. "He's the brains behind our enemy. Without him, their united front will fall apart. These two monsters attacked us because their father told them to. He's been the bane of our existence for years, just as his father Hobomok was. This must end! And we intend to end it! In the meantime, we will allow these two to live as our prisoners. That's all for now."

As the tribe dispersed to go about their usual tasks, a group of them pushed the cage with the two captives into a pit. Two sentries were ordered to stand guard while Kia used her shamanic powers to create an invisible barrier over the pit. Objects could be tossed inside, such as food and pots of water, but nothing could get out. There was no way for the two prisoners to escape.

Afterward, Kia had to get the message to Hayoka. Finding a quiet spot inside the Cliff Palace, she sat cross-legged and closed her eyes.

There was severe apprehension in the House of Many Hands in the Valley of the Blue Mists. The lack of chanting was ominous. The dim candlelit gloom matched the mood of the female shamans of the House of Many Hands. The Breathing Shaman and the Keeper of Sacred Objects kneeled in front of a rock cairn, surrounded by formerly tall candles that were mostly melted.

A cheerful Hayoka entered the chamber where the two sisters were meditating. He was brashly strutting like a rooster while softly warbling a sing-song chant. His mood was bright as he plopped comfortably down onto a seat made of leaves, grass, and feathers.

The Breathing Shaman looked over her shoulder, scowling with disapproval at the intrusion. If Hayoka noticed her glowering gaze, he made no acknowledgement of it. He just continued his melodic chant.

"We are meditating!" the Breathing Shaman snapped.

"And you do it very well," Hayoka said with mock politeness. "I admire your dedication."

The Breathing Shaman stood up. "What is it that's leading you to be so merry? We're deep in the middle of a war, and you dragged us into it."

Hayoka was calm and smiling. "And we'll win. That's why I'm happy. You should be too. Think about the victory to come and share my joy."

Narrowing her eyes in anger, the Breathing Shaman clenched a fist tightly. "Why are you so sure? We underestimated the Itiwana on previous occasions and we lost. We dare not be overconfident again. They are dangerous foes. Especially that Kia witch. Too dangerous."

"Not as dangerous as my children," Hayoka said boastfully. "Just the two I've unleashed are enough to terrify the Itiwana and cause chaos. And I've yet to bring my Skadega-Muth into the fray. When I do, the devastation will be so beautiful."

"Then why wait if she's so powerful?" the Keeper asked.

"I'm giving her more time to learn," Hayoka said. "As powerful as she is, she has a teacher who is making her more lethal, more unbeatable than you could possibly imagine."

"And who is this teacher?" the Breathing Shaman demanded to know. "Why will you not tell us?"

"Don't you like surprises?" Hayoka mirthfully answered.

The Breathing Shaman waved her fist in front of him. "Your frivolity is infuriating. I'm beginning to regret allowing you to remain here with us."

"Now, now, don't be that way," Hayoka said. "Don't let fear rule you. I promise..."

A sudden bright light startled the three plotting allies. Hayoka closed and covered his eyes. The Keeper squinted, while the Breathing Shaman looked directly into the light, even though it hurt her eyes.

"Don't make promises you can't keep, Hayoka!" a fourth voice said as the transparent image of a woman materialized in the House of Many Hands.

The Keeper hadn't seen her in many years. This intruding woman was not much more than a child when they last spoke. Still, the Breathing Shaman recognized her instantly.

"Kia," the Breathing Shaman said nervously. "I didn't imagine that even you were powerful enough to breach the mystic defenses we've formed around this place. The Blue Mists should have stopped you."

The blinding light faded, allowing Hayoka and the Keeper of Sacred Objects to see Kia. Both were shocked at her ability to breach the House of Many Hands.

"You misjudged my power eighteen winters ago," Kia said. "I would have thought you'd take the intervening time to learn a lesson. It seems while you were underestimating me, I was over-estimating you."

"What do you want?" the Keeper asked.

Kia looked at Hayoka and pointed. "My purpose here involves this rodent. It doesn't concern you."

Hayoka did his best to be calm and confident, although Kia unnerved him. "To what do I owe the pleasure of a visit from the Cacique of Kolhu?"

"I'll say this plainly and quickly, because I do not enjoy conversing with the likes of you," Kia said. "We have your children! We captured them both!"

Hayoka's smooth demeanor turned to dread, and his face went pale. "I...I don't believe you. My children are too powerful."

"So was your wife," Kia said, knowing it would provoke further emotions. "If you don't believe us, let your shaman friends use their abilities to locate you children. After you verify I'm telling the truth, remember these terms we now insist on. We'll release your children if you will surrender yourself to us. No second option is acceptable. We'll give you until the next full moon. If you haven't arrived in Shipapa-Lina by then, your children will join your wife in whatever dark demon realm she rots in. It's your choice."

The image of Kia disappeared, and immediately, Hayoka asked the two shaman women to determine the truth in Kia's statement. The two sisters agreed and sat down to meditate again. They chanted in front of the cairn, and the Keeper tossed some sort of dust onto the flickering candles. A waft of smoke drifted upward and swirled, becoming silver and bright. An image formed in the smoke.

Hayoka was able to see his two children, trapped and miserable in a cage, down in a dark pit. He could see the physical injuries and dismemberments. The sight of it brought back the moment when he dug his beloved Dagwona's body out of the dirt after Kia killed her.

"My sons!" he whispered.

Abruptly, the image of Kia appeared in the cloud, glaring with a piercing stare. "And now you have your proof. Their injuries were justice for all the lives they've taken. Be thankful we're in a merciful vein. Remember Hayoka ... you have until the next full moon."

The shaman sisters ended their enchantment and the cloud disappeared, along with the image of Kia. The three of them remained silent for a minute, processing the situation. Hayoka initially looked pitiful and defeated, but his face then changed into a veneer of cold wrath.

"It's them who've underestimated someone," he growled. "They underestimated me! No one threatens my children! This is the biggest mistake they've made since killing my wife. They'll regret this!"

"What will you do?" the Keeper asked.

"I'm going to rescue my children!" he stated emotionlessly. "And my first move will be to summon my daughter. Help me contact her. She has to be told that her family needs her. She was raised to kill the Itiwana, and its high time she begins that worthwhile goal!"

CHAPTER SEVENTEEN

The Tunerak Destroyers had once been a threatening force in Ulah-Nane. Centered mostly in the Big Sand, they were adherents to the old Aztec ways but later became worshippers of Malsumis. They followed the instructions of Dagwona, the Witch of the Whirlwind, and her student, the Salt Witch. It was the Salt Witch who taught certain members of the Tunerak Destroyers to transform into the deadly Skinwalkers. When the Salt Witch died, they waited for Dagwona to lead them, but she was more concerned with personally avenging her pupil, so she had little use for the Destroyers or Skinwalkers.

After both of those powerful mystic women were slain, the Tunerak Destroyers broke off into small, independent splinter groups, with a variety of competing new leaders. A few still practiced the transformation into Skinwalkers, but that ability was becoming forgotten. The new leaders were more concerned with petty attacks on local tribes and ceremonies to worship Malsumis, hoping their devotion to him would put them into his good graces when he returned.

In the recent years, each of those leaders had all been killed. They were slain by Skadega-Muth, heir of the Witch of the Whirlwinds. The daughter of Dagwona was intent on reclaiming her place as the Mistress of the Big Sand, which she now called the Desert of Death. She challenged the new leaders of the Tunerak Destroyers and easily killed them and any of the followers who supported them.

The majority of the warriors of the Tunerak Destroyers were all excited by the return of the heir of the Big Sand and so fell in line behind Skadega-Muth when she destroyed the leaders, especially after seeing what she did to anyone who took their side in the challenge. It had taken Skadega-Muth several years to reunite all the fragments of the Tunerak Destroyers. She now had the united army of the Desert of Death behind her.

Skadega-Muth summoned all the warriors of the Tunerak Destroyers to the Sand Alter, where the Salt Witch once used to rule the arid desert realm. She stood on a dune, looking out over a thousand loyal warriors, each garbed in the old attire of jaguar skins adorned with eagle feathers and cactus spikes. They carried wooden swords and shields. All of them kneeled in honor and fearful obedience of their new ruler, Skadega-Muth, Queen of the Desert of Death.

"I am pleased with your fealty and your fighting prowess," Skadega-Muth said to her forces. "Taxet is pleased with you, as well. You have kept the faith and honored my venerated mother. Those of you who have been chosen to carry the honor of becoming Skinwalkers are learning well. The sacrosanct secrets Taxet has passed on to me are being employed very well. Now, it is time for you to do your duty to Malsumis and to me."

She walked down the dune, followed by a small swarm of tiny, carrion-eating flies. As she moved among her warriors, even the most loyal felt a chill. "I have been contacted by my father. It is time for us to avenge the deaths of my mother and the Salt Witch. We will travel far, but when we reach our goal, it will be time to be of service to Malsumis. It will be time for you to prove yourselves to me. Soon we will provide many sacrifices for Taxet. The unseen walls between worlds will grow thin and the limitless power of the underworld will flow across all Ulah-Nane like a delightful wave of scarlet blood. By all the elders, it will be glorious!"

The warriors of the Desert of Death raised their wooden swords and cheered in loyalty to their mistress. She was impassive, staring with eyes that seemed as lifeless as glass.

"And now we go," she said. "And I predict that bringing death will make you feel so alive!"

She began her long march to the Land of Everlasting Summer, followed by 1,000 men.

In a time of trials, any opportunity to celebrate was taken. After the successful capture and imprisonment of Stikini and the Wampus Cat, some of the warriors decided to take a night to savor their deeds.

Calian, O'Yewa, Masewa, Naya-Nazgani, and Gluskap gathered in one of the pit houses. They were joined by Yoki of the Moon Clan and a few other warriors of the Two-Horn Riders. They passed around a pipe containing certain weeds that eased their mood, as well as drank a fermented alcohol beverage. They laughed as they related the stories of their adventures while pursuing and capturing the children of Hayoka.

Gluskap found himself as the guest of honor at the gathering. Masewa and O'Yewa sang his praises as they related the story of Stikini's capture.

"You should have seen the boy, holding tight to that damned bird beast as it tried to shake him off," O'Yewa said. "Such pluck! And then he froze the damn monster! I've never seen any such thing before."

"I must agree," Masewa said. "I was wrong about you, Gluskap. You saved me from almost certain death. I owe you."

"I ask no favors," Gluskap said. "We're kin."

"More than that," Calian said. "You're one of us now. As the War Chief, I officially declare you as one of the Two-Horn Riders of Shipapa-Lina."

The assembled warriors chanted "Gluskap, Gluskap," over and over. The young man savored the moment. Finally, he was accepted.

A lambent small flame danced, illuming the ruling chamber of the Cliff Palace. Pahana and his grandmother, Atira, were alone in the dim chamber, sitting in their usual places late in the evening. The chieftain had his headdress from the earlier ceremony hooked over the Dragonfly, whose tip was imbedded in the ground.

"The village is buzzing about Gluskap's battle with Stikini," Atira said. "It seems he has a warrior's heart, after all."

"Why did you doubt it?" Pahana said, gently but also scolding. "He's the blood of Tawa and Yana-Luha and Morning Star. And myself."

"Are you waiting for me to say I was wrong?" Atira asked grudgingly.

"No," he replied. "I'm waiting for you to say I was right."

"Must you hear the words?" she asked. "Hear them then. You were right about him. He'll be a great warrior someday. I hope this will make the tribe more apt to accept him as a possible future chieftain. But I still question your decision to hide him from us. I wonder about your secret life outside Shipapa-Lina."

"A vital part of my plan," Pahana said. "And one that is not over yet. In fact, now that we've broached the subject, I'll need to leave again soon."

Atira felt anger again, as she did any time he announced an absence from the Land of Everlasting Summer. However, she made an effort to control herself, since she had been wrong about Gluskap.

"To go where?" she asked. "Back to your Earth Goddess?"

"If I do, that's my concern," he insisted. "But I have other reasons to trek from the Land of Everlasting Summer."

"And I imagine you can't tell me what those reasons are," Atira said, exasperated.

"We've discussed this before," Pahana chided. "You will know what you need to know when I decide you need to know it."

"I won't argue further because it's pointless," Atira said with a bit of resentment. "When are you leaving?"

"Tomorrow at midday," Pahana said. "I was going to announce my departure in the morning. The Shakowin will be left in charge, of course."

"And who will sit in the chieftain's seat?" she asked. "Someone has to make the final decision should the Shakowin be divided."

"I have decided on Aholi," he replied. "Unless you have some objection."

"No, none at all," she said. "He's a worthy man, with much knowledge and experience. I've always liked and respected Aholi. He was close to my dearest Yana-Luha. He'll be honored to know that you're placing this trust in him. How long will you be gone?"

"I'll return before the full moon," Pahana said. "I certainly don't want to miss Hayoka crawling back here to surrender himself. That's a day I look forward to."

Pahana left the following afternoon without much fanfare or ceremony. He knew the word of his departure would quickly spread and that the Itiwana had become so accustomed to his comings and goings, there would be no major disruption in the daily life of the tribe. Aholi had the trust of the people. He had been the War Chief of the Two-Horn Riders for many years before he stepped down due to age, allowing Calian to replace him. Aholi had served for a full season on the Shakowin council, which added to his stature as a man of wisdom and authority. Beyond that, everyone liked Aholi due to his good nature, humor, and patience. The mere fact that he could get along for years with his depressingly pessimistic wife, Evaki, proved that he had extraordinary tolerance for human failings.

Aholi, with Atira and Pinga, were the ones to see him off. Aholi was effusive with gratitude about being named temporary chief. "I am over-whelmed by this great honor. I swear on our family name I will do you proud, Kik-Mongwi. You'll have no reason to regret your decision. I promise..."

Pahana held up a hand to silence him. "Gratitude is unnecessary. If you wish to thank me, just take care of Shipapa-Lina while I'm gone. Consult the Shakowin and keep constantly vigilant. I must be away swiftly. I have a long journey and much to do when I get there. I go now."

"This One wishes you safety and success," Pinga said.

"Thank you, Mother," he said. "Goodbye, Grandmother. Guard Shipapa-Lina well."

World Giant cantered forward, carrying Pahana out of the village. Various tribesmen waved and wished him well as he rode away. The sight of their leader leaving always demoralized the tribe.

"I should go now," Aholi said. "I must meet with Calian about the Two-Horn Riders, and then I need to check on the progress of the workers building the new wall. Excuse me, good ladies."

Pinga and Atira stood pensively, watching Pahana ride away. Atira was scowling. Pinga noticed her vexation.

"You're troubled by this," Pinga said. "Talk to This One."

"He should tell us where he's going!" Atira said. "If something should happen to him when he's gone, we need to know. What if we need him imminently? If he doesn't return by the full moon, how long should we wait, not knowing where to look for him? Shouldn't he at least take someone with him?"

"This One also wishes he would not go off alone to undisclosed places" Pinga replied. "But she feels we must trust Pahana, as we did Tawa."

Atira was not convinced. "I have lived through four generations of chieftains. From my husband's mother to my grandson. Never before have I questioned or doubted or disobeyed my Kik-Mongwi. Not even when I was wed to one. But now..."

"You must trust my son," Pinga insisted. "He is your blood."

Atira gazed sternly into Pinga's eyes. "I must know where he's going. I will not be at ease until we settle this. The Itiwana must know where our leader is at all times. We are under siege! We are at war! He should never be missing. Tawa would never have done this. You, above all people, know that."

"This One understands your concerns," Pinga said. "It's true that This One shared complete trust with Tawa. What do you think should be done about Pahana?"

"Someone should follow him," Atira said. "Covertly. He doesn't need to know. We just need to know where he is."

Pinga shook her head indignantly. "That is a betrayal of trust. This One disagrees with you. She does not condone using such guile against her son."

Atira put her hands on Pinga's shoulders. "Dear Pinga. I have always cared for you. You were a good wife to Tawa and a good mother to Pahana. But I will see this done. If I must, I will call a vote of the Shakowin. You already know how the rest of us stand on this. Aholi, the acting chieftain, agrees with me. You will be outvoted. However, I don't wish to do that to you. Believe me when I say I love you like my own blood. Regardless, I am going to find out where Pahana is going, even if you fight me on it."

Pinga's face, normally an image of Zen-like calm, became a mix of sadness and resentment. "Very well. This One cannot fight you. If this treacherous thing must be done, This One asks that she be the one to do it."

"You surprise me," Atira said. "But you're a sensible choice. T'Soona and I are too old. Aholi must remain here as leader, and Calian is needed to oversee the Two-Horn Riders. Manabazo is missing again, so that leaves you. If you're willing, I agree."

"This is a sad day for the Itiwana," Pinga said, turning her back on Atira. "This One hopes you will soon realize the imprudence of this. Excuse This One. She must find herself an escort."

Atira watched dejectedly as Pinga walked away. *I hope this doesn't create a permanent rift between us. I do love her like a daughter. Even if she is centuries older than me.*

As for Pinga, she walked the length of Shipapa-Lina for a time, struggling with what she had to do next. The sun glinted off her argent skin as she meandered across the busy village. People around her were renovating Shipapa-Lina for defense or repairing damage from previous battles. Most of the women were either at the cornfield, working on the crops, or practicing their archery for the Bow Sisterhood. The young men were training with Calian in the Two-Horn Riders.

Pinga then spotted Naya-Nazgani and Faw-Faw carrying firewood. She noticed Naya-Nazgani staring at her, but he turned his face away when she caught him looking. This was not the first time she had spotted him admiring her from afar. She usually took his longing gaze as a compliment. Just now, she saw it as an opportunity.

Perhaps it's improper for This One to take unfair advantage of his obvious attraction to her, Pinga thought, *but she must do this for Pahana.*

She glided gracefully to the spot where the monster slayer and his towering friend were putting the timber down in the woodpile. Naya-Nazgani was wiping wood chips from his hands when he realized Pinga was coming his way. His heart beat a bit faster, and he jumped to attention, striking a manly pose, arms akimbo.

"Pleasant day to you, worthy lady," Naya-Nazgani said.

"This One is pleased to see you, warrior," Pinga said with a kittenish smile. "And good day to you, Faw-Faw. This One hopes you are recovering from your wounds."

"Gug!"

"Is there some way I can be of service?" Naya-Nazgani asked.

Pinga struck a seductive pose. "This One is reluctant to ask, but she requires a considerable service from you, and she fears it will be a great burden to you."

Naya-Nazgani answered immediately. "Feel free to ask any task or errand of me. I'm happy to be useful to ... uh, to the Shakowin."

She gazed at him with sultry eyes. "This One appreciates your courtesy. She has a journey to make, and she needs someone to provide safe escort. She no longer has the power she once had. Would you do This One the kindness of accompanying her on a trip out of the Land of Everlasting Summer?"

"I would consider it a great honor," he told her exuberantly.

Pinga flipped her white hair with a coquettish flair. "Your kindness and boldness are most prized. This One hopes to leave before sundown. Can you do so?"

"I'm ready whenever you need me," Naya-Nazgani said.

She touched his arm flirtatiously. "This One knew you were a warrior she could depend on. You have her gratitude."

"Unnecessary," he replied. "I require no thanks. I look forward to the adventure."

"Wonderful," she said. "See to whatever affairs you have pending and then meet This One at the aqueduct. She will be there presently."

"Agreed!"

Pinga walked fluidly toward the cliff housing to prepare for her journey. She felt Naya-Nazgani's admiring eyes on her back as she walked. She knew she had him ensorcelled by her charms and was confident of her ability to induce him to do what she wanted. Her deific ears overheard the monster slayer speaking softly behind her.

"Faw-Faw, my friend," he said. "You never know what the new day will bring. Some days deliver sublime surprises."

CHAPTER EIGHTEEN

Skadega-Muth and her army marched out of the desert and into the sacred area known as the Canyon of Legend. Often called the First of Sitting places, it was the location where the Sky Elder, Kokopelli, had used his magic flute to lead Morning Star to the Land of Everlasting Summer.

Striding with a long gait that was both confident of herself and dismissive of everyone else, Skadega-Muth passed the Pisas Vaya River, which was teeming with fish. Sadistically, the cadaver-like Skadega-Muth trod ankle deep through the shallows of the river. Minutes after she passed through, dead fish were washed up on shore. The blue water was tinted brown and gray as she passed through.

Her own followers looked disconcertingly at the floating fish, unsettled by the frightening fatal power their leader possessed. Even though many of them were unnerved enough to consider fleeing from this lethal lady, none of them dared to desert from her ranks. She was so terrifying that all agreed it was better to be her ally than her enemy.

Pinga and Naya-Nazgani had ridden through the evening and well into the silent night, nestled atop his bison, War Runner. The intrepid pair had left the region of the Land of Everlasting Summer and were moving northwest. A bright moon illuminated Pinga's toneless, monochrome white skin.

Pinga had her arms wrapped around Naya-Nazgani's waist to secure herself on the bison. Naya-Nazgani enjoyed the sensation of her arms and the feel of her body pressed behind him. He noticed she was beginning to nod off, and her head was resting on his shoulder. He hoped this trip would be a long one.

When War Runner leaped with dexterity over an obstacle in his path, Pinga was awoken. She looked around to get her bearings but couldn't find any identifying landmarks in the darkness.

"We should stop for the night," Naya-Nazgani said.

"Don't stop on her account," Pinga said. "This One can go further without sleep."

He pulled the reins and brought War Runner to a stop. "I've lost the trail in the darkness.

There's no point in advancing further, or we'll go astray from Pahana's path. We should rest until morning."

"This One acquiesces to your advice," Pinga said, stifling a yawn. "She would not be averse to a short lie down."

Naya-Nazgani slid off the bison. "This is as good a spot as any."

Before Pinga could climb down from the mount, the powerful hands of Naya-Nazgani grabbed her firmly, lifting her as if she were a wispy little night bird. She didn't seem to mind. He placed her gently on the ground.

"This One thanks you," Pinga said. "You spoil her."

Naya-Nazgani began pulling objects from his saddle. "If the Gods didn't want you to be spoiled, they wouldn't have made you so lovely."

He wasn't sure, but he thought he saw a touch of color in her colorless face, as if she were blushing. *I didn't know a quondam deity could be embarrassed.*

"You flatter This One," she said, looking away coyly.

"Merely being truthful," he said as he laid some animal skins on the ground.

"Most kind," Pinga replied, placing her pale, bare feet comfortably onto an animal skin.

"Relax yourself now," he said, looking around for some wood. "I'll build a fire."

"This One does not get cold," Pinga said. "She was a winter Goddess once. However, if you would prefer a fire, This One has no objection."

"In that case, we can do without the fire," the monster hunter said. "I don't need one either, and there's no reason to signal our presence to an enemy."

Pinga scanned the darkness nervously. "Do you think there are enemies near?"

"Possibly," he said as he unhooked his heavy ax from the bison harness, while War Runner grazed peacefully. "The Itiwana have no scarcity of foes in these perilous times. And we don't know what sort of danger Pahana is riding toward or what to expect on this trek. We can't disregard the possibility a follower of the Enemy Way might come upon us."

"A chilling thought to fall asleep by," Pinga responded.

He sat with his ax on his lap. "You have nothing to fear. I'm here and I fear no warrior, monster, or witch the enemy might send. I'll kill anyone foolish enough to threaten you."

He tried to read her expression. He was unsure, but she seemed to be suppressing a smile. He wished he knew what she was thinking.

"Such confidence is heartening," Pinga said. "But don't you need to sleep?"

"I don't sleep," he said in a matter-of-fact way. "I haven't slept since the World Tree was a sapling. I will remain on guard as you sleep."

She sat on the furred animal skin, close at Naya-Nazgani's side. "This One is reassured."

"Do you want me to hunt for some food?" he asked.

"No," she said with a slight headshake. "This One would prefer you stayed close. She no longer has the power she once had to defend herself. This One is trusting you for that."

"You can trust me completely for that," he said boldly. "You could not be safer if Awona'Wilona himself were protecting you. When I fight, my ax is the lightning in the sky and the fangs of the wolf and the fire of the volcano. My enemies have only three choices: run, surrender, or die."

She patted him softly on the knee. "This One will sleep contentedly with you on guard."

Pinga laid down on her back, with her hands behind her head. She looked at the moon. "Would you believe that This One has visited the moon?"

Naya-Nazgani's eyes widened in surprise. "You're not serious?"

"No, she is not," Pinga said. "It was a jest. She is teasing you. She has only been there in dreams."

Naya-Nazgani allowed himself to indulge in a rare snicker. "A dream. More than 300 summers and winters have passed since I dreamed. I've forgotten what it's like."

She looked sympathetically at him. "The nights must seem long without sleep or dreams."

"You get used to it."

"How long does such an adjustment take?" Pinga asked.

"It took more lifetimes than I care to remember," he told her.

"This one understands the trials of a long life," she said soothingly. "She sympathizes."

"The Uwanami chose me for a reason," Naya-Nazgani answered. "I am what I am. I accept my situation."

"She admires your bravery," Pinga warmly replied. "Both in battle and otherwise."

Naya-Nazgani did not know what to say to a compliment, especially from this woman who he was so attracted to. "You should get some rest. We have a lot of ground to cover come morning."

"True," she said, and rolled over onto her side. "Have a pleasant night."

"Have good dreams," he said, looking at her longingly.

She smiled. "If anyone should try to attack This One in her sleep, would you be good enough to kill them?"

"That's a promise," he said.

He kept watch throughout the night. As he listened to her softly breathing, it was the first time in more years than he could remember that he wanted the night to last longer.

Revenge! the little man said as he stealthily crawled through the darkness of the Land of Everlasting Summer.

Carrying a clay jug, he moved like a feline, barely making a sound. That was the gift of a Yehasuri. The furtive Yehasuri was a caste of Puk-Wudjie, known for their agility and skill at moving silently. They were trained as hunters, infiltrators, and covert killers. The diminutive man had made his way deep into the Land of Everlasting Summer, managing to avoid detection, and had reached the village of Shipapa-Lina. He spotted the rows of corn crop and allowed himself a toothy smile of satisfaction.

Looking cautiously around him for any of the Two-Horn Rider sentries, he opened the jar which contained a malodorous brown liquid. As he prepared to spread the putrid fluid across the corn crop, he was startled when a youthful face with beige colored skin popped out from behind the stalks.

"Who might you be?" Gluskap asked.

The Yehasuri jumped back, accidentally spilling his mysterious potion in one spot instead of all over the cornfield. The small man hissed threateningly at young Gluskap.

"You're a Puk-Wudjie, aren't you?" Gluskap asked. "I've been told about you. What are you doing here?"

The Yehasuri had his bolas wrapped around his arm, made of animal skin and tendons. He tried to quickly unwind the bolas cord. He succeeded, but before he could throw the weapon, Gluskap tackled him to the dirt. The two scuffled for a few moments before Gluskap managed to get the bolas away from him and wrap it around the Yehasuri's throat. He began to choke the tiny man with his superior strength. The Yehasuri thrashed and clawed wildly, before he began to weaken and pass out from lack of air.

"Don't kill him!" a voice shouted.

Gluskap looked beyond the rows to see Calian sitting upon Walking Storm, who was trotting in their direction. Calian had an arrow in his bow. He lowered the weapon when he realized that Gluskap had the situation in hand.

"Let him live!" Calian ordered. "I want to question this miscreant."

Gluskap untied the cord from the Yehasuri's neck but unleashed a final punch that left the intruder unconscious. Gluskap examined his sore fist. He had never punched anyone before. "Painful."

"I heard the struggle while I was patrolling," Calian said. "You did excellently."

"Thank you," Gluskap said. "It's a pleasure to be of service."

"What are you doing out here?" Calian asked.

"Meditating among the crops," Gluskap explained. "I do so every night. I like to be amongst growing things. It's a custom I've practiced since I was smaller than this despicable creature."

Calian dismounted and examined the spilled liquid. "This substance contains considerable venom. I believe it's taken from snakes, with perhaps some spider venom included, as well. He would have killed many of us and sickened the rest. It would have made an attack by Hayoka and the Puk-Wudjies much easier for them. It's fortunate you were here. As for this wretch, he will not be so fortunate!"

Vociferous chants rang out in the modest, unremarkable hogan. The people inside the hogan, however, were an unusual sight to behold. The structure was teeming with incense. Sitting in a circle, they were chanting to a totem with carved faces representing Awona'Wilona and Manitou, the most powerful of the summer Sky Elders. The twelve people involved wore ornate wooden masks trimmed with animal hair. They had painted skin and wore the pelts of large game. This group, known as the False Faces, sang, chanted, and shook rattles for hours.

After a time, they all moved outside to perform a ritual dance in the night air of the Red Sky Forest. The hogan was not far from the domain of the Wood Men. The False Faces lit some torches, but before the masked men could begin their dance, they noticed another man approaching. They all stopped, watching the newcomer as he neared the hogan.

"He's back," one of them, named Hototo, said. "The Husk Face Man."

The man wore a mask made of corn husks and red clay, crowned with a feathered headdress. His body was covered with hairy buffalo skins. What little skin he'd left exposed was covered in dry mud. The man carried a hoe which he used as a walking stick.

"Hello, my friends," the Husk Face Man said. "I told you I'd be back. May I join you this time? You said I might be allowed."

The False Faces all looked to Hototo for a decision. He paused with uncertainty and suspicion. "Very well. You may join us for this night. I don't promise any future such privileges. But you are our guest tonight."

"Most grateful," the Husk Face Man said.

Tossing his hoe aside, he retrieved a rattle from the hogan and lined up with the others. They began the ritual, which consisted of dancing the Father Dance, circling the hogan and chanting.

CHAPTER NINETEEN

At dawn the next day, the Yehasuri was bound hand and foot. He lay on the floor of a damp pit house. Above him, glaring down in judgmental anger, were members of the Itiwana Shakowin. Aholi had been summoned, along with Atira and T'Soona. Calian and Gluskap were also present. A large, gray wolf came into view and sat near Aholi.

"Suffering is a fact of life," Calian said to the little man. "How badly we suffer can be an act of fate or it can be a result of our decisions. The decision you make now will determine whether or not you suffer. And how badly."

The Puk-Wudjie merely hissed up at them, defiant despite his situation. He tried to squirm out of his bonds, but they were far too tight. He spit disrespectfully.

"We have two questions for you," Aholi said. "I sincerely hope you will make a wise decision, although I would not be surprised if you were to act the fool. The first query is to verify that Hayoka planned this affrontery. The second question concerns a weapon. A certain tomahawk that the Puk-Wudjies possess."

The Yehasuri's expression showed that he knew very well what Aholi was talking about. Gluskap, on the other hand, did not. He leaned to whisper to T'Soona.

"A tomahawk?" he asked.

"Indeed, a tomahawk," the old medicine man whispered back. "It's the source of the hostility between the Itiwana and the Puk-Wudjies. They have in their possession the Utlunta: the sacred tomahawk that your descendant Morning Star used long ago. Pahana failed to retrieve it once, and the Puk-Wudjies haven't forgotten our little attempt at theft."

"We require the Utlunta in our battle with the Enemy Way," Aholi said. "Tell us where it's hidden, and we'll show you mercy. If not ... well, unpleasantries await you."

"The Puk-Wudjies will see your people dead for your transgressions," the Yehasuri growled.

"I see persuasion is necessary," Aholi said. "Manabazo! Go!"

The big wolf, which was another animal form of Manabazo, leaped into the pit. Snarling and baring its fangs, the wolf crept toward the

Yehasuri, who stared in fixated fear. Still, he didn't speak.

"Faw-Faw!" Aholi called.

The immense form of Faw-Faw came into the Yehasuri's view. He was carrying the metal hammer he'd won from the Vykans many years ago. Faw-Faw jumped into the pit. Lifting his hammer, he slammed it down on a stone, breaking it into pieces. Faw-Faw then emitted a fearsome roar and stalked closer to the Yehasuri, hammer held high, ready to strike.

"The wolf will chew pieces off your flesh," Aholi said. "And the Wood Man will crush your limbs, one at a time. The pain you'll experience will be unimaginable. I pity you."

"But what must be done, will be done!" Atira said.

The Yehasuri looked back and forth between the two lethal threats. A slavering wolf on one side and an angry, club-wielding giant on the other. He trembled, his bravado gone.

"Wait!" the Yehasuri yelled. "I am no fool. I will converse with you."

Aholi held up a hand for Manabazo and Faw-Faw to stop. "I'm happy you chose reason. Was this the plan of Hayoka?"

"It was," the Yehasuri replied. "He despises you for the death of his woman."

"We know what he despises us for," Atira said.

"I knew this was his doing," Calian cried. "By the Elders, I dream of the day I will have my hands around his throat!"

"And the tomahawk?" Aholi asked.

"We moved it to a safer hiding place after your last attempt to steal it," the Yehasuri said. "It is in a jar, hidden beneath Beaver Creek, in the domain of Mishepishu the Water Panther, who protects it."

"Thank you," Aholi said. "You've been very reasonable and cooperative. Now, what should we do with you?"

"I have a suggestion," Atira said. "Let's put him in with the children of his ally. Lock him up with Stikini and the Wampus Cat."

"No, not there!" the Yehasuri yelled. "Those savage children have no kinship or mercy on anyone except their father!"

"Then you had best do some clever talking," Atira said. "Maybe you can convince them to be reasonable. If not ... you'll learn the consequences of being an enemy of the Itiwana. We always win."

"No, you mustn't..." the Yehasuri yelled in terror.

"Faw-Faw," Aholi said. "Bring him."

Big Faw-Faw slung the Yehasuri over his shoulder effortlessly as the little intruder shouted for mercy. Faw-Faw sprung out of the pit.

"Follow me," T'Soona said. "We're taking a walk. Our visitor will get to see some old friends."

The shrieks of panic continued as T'Soona led the Wood Man away. Gluskap, who had been silent all this time, addressed the Shakowin with enthusiastic boisterousness.

"Let me retrieve the tomahawk!" Gluskap asked. "If my father failed to bring it back, it's a matter of honor for our bloodline. Let me prove myself. I can do this thing. Please permit me!"

Aholi hesitated, scratching his head. "I'm not sure Pahana would approve. He has his plans, and this may not fit into his grander vision. Also, he may not appreciate us sending his son on a deadly mission before his training is done."

"I'm prepared!" Gluskap said. "I am not afraid."

Manabazo had jumped out of the pit. "The Utlunta is valuable indeed. It is a weapon we sorely need. Its retrieval has long been due. I think he would approve of sending you."

"I agree!" Gluskap said. "Manabazo is wise."

"I don't object," Calian said. "I was with Pahana on that day, and we both failed to retrieve the tomahawk. I would wish to accompany him on this venture. It is a matter of honor for me, as well."

Aholi looked at Atira, who was deep in thought. "What do you think, wise woman?"

She mused for a few moments more. "I think it's a good suggestion. I feel matters are coming to an aggressive conclusion and we'll need that weapon. My departed husband Yana-Luha used to talk about regaining the tomahawk of his ancestors but never knew where it was. And if Gluskap is potentially to be our future chieftain, this will be a chance for him to prove his worth to everyone and erase all doubt from the tribe. And from me, as well."

"Then we are decided?" Gluskap asked.

"We are decided," Aholi told him. "Calian, you will lead this zealous youth to Beaver Creek and procure the weapon. My sons, O'Yewa and Masewa, will replace you as War Chiefs until you return."

"Hmmm," Calian thought. "That should be interesting. I hope you can get those two scamps to act responsibly for the duration."

"Have faith," Aholi said. "My boys know when to be men."

Gluskap was bursting with the desire to begin his adventure. "When shall we set forth?"

"By midday," Calian said. "This should be a notable day for the Itiwana."

War Runner trotted over a hill in a picturesque, sunny countryside. Pinga was again seated behind Naya-Nazgani, looking around and stabilizing herself by gripping Naya-Nazgani's broad shoulders. She hadn't left the Land of Everlasting Summer in so long, she found herself enjoying the exploration of Ulah-Nane. She was seeing parts of the continent that she had never visited in her long life.

Her enjoyment of the trip was diminished by her regret that this trip was necessary at all. She felt like a traitor to her son by coming all this distance to pry into his affairs. It was clear evidence that he did not share the complete trust of the

Shakowin. If Pahana were to find out about this, what could she say to him about this disloyalty?

The monster hunter Naya-Nazgani was more exuberant and upbeat than he'd felt in many human generations. The combination of Pinga's company, as well as this new adventure he had embarked on, made him uncharacteristically chipper.

Naya-Nazgani made War Runner stop and then hopped down to the grass. The monster slayer kneeled down beside some tracks which Pinga had not noticed until now. The muscular man studied the tracks thoroughly.

"It's World Giant," Naya-Nazgani said. "The hoof size and stride length are consistent, and the depth of the tracks indicates the weight of a very large male bison, with a man riding him. Who else rides bison other than the Itiwana? The hooves have been recently trimmed. I saw that Pahana had just had World Giant's hooves done the morning before he left. It's most definitely him. We're on the right trail."

"How far ahead is he?" she asked.

"These are very fresh," Naya-Nazgani said. "We're close on his tail. We'll either overtake him or find him stopped before sundown."

Shielding her eyes from the sun, Pinga squinted to examine the horizon. She saw the tall trees in the distance. "What timberland is that?" she asked, pointing.

"It's the Red Sky Forest," he said. "It seems as though Pahana is headed there."

What could Pahana need so urgently in the Red Sky Forest? she wondered.

"Do you want to stop for a meal?" he asked. "There is fruit here, easily collected."

"No, she wishes to go on," Pinga said. "This One wants to finish this distasteful quest as soon as we're able."

Rejoining her on the bison, he took the reins. "As you wish. Onward, War Runner. We're very near the end."

She hugged him around the waist again, thinking about her son, as War Runner cantered forward toward the nearby forest.

CHAPTER TWENTY

The Faces on the Trees were frightening. When those eerie, otherworldly faces appeared on the trees of the Red Sky Forest, howling with anger and hatred toward all humans, death often followed. Mortal men who saw the faces often died of fright, or otherwise were stricken with some sort of disease. The Faces were the earthly manifestation of the Soyoko; evil Kachina who serve Matche-Monedo, a dark Kachina who despises humans and who preys on them for sport.

The Wood Men had become accustomed to the Faces in the Forest. Innocent and brave, the hirsute, looming Wood Men were not like mortal men. Bigger and stronger, although considerably less intelligent than humans, they were not targets of Matche-Monedo. Even if they had been, the Wood Men seemed immune to the deadly power these hateful beings possessed.

A group of Wood Men, both male and female, sat indolently in the Red Sky Forest. They were wiling the day away, as they frequently did. Left alone, they wanted nothing and harmed no one. Aside from Faw-Faw and another named Ko-Ko, no Wood Man or woman had left the Red Sky Forest in over a century. In recent years, they had only been threatened by the cult-like society known as the Ghost Men; secretive men who painted themselves like skeletons and worshipped the Matche-Monedo.

The Wood Men's keen senses detected the scent of a human coming their way. They stood on alert, always unsure of what the arrival of a human meant. They feared it might be the Ghost Men. Some concealed themselves, while the two largest stood, tall and imposing, to show that they had no fear of strangers.

Stepping out of the foggy mist of dusk came the Husk Face Man. His hoe in hand, he walked directly to the two tallest Wood Men. He stopped in front of them, fearlessly meeting their suspicious gaze.

One of them, named Ko-Ko, who was more familiar with humans than other Wood Men were, sniffed the Husk Face Man. The visitor made no threatening moves. After allowing them to examine him, the Husk Face Man produced an apple and held it out to the Wood Men. This offering of fruit was a gesture of friendship to the simple woodland dwellers.

"Gug," the Husk Face Man said loudly.

"Gug," Ko-Ko replied, taking the apple. Sniffing it, Ko-Ko bit it in half with one bite.

Using his hoe, the Husk Face Man began drawing pictures in the dirt as a way of communicating with the Wood Men, who had no spoken language beyond 'Gug.'

"I hope I can make you understand," the Husk Face Man said. "I have need of you."

At sundown, the Ghost Men came out from the cave they used as their shrine to Matche-Monedo. In their skeleton paint and loin cloths, carrying stone-tipped spears and wooden swords, they stepped out into the night. Their leader, whose painted skeleton was gray instead of white, was usually called "the Gray Man."

"Come," he said to his thirteen companions. "It's time we did our duty."

"Are we going to the Wood Men again?" one of the Ghost Men asked.

"Where else?" the Gray Man said. "One day, if we're dedicated, Matche-Monedo's prediction will come true. One day we will find the beautiful silver Goddess among them, and when we do, we'll give Matche-Monedo exactly what he wants."

###

Walking Storm grunted as it cantered through a stream. Flying Courage was close at his side. Calian and Gluskap rode at a brisk clip. The moon was rising, and they wanted to cover as much distance as possible before finding a concealed, defensible place to camp for the night. With so many of the Itiwana's enemies lurking in every shadow of Ulah-Nane, they didn't want to be caught sleeping and vulnerable.

"I hope you don't take this amiss, but I was greatly hoping I could perform this feat alone," Gluskap said. "Although I confess, I never would have found this Beaver Creek on my own, having lived on a mountain my entire life. But I know I have the power to succeed and bring honor to my father."

Calian's face showed sympathy. "I understand your passions. I also stand in the shadow of a great man. My father Pogum was the greatest among the Itiwana. I know about the need to fulfill a legacy. But you'll soon be hoping for even greater power when the conflict you desire arrives. It's always that way. We believe we can do everything alone until we see the forces aligned against us. That's when we look around for our friends and family and fellow warriors."

Gluskap took these words to heart. "You're probably right. I hear you usually are. I shouldn't be so haughty when I've only fought one battle. I take back my careless words and welcome your company."

"You're a fine young lad," Calian said. "You've impressed many among us so far. I predict you'll do great things."

"I pray I won't disappoint," Gluskap said.

The sound of bison hooves on grass mixed with the chirping of crickets. War Runner casually pushed his way through thick bushes and shrubs. Naya-Nazgani and Pinga had been trailing Pahana's tracks for hours. Night was falling and Pinga feared they would lose the trail again.

Naya-Nazgani halted his mount. "Do you smell that?" he asked, sniffing.

"This One smells nothing different," she answered.

"A bison," Naya-Nazgani said. "A different one. Not War Runner. It's close."

"This One does not see any bison," she said.

Naya-Nazgani sniffed again and pointed. "There. That way."

After a short canter, they reached a small cabin made of stones and clay. Outside was a little girl and a very old man. The girl was grooming a rather large bison, while the old man smoked a pipe.

"That's World Giant!" Pinga cried. "Unmistakable. This One knows her son's mount."

"This is not what I expected," Naya-Nazgani. "Let's find some answers to vexing questions."

Dismounting, they walked to the cabin. The old man and the girl watched them as if they were wolves stalking the house. The old man grabbed a bow and arrow, but he seemed to have trouble standing. "Who are you?"

"Be at peace, my friend," Naya-Nazgani said. "We're just travelers. We're of the Itiwana tribe."

"I am Luls Juk," the elderly man said. "This is my granddaughter, Bitsitsi. We are of the Juk clan. This land is ours. We Juk's have lived here for many seasons. My children are away at the moment."

"This One greets you in peace," Pinga said. "We are looking for someone. His name is Pahana of the Itiwana tribe. Can you tell us where he is?"

Naya-Nazgani moved forward to pet World Giant. "We assume you know where he is to be found. You have his bison. Hello there, big fellow. Where's your master? Why did he leave you here? Where did Pahana go?"

"He asked us to take care of his animal," the little girl said. "He gave us lots of corn seeds and delicious nuts. And some feathers for my collection."

"This One is Pahana's mother," Pinga said passively. "We need to find him. It is important. Please tell us ... where is Pahana?"

Finding their way in the dark was difficult. Naya-Nazgani had not been to the Red Sky Forest in over fifty seasons and Pinga had never been there. Following the verbal directions of an elderly stranger and a child through the dark woods was challenging.

"This One feels we are lost," Pinga commented.

"I will get you there," Naya-Nazgani said, a tad embarrassed. "I brought you this far. Trust me."

"This One does," Pinga said. "Her faith in you is unwavering."

"As is my loyalty to you," Naya-Nazgani replied. "I..."

The pair were interrupted by an angry wailing sound. The macabre din chilled Pinga to the soul. She had never heard anything so bloodcurdling. Filled with terror, she tightened her grip around Naya-Nazgani, squeezing him closer.

"What is that sound?" she asked. "It frightens her."

"It's the Faces of the Forest!" Naya-Nazgani replied. "I encountered them here, long ago. Their voice instills terror. Be strong, Pinga. It will get worse!"

The Faces began appearing on the trees. Their twisted, grotesque faces stared at the two riders. Pinga saw the horrific visages surrounding them and she had to stifle a scream of pure panic.

Naya-Nazgani urged War Runner to do as his name implies and run. Moving as fast as it could, the bison charged through the forests. Even the animal seemed agitated by the terrible sounds.

"Brave heart, Pinga!" Naya-Nazgani said. "Don't let them overcome you! Persist and we will prevail!"

Closing her eyes and biting her lip to keep from screaming, Pinga desperately hung onto her monster hunting companion as they darted through the woodlands. The next few minutes seemed to be an eternity of dread, and Pinga trembled in distress.

Abruptly, they found the hogan in front of them. Naya-Nazgani jerked the reins, stopping War Runner. He presumed they had found the place they were looking for if the Juks were telling the truth. The sound of chanting came from inside.

"Pahana! Are you here?" he shouted, to be heard over the spine-chilling voices.

Pinga seemed to be frozen, so he scooped her off the bison and carried her toward the hogan. As he did so, Hototo stepped out of the hogan, adorned in his wooden mask. Having heard Naya-Nazgani yell, he came to see who was out in the woods while the faces screamed.

"Bring her inside!" Hototo ordered.

Naya-Nazgani easily carried her into the hogan, to find a group of painted people in wooden masks and furs inside. One man had a mask made of corn husks and a headdress. The voices from outside were still audible.

While most of the masked people continued chanting and using rattles, the man in the corn husk mask hopped to his feet and rushed to check on the insensate woman.

"She's being affected by the Faces in the Forest!" Naya-Nazgani shouted.

"We know," Hototo said. "We will attend to the forest demons."

He sat to join the others in their ceremony while the Husk Face Man examined Pinga. "Put her down here."

He pointed to a bear skin in the room, used as a spot to kneel before their totem. Naya-Nazgani placed the disoriented Pinga onto the bear skin. The Husk Face Man looked into her eyes.

"She's shocked from fear," he said. "With luck, she'll recover when the voices stop."

I know his voice, Naya-Nazgani thought.

The awful voices outside began to fade and became silent. Hototo stood up and walked to the entrance, gesturing for the others to follow him. "Let's finish our work."

All the False Faces hurried outside to do the Father Dance around the hogan. The Husk Face Man remained inside with Pinga and Naya-Nazgani. The Husk Face Man kneeled to whisper into Pinga's ear.

"It's over," he said. "There's nothing more to fear. Rest now. Sleep."

Whether she was responding to his voice or just overcome by the ordeal, Pinga seemed to lose consciousness. Naya-Nazgani was concerned.

"Is she harmed?" the monster hunter asked.

"She'll sleep for a time," the Husk Face Man said in that familiar voice. "We can only hope that there are no lasting effects. If there are, the False Faces should be able to exorcise the evil from her. For now, we must wait."

Standing over Pinga, Naya-Nazgani took a closer look at the Husk Face Man. "I recognize your voice. We've been looking for you, Pahana."

The Husk Face Man removed his mask, revealing his bright white face. "Why are you here? Why has my mother been brought into danger?"

"It was a decision of your grandmother," Naya-Nazgani replied. "Take her to task for it, not your mother. Pinga was chosen to find out where you were."

With a sigh, Pahana tapped his mask. "I should have anticipated this. My grandmother made no secret of her anger at my absences. It was only a question of time before she did something like this. I'll need to settle this with her upon my return. And what of you, Naya-Nazgani? What's your part in this?"

"I came along to protect her," he answered.

"Then I am once again in your debt," Pahana said. "You did a good service for my father before his death. You helped defend Shipapa-Lina, and now you've defended my mother. I feel I have an obligation to you that even a chieftain cannot recompense."

"I may hold you to that in the future," Naya-Nazgani said, looking around the hogan. "What is this place? Who are those people?"

Pahana sat on the floor beside his mother. "The False Faces are the disciples and worshippers of Katche-Monedo, a benign Kachina eternally at odds with his vile brother, Matche-Monedo, who rules the Soyoka. The False Faces help to ward off the Soyoka."

"I know of the Soyoka and the Faces in the Forest," Naya-Nazgani. "I know that encounters with them can be lethal."

"Sadly, yes," Pahana said, brushing a hair out of his mother's face. "If their fear attack doesn't kill, their victim can later develop an ailment of some type. Fortunately, my mother is not a mortal, and so she should survive. Time will tell whether or not there are any aftereffects. It appears you are sufficiently immune."

"I was born a Mastop-Kachina and the Uwanami made some ... alterations," Naya-Nazgani said. "Creatures like the Soyoka hold no threat for me. But if I may ask, why are you here?"

"I am here to make an alliance with Katche-Monedo," Pahana said. "The specifics of my plan are not for you or anyone else to know at the moment. Just know that Katche-Monedo can be valuable to the Itiwana in the future. On a previous visit, I discovered several unfortunate pieces of information. His brother Matche-Monedo has servants called the Ghost Men, who apparently have the unpleasant idea to break down the walls between realms and free Katche-Monedo and his Soyoka servants. They will cause devastation among the mortal men of Ulah-Nane if that should happen. I have reason to believe they will also target the Wood Men, who are long-time allies of ours."

"Faw-Faw is my close friend," Naya-Nazgani said. "I would be loath to see his people destroyed."

"I intend to stop this from happening," Pahana said. "Not merely because it's the proper thing to do, but also because Katche-Monedo will never be free to focus on what I need him to do if he is battling an invasion of the Soyoka. Therefore, the Ghost Men must be stopped."

"I understand," Naya-Nazgani said. "Do you require assistance?"

"If I had wanted assistance, I would have brought assistance," Pahana replied. "I will do what must be done without you or the Itiwana. I have made arrangements with the Wood Men and the False Faces to help me. That will be enough. All I ask of you is to make certain my mother gets safely back to Shipapa-Lina."

"That much I promise," Naya-Nazgani vowed. "We've accomplished our goal. As soon as your mother recovers, I will escort her home. No harm will befall her."

The sound of the False Faces returning caused Pahana to quickly replace his mask onto his face. "Do not tell them who I am. Don't ask why. I have no time to explain."

"As you wish," Naya-Nazgani replied.

The False Faces reentered. They looked curiously at Pinga. Hototo took off his mask and regarded her with great interest. Naya-Nazgani stood guard over her, not trusting anyone where Pinga was concerned.

"The Faces in the Trees have been driven away for now," Hototo said. "This woman is fortunate to be alive. She cannot be a mere mortal."

"I think she will recover soon," Pahana said under his Husk Face mask. "I believe she is a Goddess. We should treat her well, to please the Sky Elders."

Hototo turned to Naya-Nazgani. "Odd that you are completely unharmed. How do you explain this, stranger?"

"Perhaps I am just fortunate," Naya-Nazgani replied. "Or it may be that I am too obstinate to be defeated by a tree."

"I find you suspicious," Hototo said. "Who are you?"

"I am Naya-Nazgani. Hunter of monsters. Ageless slayer of beasts."

The False Faces responded with excitement. Some of them bowed with respect. Even Hototo was impressed.

"The great Naya-Nazgani stands among us!" Hototo said. "This is an honor. We are but novices in battling the creatures of night. You are the master of it. You must have many stories and much wisdom to impart. Can we impose on you to remain for a time? We would deem it a privilege."

"I'll remain until my lady Goddess is ready to travel," Naya-Nazgani said. "Until then, I will be here, at her side."

"And you will both be honored guests," Hototo said. "Consider this your home for as long as you like."

CHAPTER TWENTY-ONE

Near the Bitter Root Valley, Calian and young Gluskap had reached Beaver Creek. Calian hadn't been to this region since he was a youth. But failures of the past didn't mean anything at present because Calian was a different man now and he didn't intend to fail twice.

They dismounted and led their mounts to a place to graze. Calian led Gluskap to the sandstone cliffs over the pristine water. The long creek cut through the rocks, making this area convenient to jump in and swim. Below was an inviting swimming hole, offering relief from the heat.

"This is it?" Gluskap asked.

"It is," Calian answered. "If that Puk-Wudjie is accurate, what we want is just below. As is the deadly Underwater Panther."

Gluskap was too excited to be nervous. "Shall we proceed?"

"I see no reason to hesitate," Calian said. "I want to quickly return to Shipapa-Lina and resume my position as War Chief before my two rascally friends undo all my work with their foolishness. Let's begin."

The excited Gluskap immediately dived from the sandstone rocks, not waiting for Calian. As the young man disappeared under the surface, Calian sighed and shook his head.

"Just like O'Yewa and Masewa," he mumbled. "More courage than wisdom."

He leaped from the rocks and splashed into the creek. In the mostly clear water, he could see Gluskap swimming downward, without fear. Calian looked around him, wary of the imminent arrival of the Underwater Panther.

Gluskap swam along the bottom of the creek, unable to find the jar the Yehasuri spoke of. He had to return to the surface several times to fill his lungs. Calian allowed him to do the searching, preferring to float near the surface, waiting for the Underwater Panther to arrive. He had a stone knife latched to his clothing of sewn yucca fibers.

Gluskap began to gesture as if he'd found something. He dug out an object, half buried in the creek bottom. Calian bobbed to the surface to get another supply of air before swimming down to assist his young friend.

Before he could get to the bottom, he saw the silhouette moving quickly toward them. As the dark figure came closer, Calian got a look at Mishebiju, the Underwater Panther. It looked much like a black panther except that it had a long tail which was a wriggling eel. The tail had a face whose teeth were almost as intimidating as those in the panther's head. The creature had gills on its neck and a dorsal fin on its spine. The eyes shined in the darkness like fireflies in the night.

Despite being underwater, the beast made a threatening sound that could only be described as a roar. Gluskap noticed the panther also and swam upward.

The two warriors of the Itiwana battled fiercely against Mishebiju. Calian and Gluskap were at a great disadvantage underwater. Aside from the panther being quicker and more maneuverable under the surface, the Itiwana needed air. The possibility of drowning was just as much a danger as was the threat of those panther fangs tearing out their throats.

At first, the two together put up a good fight. Calian held off those teeth and fangs with his stone knife, while Gluskap came up from behind, wrestling with that strange tail and the mouth that snapped at Gluskap viciously. But the tide of the battle changed when they began to run out of air. Calian went up for air, leaving Gluskap alone with the beast. He barely returned in time to save Gluskap from a lethal bite. Next it was Gluskap's turn to go up for air. This strategy of alternating in combat against their powerful foe proved futile, because neither of them could contend with the creature alone. They received several claw wounds, and blood flowed into the creek water.

Calian felt the water becoming cold and witnessed ice forming around the Underwater Panther. He then remembered that Gluskap had inherited the same natural powers Pinga and Pahana had. Gluskap pointed to the jar at the bottom of the lake.

Calian decided to risk leaving Gluskap to contend with the Underwater Panther while he saw to the retrieval of their prize. Diving down, he uncovered the sunken object and saw that it was, indeed, the jar that the Yehasuri had described.

Mishebiju the Underwater Panther instantly forgot about Gluskap and dived furiously toward this man who dared to touch the thing it protected. Gluskap grabbed the panther from behind, increasing the rate of ice that covered the beast. That eel-like tail had become incased in a block of ice.

Calian tried to avoid the diving beast, but its powerful paw swiped at his face. He felt the skin on his face tear as the impact knocked the air out of him. Stunned, he dropped the jar and sank to the bottom. He knew he was drowning.

His last thought was a strange peace that his death had been as noble as that of his father Pogum.

CHAPTER TWENTY-TWO

I*'m alive!* Calian thought.

The Itiwana sat up, surprised that there was no pain. He touched his cheek and didn't detect the blood or facial injury he had previously received.

Calian surveyed his surroundings. He sat in an eerie landscape of dark skies, black sands, ominous gray mists and an obsidian river. There was a dread feeling of foreboding permeating the strange land. He could hear faint screams and cries of battle in the distance. All his instincts told him that this was a very dangerous place.

"Where in Awona'Wilona's name am I?" he asked. "Where's Gluskap? And that monster?"

"Monsters are common here," a female voice said.

Jumping to his feet, Calian saw a tall woman with mahogany skin, covered with a cloak and hood. She had strange eyes that seemed to see too much, and yet there was something tranquil about her. "We know all about monsters in this place."

Calian cautiously approached the hooded woman. "Who are you? What is this place?"

"Be at peace," she said. "I am Tiya, and we are on the banks of the river of death. This is the second world... A place between the first world of physical sorrows and the third and fourth realms of death."

Remembering his battle with Mishebiju, he realized what had happened to him. "I have fallen, haven't I? I am dead."

"You are in the place where souls are transported to their final destination," she answered with a soothing voice. "Some will come with me to the third world, called the Holy Hunting Ground, and enjoy their eternity. I am the Goddess of peaceful death. Others will go to the fourth world with Taxet, the God of violent death. We have a long-standing animosity."

"And where am I to go?" Calian asked. "I died a violent death."

Tiya held up a finger. "But not so hasty. You are not, in your heart, a violent man. You are brave and noble just like your father was."

"You know of my father Pogum?" Calian asked eagerly.

"Indeed, I do," Tiya said. "He has been a warrior here in the second world for many of your seasons."

Calian remembered a story Kia had told him and his mother years ago. A story of meeting Pogum on a journey to the world between worlds. "I owe Kia an apology. I thought it was simply the fanciful tale of a child. My mother thought she was merely attempting to make us happy with her incredible story. I wish I could beg her clemency, but I don't imagine I will see her again in the world of the living. Where, then, shall I go?"

"That is yet to be decided," Tiya informed him and gestured toward the lake. "Here lay the River of Death. Soon, the Ferry of Fallen Souls will sail past. It returns here after sailing the river, like an ouroboros. The ship has a grand purpose."

"I'm afraid to inquire what that may be," Calian said.

"And well you should be," Tiya said. "This ship transports the dead from here to the third and fourth realms. The decision is declared by great Manitou regarding which land the soul will ultimately reside. In some cases, the decision is not made until the ship has already sailed."

"As in my situation?" Calian asked.

"Perhaps," she said. "But perhaps you are too cold to yourself. You underestimate your goodness."

"Then I will go to the Holy Hunting Ground?" he asked.

"As with every other soul, you will learn your fate as we travel," she said.

Calian looked around again. "If this is the method of transporting the dead to the afterworld, where are the other souls? Why am I the only one here?"

She smiled and touched him gently on the chest. "Because I need your assistance."

"Mine?" he asked. "What help can I be to a death Goddess?"

She looked at the river. "The ferry is not merely a way to transport dead to their reward, but also a way to defend against the opposite."

"I don't understand."

"Many evil and determined souls reside in the harsh, merciless fourth world of Taxet," she explained. "And many of them try to escape. This ship patrols the river like one of the sentries of the Two-Horn Riders, ensuring that these menacing ghosts do not succeed in finding their way back to the first world of the living. If this ferry ever ceases its endless journey, the souls of the evil dead would escape back to the mortal realm. Think of the chaos if that were to happen. So, the ship still sails eternally, standing guard."

"Just you alone?" Calian asked.

"You've discovered the reason I need your assistance," Tiya said. "I usually share my voyage with a strong and formidable warrior of endless courage and limitless nobility. However, on this occasion, he was summoned away by Matche-Monedo due to an event in the Red Sky Forest of your world. That leaves me to do this task alone. You were ... suggested as a fleeting replacement for this latest trip. That's why we are traveling alone. Since you are unfamiliar with the threats you will face, we felt there was no need to subject you to a possible mutiny of the evil souls being delivered to Taxet. It's happened before, and you will have enough to contend with."

"But why me?"

"You'll know in time," she said. "I assume you will cooperate."

"Of course," Calian replied. "Like my father, I wish to be of service in whatever world I reside in."

"As expected," Tiya said. "Look, the ferry comes."

The bloodred ship sailed out of the mists. It had no visible propulsion, since the mast had no sails. It moved because it was meant to move. Calian watched the spectral ship come closer, until it came to a sudden stop near Tiya and Calian. A ramp was extended as an invitation to come aboard.

"Follow," Tiya said as she ascended the ramp.

Calian, feeling overwhelmed, walked behind her. Once onboard, he saw another robed individual standing near a circular object. Calian couldn't see his face. "Who is that?"

"That is Make-Taori," she said. "He controls the ferry, steering it in the proper direction. Pay him no heed. He will not interfere. He only does what he's meant to do. Expect no help from him."

The ramp withdrew itself and the Ferry of Fallen Souls began moving once again, sailing down the river of death. Tiya walked to a seat and made herself comfortable. She gestured to Calian to join her.

"You may as well sit and be at peace," she said. "Soon you will need all your strength, intelligence, and willpower to contend with what will come next. If the dead souls are able to sense that my usual companion is not with me, we may face more escaping souls than usual."

"Any other ill news to share?" Calian asked.

"I'll leave you to discover the rest," she said.

Time passed differently in this realm of the undead and unalive. Calian tried his best to perceive the length of his trip. The travels of the Ferry of Fallen Souls passed uneventfully for a period that seemed to Calian like a full day. He studied the foggy shore landscape, listening to the unnerving sounds in the distance. The ferry cruised neared the sargasso of fire, where flames burned over a whirlpool. Calian was nervous as the ship sailed over the fiery swirl, but the ferry got through the obstacle safely. He was relieved that so much time had passed quietly.

"No danger so far," Calian said. "Perhaps this won't be so arduous."

"Keep your mind focused," Tiya said. "We are passing closer to Taxet's fourth world. I doubt that peace will reign much longer."

"Look there," Calian said, as if on cue. "What's that ahead?"

An ice flow was drifting toward the ferry. Standing on the burg was a large, furry, white creature, with noticeable claws. The frost conveyance moved to intercept the Ferry of Fallen Souls.

"It is Giwakna, the Ice Wendigo," Tiya said.

Calian knew the name and the stories he had grown up with. "Giwakna? My father killed that creature."

"Yes, it comes to our ship quite often," Tiya said. "But we seem to have a second problem!"

The water began to bubble up, as if a large creature was under the surface. The colossal horned serpent, Uktena, rose from the black river. Rising upright, it towered over the ferry. Its jaws were immense when expanded.

"Uktena was killed in battle with the Great Turtle, in the days before your tribe existed," Tiya said.

Calian watched the salivating, venomous monster rearing for an assault. "We're being attacked from the front and the side!"

"We need a clever tactic," Tiya said.

Giwakna began to climb on board the ferry, using its claws. Calian's eyes scanned the ship, looking for a weapon. He noticed a rigging rope dangling from the mast, which contained no sails. Calian scampered part of the way up the ramp, grabbed the rope, and then leaped. He swung, getting as much momentum as he could, aiming for the front of the ferry. Just as Giwakna was climbing onto the deck, Calian slammed into him. The wendigo roared as it lost its balance. Giwakna fell into the water. While Giwakna splashed around, Uktena was moving toward the ferry.

Tiya lifted her hands and utilized some hitherto unrevealed magical power. She created a realistic image of the Great Turtle, which had destroyed

Uktena. Uktena suddenly backed away, frightened by the sight of its murderer. It descended back into the deep water. As it did, the serpent displayed its anger by grabbing Giwakna in its teeth, chewing and swallowing the screaming wendigo. Uktena vanished into the river.

"Very well done," Tiya said. "One crisis averted."

"I hope the rest of our trip will be as successful," Calian replied.

CHAPTER TWENTY-THREE

*H*ow long have I been here? Calian wondered. His pondering was interrupted by
Tiya, who rose to her feet, clearly sensing something. Calian moved to her side.

"Where?" he asked.

"There!" Tiya said, pointing. "The atoll of the
grasshopper."

A grasshopper larger than a bison sat on an
atoll in the river. A hoard of dead but flying bugs
flew in circles around the giant insect.

Calian leaned over the railing, studying the
creature. "That must be the giant grasshopper
that sent the plague of locusts to Shipapa-Lina.
He was destroyed by Mapingwari and Faw-Faw.
He has an even larger swarm here."

"The grasshopper can't leave the atoll, but we
still must be cautious as we pass, lest the insects

overcome us," Tiya said. "The ferry must remain guarded! Light the torches."

"Do you have any other suggestions?" Calian asked.

"Yes. Look above," Tiya said. "Another threat has arrived."

From above, a slim, bronze-skinned sorceress sailed through the dark skies, gliding on the winds from a cyclone of her own making. She laughed a heartless laugh as she swooped over the ferry. Calian recognized her immediately.

"Dagwona!" he said. "Even in death, the Witch of the Whirlwind is as murderous as ever."

"Dagwona destroys!" the witch shouted, excited for revenge.

From the mists of the River of Death, an army of Skinwalkers floated into view on a grouping of rafts and driftwoods. They tossed vines with wooden hooks onto the ferry and proceeded to climb up to the deck.

"Eliminate enemies!" Dagwona yelled. "She slays! Winds will whip wildly!"

"I must fight her," Tiya said to the Itiwana warrior. "Only by defeating her can the Skinwalkers be stopped. You must attend to the swarm while I battle her!"

"I'll do my finest," Calian said.

While Calian attended to the torches, Tiya raised her hands to begin her battle. She wasn't overly confident. Even in death, Dagwona was as ferocious as she was powerful. Tiya was also being battered by the winds. Her strength was fading.

Calian had lit all the torches, but it only slowed the swarm. Looking behind, he saw that the Skinwalkers were climbing over the railing. They closed in, growling and hissing. With Tiya occupied, he had to come up with something alone.

"Look at the basket," a voice said.

Calian realized that Make-Taori had finally spoken. The man at the wheel pointed to a greenish basket. "Open it."

With no other options, Calian lifted the top of the basket off. From out of that emerald basket came a multi-colored crow. Calian was confused as to how this strange creature could help. He wasn't familiar with the legend of the Rainbow Crow; a nature spirit who saved the Lenape Tribe from a forest fire by taking the fire into itself, sacrificing himself in the process.

The colorful crow flew out of the basket and circled around the deck. It suddenly burst into a scorching fireball. Flying in an oval shape, the Rainbow Crow flew through the swarm of insects, instantly scaring them away. The crow also startled the Skinwalkers.

Make-Taori slid two pieces out of the ferry helm wheel. The removed pieces now served as two heavy clubs. He tossed one of the clubs to Calian. Make-Taori began battering the Skinwalkers with surprising speed and considerable force. Calian joined him, smashing the animal-men with unrestrained brutality.

As a result of the combination of the fire and the painful clubbing, the Skinwalkers retreated, jumping back into the water. Above them, Dagwona was distracted by the retreat of her Skinwalker servants. Calian and Make-Taori stood at Tiya's side, ready to resist the Whirlwind Witch.

"You won't win, Dagwona," Tiya said to her opponent. "Don't die again!"

The Witch of the Whirlwind hesitated, sneering at the trio, but finally, she began to drift away. "Dagwona delayed!" she said. "Witch will wait. Revengeful return!"

The Witch of the Whirlwind departed into the mists. As for the giant grasshopper, it merely watched the ferry sail passed. The ship left the creature behind.

"Well done, both of you," Tiya said.

Calian put his hand on Make-Taori's shoulder. "And thank you my unseen friend. I am grateful for your help. I'm indebted to you."

"And I am very proud of you," the man known as Make-Taori said as he pulled down his hood, revealing his face. "Very proud of you, my son."

Calian had never seen the face of his father before, but he had stared at the painted image of Pogum on the rock wall many times. He listened to his mother's description of Pogum countless times. Calian looked into eyes that had always been reflected back to him from the aqueduct water. Beyond that, all his instincts told him who this was.

"Father?" Calian asked. "Is it you?"

"It's me," his father said. "I am Pogum. It's a blessing from Awona'Wilona to finally meet you."

After a moment of silent amazement, Calian wrapped Pogum in a tight hug. "Father!"

"Just let me look at you," Pogum said.

Pogum stared at Calian for a few moments while his son stood flabbergasted. He had never thought this moment would ever come. *It's really my father!*

"Ah, you've become a fine form of a man," Pogum said. "My greatest tragedy was that I didn't get to see you born and watch you grow up. I wish I could have been there to be a father to you."

"Yes, I wish we could have spent all those summers and winters together," Calian said. "Every story our people told me about you filled me with pride but also shattered my heart that I would never meet you."

"I'm sorry I wasn't there for you and your mother," Pogum said.

"You died a true hero," Calian replied. "You were the greatest Itiwana of all."

Pogum put a hand on the nape of Calian's neck. "I wish we had more time. I want you to know that I've been able to see you on occasion. Not as much as I'd like but there are times when the veil between worlds opens and Tiya helps me to envision Shipapa-Lina. I have such pride that you're the War Chief now. Just as I once was."

"I can never be as good as you," Calian said. "I can only aspire to be half the War Chief you were."

"Don't doubt yourself," Pogum said. "Trust that you'll do miracles. And remember this: the end of the God war is coming soon, and you will need to exceed yourself. You have much to do."

"But ... aren't I on my way to the third world of death?" Calian asked.

"You're returning to the first world," Pogum said. "You have a vital part to play."

"You passed your test," Tiya said. "You win a reprieve."

"I requested to great Manitou that you have a second chance at life," Pogum said. "Use it well. Be as strong and loyal and fearless as you've ever been. You must protect your chieftain, and you must slay that venomous fiend, Hayoka. I know you'll do it like a great warrior."

"I'll be my father's son," Calian replied, teary-eyed.

"You'll be spectacular!" Pogum said, lovingly. "You must go now."

"But it's too soon!" Calian said. "I want to..."

"What we want comes second to duty," Pogum said. "Our family has always lived that way. Go and be a hero. And give my deepest love to your mother. Goodbye, son. I love you."

"And I you, Father."

They embraced once more. And Calian was gone...

I'm alive! Calian thought.

He felt the ground against his back and the sun on his face. Opening his eyes, he saw Gluskap kneeling over him. The son of Pahana was tending to his face. Gluskap had created some ice to use on Calian's wound.

"Thank the Elders you're alive," Gluskap said. "Lay there. Rest. You had a near fatal encounter."

"I'll survive," Calian said. "Are you well?"

"I'm hail and well," Gluskap said. "Other than a few deep cuts from those claws, I'm perfectly intact. You have a face wound. The ice has stopped the bleeding. But you'll have scars."

Calian chuckled. "Just like my father. I'll wear them with pride. But what happened to the Underwater Panther?"

"Not a problem for the present," Gluskap said. "He's frozen in the lake. It will take quite some time for him to thaw out."

"And the tomahawk?"

Gluskap cocked his head toward the shattered remains of the jar. Next to the pieces was a golden tomahawk sticking into the ground. Gluskap pulled it from the dirt and handed it to Calian. "Success!"

Calian's face lightened into a weak smile. "Success. I've waited ages for this."

"My father will be proud," Gluskap said.

"As will mine," replied Calian. "As will mine."

CHAPTER TWENTY-FOUR

For several days, the False Faces made Naya-Nazgani feel welcome. He entertained them with tales of his adventures across Ulah-Nane, giving vivid descriptions of all the creatures he'd battled over the years, including more recent ones in Shipapa-Lina.

Pinga was recovering slowly. Although her life was not in danger, the aftereffects still plagued her. The lingering illness that the Faces in the Trees inflicted on her was a lower-body paralysis. For the first day, she couldn't move her legs at all. Over the course of two nights, the feeling came back to her legs, and she was regaining the ability to move them ever-so-slightly. Her legs were still too weak to support her, but every day, she was hopeful that she would soon be able to walk again.

Naya-Nazgani attended to her at all times, unwilling to let her out of his sight. Pahana, still dressed as the Husk Face Man, checked on her occasionally but didn't want to be obvious because it would give away his identity. He still had not told Pinga or Naya-Nazgani why he wanted to remain anonymous, but they respected their chieftain's wish.

Naya-Nazgani wasn't the only one to nurse Pinga back to health. He was disturbed to see how much time Hototo spent attending to Pinga. Hototo brought her food and water, talking to her at length. Hototo smiled at her a little too much for Naya-Nazgani's liking. It was clear the leader of the False Faces was as taken by Pinga's charm and beauty as Naya-Nazgani was.

"How are your legs today, my lady Pinga?" Hototo asked her.

With a warm smile, she pointed at her feet. "This One can now wiggle her toes. She expects to be walking again by the rise of the crescent moon."

"Only seven more days," Hototo said. "Would you find me cruel and selfish if I said I was disappointed to hear you will be recovered so soon? That means you'll be leaving us. This news makes me sad. Your beauty has made the days brighter."

She smiled sweetly at him. "She is very pleased by your tribute and your honesty. Perhaps she will return to visit you in the future."

Naya-Nazgani burned with resentment at the idea of a rival for Pinga's affections. He was tempted to challenge Hototo to a fair, man-to-man battle for Pinga's hand, but resisted the urge because he knew the stakes were very high. The plan Pahana had for Katche-Monedo and Matche-Monedo was somehow vital to his overall strategy to battle the Enemy Way. Naya-Nazgani couldn't risk ruining the alliance between Pahana and the False Faces because of jealousy.

And he wasn't the only one who was feeling jealous. The sole female member of the False Faces was Cheraya. She was very devoted to the cause. She also had a sexual attraction to Hototo. She witnessed how attentive Hototo was to this snow-skinned woman. So attentive, in fact, that he chose not to participate in the nightly Father Dance.

Naya-Nazgani had quickly built a special chair with a high back for Pinga to sit in, so the former Goddess could be comfortable until her partial immobility passed. Cheraya watched fuming while Hototo and Naya-Nazgani competed to see who could spoil her the most.

She tried to point this out to the other members of the False Faces, but they didn't seem to share her concerns. Cheraya was outraged at how no one else could see that Pinga was a dangerous distraction from the big picture. Cheraya wondered if the men among the False Faces would be so tolerant of this disruption if Pinga weren't so stunning.

On the fourth day, the mysterious Husk Mask Man was absent again, as he was so frequently prone to do. The legendary Naya-Nazgani kneeled dutifully beside Pinga's chair, trying his best to keep her spirits up during her convalescence.

"This One feels very guilty," Pinga said. "She knows you are a man of action. Because of her, you are induced to play sedentary caretaker for all these days."

"Nonsense," Naya-Nazgani replied. "This has been a fine, relaxing visit. I enjoy a bit of quiet on occasion."

Pinga put her finger over his lips. "You are too noble to lie, warrior. This One knows you live for the siren cry of battle and thrill of danger. But she thanks you for lying to spare her feelings. It's kind of you. You've done so much for This One. She doesn't know how to thank you."

"I told you, that's unnecessary," Naya-Nazgani said. "It's my honor and privilege to serve you."

With a tender smile, Pinga stroked his large bicep. "This One is lucky you came to Shipapa-Lina. May she ask you another boon?"

"Anything," he said eagerly.

"This One is hungry," she replied.

He immediately hopped to his feet. "Do you prefer a rabbit or a bird? Or shall I bring you both?"

"Some fruit and nuts would be lovely," she said with a flirty flutter of her eyes.

"As you wish," he answered. "I'll be back presently."

Only minutes after he was gone, Hototo was reminded that it was time for their weekly excursion to study the trees which were used by the Soyoka to create portals for the Faces in the Trees.

To the surprise of the other False Faces, Hototo attempted to avoid his responsibility so he could stay with Pinga.

This raised some concerns by Cheraya. Beyond her jealousy, she feared this woman was distracting the leader of the group away from his vital duties. And Naya-Nazgani was also clearly under the spell of Pinga. He should be out fighting monsters instead of nursing some silvery trollop. *That woman is distracting everyone from their proper duties.*

Hototo was dithering regarding his participation in the trek to the forest. Cheraya took it upon herself to influence him. "You know you cannot eschew your duty as leader. We all look to you for guidance and inspiration. Katche-Monedo also trusts you to be his avatar in Ulah-Nane. If it soothes your brow, I will stay and watch over Pinga for you until you return."

"Oh, very well, it seems I must," Hototo said. "Come along, brothers. Let's do what must be done."

Putting on his mask, he led his fellow False Faces out of the hogan. This left Cheraya alone with the still immobile Pinga. Cheraya stood over the Itiwana woman and sneered disgustedly at her.

"Are you enjoying your games?" Cheraya said.

"This One does not understand," Pinga replied.

She pointed an accusing finger at Pinga. "You are deliberately manipulating the men. You use your beauty and wiles to bend them to your will, and you do it well. You've even won stoic Hototo to your worship. I never imagined he could be conquered so easily. I congratulate you on your achievement. But your games of vanity are causing the men to be derelict in their obligations."

Pinga fidgeted nervously, afraid of the other woman's anger. She tried to push herself to her feet but still couldn't stand. "You have no reason for such anger. She has no evil intentions. This One only came here looking for her son."

"Your son is not here!" Cheraya cried. "And we're burdened with you."

"As soon as This One recovers, she will leave you," Pinga said.

"Not soon enough for my liking," Cheraya said. "You can do much damage in the duration."

Pinga heard a strange sound approaching. She was unfamiliar with it, but it was the sound of a squeaky old wooden cart approaching. The Itiwana did not have the wheel, but the newly arrived visitor did. Footsteps came toward the hogan.

"Who is that?" Pinga asked nervously. "Who is coming?"

"That's Navit'Ku," Cheraya said. "He's a trader from the northern regions. He brings us supplies in exchange for the healing powders we give him, which he sells to other tribes for valuable baubles and trinkets. His arrival is timely."

Pinga wondered what she was up to. Cheraya let in a hairy, slovenly, portly mountain man with a bushy beard. Cheraya greeted big Navit'Ku, whose odor filled the room. Pinga watched as they exchanged supplies for powders. She noticed, however, how they whispered to each other. *This One thinks matters are set to turn unpleasant for her.*

"You wish me to transport this woman to the Juk clan?" the mountain man said. "Indeed, Navit'Ku can do that."

"Good," Cheraya said. "Once she is away from here, the sooner the False Faces can return to our duty. I suppose you want some exchange recompense for this imposition?"

The big, burly man looked Pinga over lustfully. "Navit'Ku needs nothing else. Navit'Ku will enjoy this."

"No! This One does not want to go with him!" Pinga cried. "Leave her alone!"

Ignoring her protests, the mountain man scooped the weakened, immobile Pinga up out of her chair.

"Pretty girl," the mountain man said.

Pinga yelled in desperation, "Naya-Nazgani and Hototo will not forgive you for this! You will face retaliation."

"You're not the only one who can use her femininity to manipulate men," Cheraya said confidently. "I'll explain to them how I compassionately sent you away from the dangers posed by the Faces in the Trees. You'll be in the safe region where the Juk clan lives. Be at peace, Pinga. The Juks are fine people, and they will take good care of you. I will send Naya-Nazgani to the Juk clan cabin when he returns. As for Hototo, I will pacify him as I used to do before you came and bewitched him. Goodbye, Lady Pinga."

The big man carried her out of the cabin, while Cheraya mockingly waved goodbye. "Enjoy your journey."

Pinga struggled futilely against his great strength. He carried her back to his rickety old buggy, which was pulled by a team of large goats. The man roughly tossed Pinga into the buggy's seat. Weak from her ordeal and immobilized from the waist down, she couldn't offer any significant resistance against the burly, powerful man. *This One can't walk! How can she escape?*

Incapable of moving an inch, she could only watch as the mountain man said his goodbyes to Cheraya and walked slowly back to the buggy. He indolently climbed up, sitting next to Pinga, and grinned at the Itiwana woman. She met his eyes, sensing he was lecherous and dangerous. She feared him but couldn't make a move to flee or fight. *I'm at his mercy!*

As the goats and buggy trotted along the road, the mountain man hummed, often glancing lustfully at Pinga. She could only sit at his side and wait to see what he had planned for her. Neither she nor Navit'Ku noticed the painted man watching them covertly from the woods.

As they traveled, Pinga noticed they weren't going in the right direction to get to the Juk's cabin. "Where are you taking This One?"

"Navit'Ku has a cabin further north," the mountain man said.

CHAPTER TWENTY-FOUR

"But why?" she asked with dread. "What do you plan to do with This One?"

He just grinned a toothy grin, displaying crooked teeth. "Recompense. Heh, heh."

Pinga gasped when she realized what he had in mind for her. *By the Elders! No!*

Singing happily, big Navit'Ku directed his goat-powered cart to their unplanned destination.

Pinga continued trying to reason with him. "Please take This One back to the hogan. She can promise the Itiwana will reward you if you return This One unharmed. If you hurt This One, you'll reap the anger of Naya-Nazgani and all the Itiwana."

To her fear and frustration, Navit'Ku didn't react or respond to her pleas. *It's useless. He is too fixated on doing what he plans to do to This One, and I can't dissuade him.*

When they arrived at his ramshackle wooden cabin, he picked her up and carried her inside. She flailed her arms and pounded on his broad chest but to no avail. He dropped her on a bed of leaves and grass. She landed with a painful bump, since she couldn't use her legs to cushion her fall. Laying on the ground, she was unable to stand up. Her legs still wouldn't support her. *I'm powerless against his strengths! He's going to ravage me, and I can't run or fight!*

Before the mountain man could do what he planned to do, thirteen men painted as skeletons burst into the cabin. They swarmed toward the bed. The mountain man grabbed an ax and put up a decent fight. He took two of them down, but the superior numbers overwhelmed

him, and he fell in a pool of blood. Pinga, unmoving on the bed, watched the fight.

"Grab the sacrifice!" one of the Ghost Men yelled.

Sacrifice? Pinga thought, baffled.

Victorious, the eleven men grabbed Pinga and carried her outside. She struggled, but there were too many of them and she was too weak. Outside, near the cart, she saw a sedan chair. She had not seen one of those since she was across the sea in Europe with the Red King years ago.

What on Earth is this? she wondered, perplexed.

They hoisted Pinga into the sedan chair. Seated and unable to move, Pinga's heart pounded, wondering who they were and what they wanted. *If This One could stand, she would run like a rabbit away from here.*

Lifting the sedan chair, six men carried her in the seat while a seventh led the way. Pinga sat immobile in the chair, scared and confused.

"Who are you people?" she asked desperately. "Where are you taking This One? Let her down! You mentioned a sacrifice. Are you planning to sacrifice This One? For what purpose? This One warns you, when the people of the Itiwana hear of this, you'll all die!"

As with Navit'Ku, her captors didn't respond. With no other alternative, the weakened Pinga submitted to being carried off to her unknown fate.

CHAPTER TWENTY-FIVE

Damn her! Naya-Nazgani thought as he rode his bison across the field.

From the moment he had learned about Pinga being taken away by Navit'Ku the mountain man, he was enraged. He wanted to slap Cheraya senseless but had no time to waste. Hototo promised he would attend to Cheraya himself.

As an experienced, expert tracker, Naya-Nazgani was easily able to follow the trail of the old cart. He rode for miles, unwilling to let War Runner stop for a rest as long as Pinga was in danger. "Hurry on, large one. Hurry!"

It was obvious the mountain man was not taking her to the Juk clan. Carrying his ax, Naya-Nazgani swore he would dismember Navit'Ku if he dared do what Naya-Nazgani deduced he was planning to do to her.

Upon reaching the cabin, he saw the cart he'd been trailing. Without waiting even one second, he leaped from the mount and burst through the wobbly door of the cabin, knocking it to the ground. Bounding inside, he saw the bloody body of Navit'Ku laying alone in the cabin. No one else was present.

Pinga couldn't have done this, he thought. *And she couldn't have walked away. So where is she?*

The signs of a fight were obvious. He knew someone else had been here. Searching outside, he found multiple footprints. Whoever they were, they must have taken Pinga with them.

He jumped atop War Runner, muttering threats. "I tell you, friend, if they dare to harm her, not even the Gods will be able to stop me from slaughtering them like fat turkeys before a feast!"

Pinga was still being carried in the sedan chair. She didn't know how long or how far she had been conveyed. She tried to force her legs to move but still could do little more than wriggle her toes. She had given up trying to talk to the men. She heard the gray leader of the group mention Matche-Monedo to his followers. *Is This One to be some type of sacrifice to Matche-Monedo? But why This One?*

While they were carrying her over a hill, Pinga heard something in the bushes. She believed she saw something moving within. *Is it who This One hopes it is? She prays to Awona'Wilona it is.*

Her prayers were swiftly answered. The muscular, ax-wielding figure of Naya-Nazgani leaped out of the woods. By the time the eleven Ghost Men saw him coming and set the sedan chair down, the monster slayer was already upon them.

His ax decapitated two Ghost Men heads before they could coordinate their attack. The Ghost Men brought their wooden, serrated swords and stone-tipped spears to bear. It did them little good. Two more were disemboweled in rapid succession.

The sedan chair was left on the grass as the fight raged. Pinga was still unable to move and could only watch and worry, hoping that Naya-Nazgani could defeat so many armed foes. *If any man can win this battle, I have faith in Naya-Nazgani to be the one.*

The remaining Ghost Men were on the defensive, outmatched and intimidated by the legendary monster killer. Their leader, the Gray Man, could see that this battle was not going to end well for them, despite their numerical advantage.

He signaled to the two men closest to him, removing them from the fight. "Grab the woman!"

As the other four men fought their losing battle, two of the Ghost Men lifted Pinga off the sedan chair. She slapped and pounded on them, but without her legs, she couldn't escape. The Gray Man gestured for his allies to follow him, and they ran off with Pinga.

"Naya!" she yelled with a piercing, high-pitched cry. "This One needs you!"

Naya-Nazgani was distracted by her cry for help. Turning his head, one of them struck him with their heavy, wooden sword. The serrated edge cut his forehead. The four painted men quickly piled on him, trying to jab him with their spears.

The last sight Pinga had of Naya-Nazgani was that of him being overwhelmed by a group of armed foes. *Great Awona'Wilona! Please let him survive!*

She reluctantly allowed herself to be carried until they reached the cave to fulfill their plans for her. Toted inside, she saw that the cave had been designed as a temple. It was lit by torches. Pinga was unfamiliar with the symbols and totems within, but she could guess who this shrine was devoted to.

"Is this where you worship Matche-Monedo?" she asked.

"No time for fool's questions," the Gray Man said. He pointed to one of his two surviving men. "Go retrieve the heart from the stag we buried outside. I will ignite a fire for the sacrificial incense."

The other man placed Pinga on an altar. She tried her best to move her legs and stand. She felt them shifting but no more than an inch. She still couldn't walk. To be certain she didn't escape, they tied her wrists to the altar. *This One can go nowhere!*

Pinga looked to the cavemouth, wishing that she would see Naya-Nazgani rushing in to rescue her, but she was not even certain if he was still alive.

Pinga slumped in her seat, feeling utterly helpless. She realized that these men had brought her to the cave temple to be a sacrifice; a fate she was praying she could still avoid. Her attention was drawn to a young, slim girl, barely the age of womanhood. The girl had a small clay jar filled with some type of oil.

"You have a great honor," the young girl said. "You will be the sacrifice that frees Matche-Monedo and the Soyoka."

Pinga tried to dissuade the petite young woman. "You mustn't do this. Don't you realize what you're about to do? Please, free This One. Let her go."

The girl, whose name was Zot, ignored Pinga's words and began to rub oil on the immobile Goddess. Pinga could do nothing but protest. "Stop that! Don't put that vile stuff on her! Leave This One alone!"

Despite her threatening tone, she knew—as did the woman—that Pinga was manifestly powerless to do anything about it. The young woman continued to oil Pinga down, and the beautiful prisoner could do nothing in response as long as she remained immobilized. *The girl knows that This One can't make a move! The child won't help me, no matter what I say.*

Pinga sat resigned as Zot continued her work. After preparing Pinga's silvery skin, the young woman left Pinga alone. Pinga sat in the cave temple, unguarded yet completely unable to do anything to save herself. She looked longingly at the door which led to freedom, unable to move an inch.

The four remaining members of the Ghost Men returned, making their preparations. Pinga saw the lethal-looking dagger that would no doubt be used to kill her, and she let out a cry of alarm.

"This One does not want to die!" she cried, petrified.

"Your death is necessary!" the Gray Man said. "And at moonrise tonight, at the appointed time, you will help us raise Katche-Monedo and all of Ulah-Nane will remember this day!"

"But why This One?" Pinga asked.

"It was foretold," the Gray Man explained. "Long ago, a prophecy by the Salt Witch claimed that a beautiful silver-skinned Goddess would come to the Red Sky Forest. And on that day, she would be sacrificed to Katche-Monedo. And then the mighty one will wreak havoc!"

Pinga closed her eyes, dreading being responsible for such a calamity. But what could she do about it? She couldn't move at all. She could only hope that Naya-Nazgani or perhaps Pahana would find her in time.

As the minutes passed and sundown came nearer, Pinga sat morosely, tears forming in her lovely eyes. She kept trying to move her legs, wishing she could escape, but she was still mostly immobile from the waist down. Three of the Ghost Men left the cave for some reason, and the remaining one was dozing off.

Pinga managed to wriggle her hands free. She saw that the sole Ghost Man guarding her was asleep. *If This One could walk, she would flee quickly. Can she crawl from this place in time, before he awakes or the other two return?*

Just then, tiny 14-year-old Zot returned. The girl shook the Ghost Man who was dozing, rousing him from his half-sleep state.

"What is it, Zot?" he asked her, embarrassed to be caught sleeping.

"It's almost dark," Zot said. "The others should be back already."

The man nodded. "You're right. We have preparations to make if we're going to be ready by midnight! I should look for them. Someone should guard the woman, in case..."

"Do not bother with that," Zot said. "I can watch her. If anyone comes near, I'll summon you with the big bell. You should just find the others."

"Are you sure?" he asked.

She nodded. "Absolutely. It will not be a chore."

"Very well. Wait here and watch the woman! I'll bring the others back and get things ready!"

Zot nodded and the man left. Zot folded her arms and eyed Pinga. Taking a closer look, she noticed that Pinga's hands were free. "Don't attempt anything, silver one! I'm stronger than I look, and no half-immobile harridan is going to escape from me."

"Such large hostility from such a tiny girl," Pinga said. "If I could stand, I would fight you as an Itiwana woman should!"

"Feh!" Zot said. "Don't imagine you can intimidate me. I am not impressed by a spoiled Holy woman with nothing to offer but her pretty face."

Pinga tried to utilize her once formidable ice powers, but they had faded too much. In her weakened condition she couldn't produce a snowflake. "You are fortunate This One did not meet you at another time, little girl."

Zot suddenly slapped Pinga and then turned her back on the Itiwana woman.

"You... You...!" Pinga angrily said, unable to rise from the chair.

Zot watched the door with her back turned as the helpless Pinga could do nothing but sit still and wait.

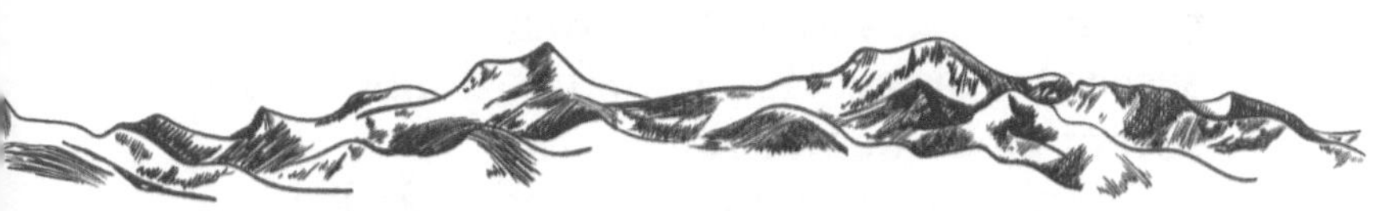

CHAPTER TWENTY-SIX

Pinga had been unwillingly prepared for the ceremony. She was decorated with wreaths of garland and flowers in her hair. She was now seated in an ornate chair, which she couldn't rise from. Pinga knew it was hopeless to think she could recover in time. She shivered with dread as the men finished their preliminary chants and announced, "It is time! Bring the woman forward!"

The chair in which the frightened Pinga sat was slid to the altar, where the stag heart was placed. She was positioned in the proper slot, still sitting in the chair. As nightfall came, the three men began their final chant to summon their master Matche-Monedo. The arrival of the creature was only minutes away, and Pinga wept, knowing the part she was unwillingly about to play in bringing this evil to the world.

She was relieved, however, by the sound of a familiar voice. Her eyes opened wide.

"I have a question for you fools!" the deep voice said.

Everyone looked toward the cavemouth and were stunned to see Naya-Nazgani silhouetted in the fading red sunlight. He was covered in blood, as was his big ax. His face left no doubt as to what sort of mood he was in.

"You're alive!" Pinga shouted with delight.

"Can your Kachina master talk to the dead?" Naya-Nazgani asked the men. "I wish to know, because I want you to deliver a message to Matche-Monedo for me. But you'll only be able to do so if your master can talk to the dead. You have only moments to live. Pray quickly."

The Gray Man grabbed his spear. "We can't let the ax-wielding buffoon stop us now! Kill him!"

"Thank you for being stupid," Naya-Nazgani said.

Pinga smiled. "Your deaths will be quicker than you deserve."

Her prediction was accurate. He swung his heavy metal ax with a fury unmatched by anything Pinga had seen in all her years. Blood splattered across the room and some of it splashed onto her fair skin. She had to turn her head away because she couldn't stomach the ferocious violence she was witnessing. With eyes closed, she heard the screams of death.

"It's over, Lady Pinga!" he said. "You can look now."

She opened her eyes. Naya-Nazgani was covered in the red of his enemy's blood. He held the Gray Man's head in his hand. The warrior looked to a shadowy nook of the cave and saw Zot crouched there, hugging herself and trembling in terror. She was also covered in blood splatter. Zot stared, overwhelmed by fear.

He pointed to the cave entrance. "Get out!"

After a moment of confusion, Zot jumped to her feet and ran with foxlike swiftness from the cave temple. She would never return. Pinga was disappointed that she wouldn't get the chance to slap that brat of a girl.

"You came for This One," Pinga said as she used the energetic elation of his arrival as motivation to push herself to her feet. She managed to stand for a moment but then toppled forward. Naya-Nazgani moved with astounding speed and caught her before she hit the ground. He scooped her up in his arms.

"Are you hurt?" he asked worriedly.

"No, you arrived in time," she said, beaming affectionately at him. "Do you ever tire of protecting This One?"

"I told you, I never get tired," Naya-Nazgani said with a sly grin.

"Please take This One away from here," she said. "Let us find a nice lake or waterfall where we can take a bath in the moonlight and be rid of all this blood."

"Ah, I like the idea of bathing together," Naya-Nazgani said.

"This One is very sure you'll like it," Pinga said. "She thinks you've earned it."

The cloudless sky allowed the luminous moonlight to brighten the serene lakeside where Pinga and Naya-Nazgani were bathing. They had rid themselves of the scarlet blood that evidenced the night's violet events.

Pinga sat naked on the edge of the lake, rubbing her legs. The cold, clear water was surprisingly therapeutic to her, and she was able to move her feet and ankles and even raise her right leg slightly. The moonlight glimmered on her wet, alabaster skin.

"This One should have realized that the cold would help her," Pinga said. "Sometimes she thinks her brain is addled. Had she done this days ago, her legs would be recovered by now."

Naya-Nazgani waded chest deep in the chilly water, looking more content and relaxed than he had been in a century. Also fully bare, his bulky muscles flexed as he stretched his arms heavenward.

"Don't chastise yourself," he said. "You were shaken by your experience with the Faces in the Forest. If you'd been thinking clearly, I'm sure you would have come to that conclusion sooner."

"It's very sweet that you're trying to protect This One's feelings," Pinga said with a twinkling smile. "She thinks that protecting her is becoming a habit for you."

He rubbed his chin with a puckish smirk. "Hmmmm. Perhaps. Do you think you're worth it?"

Giggling, she splashed water at him playfully. "She is."

"Indeed?" he answered. "Well, why didn't you tell me that sooner?"

She leaned alluringly on the shore, with her elbow on the grass and one hand in her hair. "She thought you might have realized while we were making love."

"Remind me," he said.

She gestured invitingly for him to come closer and laid down on the grass tantalizingly. He came closer and crawled atop her. "Ah, the things I do in my duty to the Itiwana," he said.

"Poor thing," she replied. "Let her know if she overtasks you."

Before they could go any further, they heard the sound of heavy footsteps coming their way. Naya-Nazgani instantly jumped to his feet and rushed to where his ax was imbedded in the ground.

"Someone's here!" he said.

"This One heard it, also," Pinga cried. "She is still unable to walk."

"Don't fear!" he said. "Just stay where you are, and I'll kill whoever it is, even if it's an army of 1,000 men!"

"This One has no fear while you're here," she told him.

Three individuals stepped out of the shadowy woods. Two of them were so large and lumbering, they were immediately identifiable as Wood Men. The third man was leading them. His pale face was clearly visible, although the rest of his body was in silhouette. The man carried a hoe.

Pinga recognized the face immediately. "Pahana!" she cried.

"Hello, Mother," Pahana said, still in his Husk Face Man guise, except without the mask. "Greetings to you, Naya-Nazgani. I seem to have interrupted a private moment. My apologies. Perhaps you wish to clothe yourselves?"

Pahana tossed Pinga's garments to her. Embarrassed, she covered herself up as best she could without standing. Naya-Nazgani was a bit more leisurely as he dressed.

"I've been looking for you ever since I returned to the False Face's hogan," Pahana said. "I stopped to recruit some assistance, thinking there would be a fight. Allow me to introduce Ko-Ko and Pom-Pom. They were gracious enough to come to your assistance, although you clearly don't need it. When I saw what was left of the Ghost Men in their cave, I knew Naya-Nazgani had been there. I've been searching all night. Perhaps my timing was imperfect."

"I would agree with that," Naya-Nazgani said.

"Are you unharmed, Mother?" Pahana asked.

"Naya-Nazgani has taken good care of This One," she said.

CHAPTER TWENTY-SIX

"So I see," Pahana replied with a double meaning. "How are your legs?"

She raised them slightly off the ground. "Much recovered. She will be walking soon."

"Excellent," the chieftain said, and then slapped a hand on Naya-Nazgani's back. "Walk with me, my friend. Ko-Ko and Pom-Pom will look after my mother."

"Very well," the monster hunter said.

Naya-Nazgani looked over his shoulder at Pinga as they strolled into the woods. She shrugged, clearly clueless as to what Pahana wanted to talk about. The two men walked a dozen yards before Pahana spoke.

"Again, I am in your debt for rescuing my mother," Pahana said.

"I ask for nothing," the monster slayer said.

"As I expected," Pahana replied. "So, did you enjoy having sex with my mother?"

Naya-Nazgani stopped. "You have no justification to ask me that."

"Do I not?" Pahana replied. "As her son, I have every cause to inquire about your ... activities."

"Is this truly the time to discuss such things?" Naya-Nazgani asked.

"Perhaps not," the chieftain answered. "But don't get heated. Actually, it's I who should be furious with the two of you."

"Why?"

He poked his finger into Naya-Nazgani's strapping chest. "Because you've blighted my well-laid plans. I had been arranging this for over two full summers. My plan was for the Husk Faced Man to become a friend and ally to Katche-Monedo by thwarting the Ghost Man's scheme to release Matche-Monedo. I had successfully recruited the Wood Men to my cause. As I told you, Katche-Monedo would have been a great asset to my strategy against the Enemy Way. I needed him to see the Husk Face Man as valuable to his own feud with his brother. This alliance between he and I was close to fruition when you two bungled your way into the situation. By killing all the Ghost Men, you've made me irrelevant to him. Katche-Monedo has no need of an alliance now."

"I was protecting your mother!" he insisted.

"Understood and appreciated," Pahana said. "But if the pair of you hadn't fumbled into this, she wouldn't have needed saving, and I would now have my alliance. You've botched things entirely."

"That wasn't my intention," the monster hunter answered. "I just came as escort for Pinga. It wasn't her idea, either. I regret to say, the blame for this falls to Atira."

"I'll have words with my grandmother when I return to Shipapa-Lina," the chieftain said. "You can be certain of that. At least your unintended interference has ended the threat to the Wood Men. That's one victory we can take from this. Although I would have accomplished that on my own."

"At least you've found something in my actions you approve of," the ax-wielding hunter said.

"If you want esteem, you can get that from my mother," Pahana said. "And while we're on the topic, I charge you with safely taking my mother back home. I know you're ... up to the task."

Naya-Nazgani ignored the inuendo. "Aren't you returning?"

"No!" he said. "The Husk Face Man must return to the Red Sky Forest. I hope to yet make some eatable sauce from the rotten apples you've left me."

"Can I ask why you require this deception?" Naya-Nazgani asked. "Why the mask?"

"I didn't want word of my presence to spread," Pahana answered. "If Hayoka or one of my enemies should learn that I was in the Red Sky Forest, they would have sent people to kill me or eliminate my False Face allies. I have many enemies. The less they know about my actions and whereabout, the better for the Itiwana."

Scratching his forehead, Naya-Nazgani gave up trying to understand the manipulative chieftain's reasoning. "If I can be so bold, Kik-Mongwi, I think you are a rather strange man."

Pahana glanced up as the stars, as if he were looking to the Gods for an equal. "You have no conception of how labyrinthine my mind is. But you'll learn in time. Everyone will see in the future... The chieftain is always correct. Now, if you have no other questions, I command that you and your weapon escort my mother home. And bring your ax, as well."

Brushing off the latest jibe, Naya-Nazgani pointed to the hoe. "Speaking of weapons, when did you replace the Dragonfly with a farming tool?"

With a wry grin. Pahana removed the false head off the long wood shaft. The metal tilling end of the hoe was just a ruse. Underneath was the sharp tip of the mystic spear known as Dragonfly.

"I'm never parted from it," the chieftain said.

"Cunning as always," Naya-Nazgani replied. "I'll leave you now to your scheming and planning. It is time Pinga and I were on our way home."

"Travel safely, my friend," Pahana said. "And keep your wits about you. I suggest you don't allow yourselves to become too distracted by ancillary activities."

"Tact is clearly not a virtue of chieftains," Naya-Nazgani said.

"Chieftains don't need to be tactful," he said.

"But you can be guileful," Naya-Nazgani replied.

"Oh yes," Pahana said. "We most certainly can."

CHAPTER TWENTY-SEVEN

"We'll be home soon," Naya-Nazgani said, impelling War Runner onward.

"At last," Pinga replied, smiling dreamily.

Pinga sat sidesaddle on the bison. She was seated in front of Naya-Nazgani, who supported her with one hand firmly around her mid-section and the other hand on the reins. She looked up at the rising sun, thinking about how her life had changed during this trip.

She also felt somewhat guilty. She originally asked Naya-Nazgani to come on this trip because she had planned to manipulate him. She sought to take advantage of his attraction to her, but after he repeatedly risked his life to protect her, everything was different now. *This One has not been in love since Tawa died. Eighteen summers have passed, and This One believed she'd never find another so special.*

"I hope you'll be able to walk when we get there," the monster slayer said. "You should walk in proudly, on your own feet."

"This One thinks she might be able to walk already," she told him. "Let This One test her legs."

After dismounting, Naya-Nazgani lowered Pinga to the ground. Her knees almost buckled, and she grabbed him for support. He swiftly put his arms around her, keeping her stable on her feet.

"Too soon, is it?" Naya-Nazgani asked.

"This One thinks she can do it," Pinga replied. "Keep hold of her hand."

Starting with tentative baby steps, Pinga slowly began to walk. With Naya-Nazgani's powerful arm for balance, she took longer and longer strides, becoming more comfortable with every pace.

"Let This One walk on her own," she said.

Without any help or support, she paced across the grass for several minutes, beaming merrily at her recovery. She even managed a light jog. She stood on her tiptoes, and then on one foot.

"This One is fully recovered," Pinga announced. "Isn't it amusing how much pleasure one can find in something as simple as walking?"

"Wonderful," Naya-Nazgani said. "I love watching you walk. You have a divine walk."

"You'll find This One can be divine in many ways," she said teasingly. "Such as in dancing. Watch as This One dances."

She sung and hummed as she slow danced in a seductive manner, intentionally enticing the monster hunter. Naya-Nazgani leaned against War Runner, staring at her with almost hypnotic focus.

But his focus was broken by the sound of footsteps. "Wait! Don't make a sound!"

Pinga froze, being as silent as possible, while Naya-Nazgani used his sharp senses of hearing and smell to pinpoint the sound. He reflexively grabbed his ax. Even War Runner seemed to detect the presence of strangers.

Naya-Nazgani shouted to the bushes and trees, "I feel I should tell you that anyone so staggeringly stupid as to attempt any harm to this woman will get to see what your own heart and guts look like as you die. Be wise and run far, far away. Don't stop running until you reach the Blue Patowa'Kacha. And then start swimming!"

Despite her nervousness, Pinga was aroused by Naya-Nazgani. *When we are safely back in Shipapa-Lina, This One is going to treat him divinely all night.*

"Be calm!" a strange voice said. "We are not here as your enemies. We're here to help."

"Come out where I can see you!" the monster hunter yelled.

Ten men stepped into view. They wore long coats with an array of buttons down the entire length of the front and with wide cuffs. The leader wore a cloth bandana. The all carried metal swords, similar to the Vykans.

"Who are you?" Naya-Nazgani asked.

"My name is Brother M'Dessun," the leader said, holding his hands up. "We're friends. You have no reason to attack us."

Before he could say another word to them, all the men unexpectedly kneeled before him. They seemed to be genuflecting in his presence. Naya-Nazgani raised his eyebrows. Both he and Pinga were taken aback by the sudden show of reverence.

Brother M'Dessun spoke respectfully, with head bowed. "We are the Thunder Dancers, the fist of the Thunder Beings, and we are devoted to the Eternal Savior."

"The who?" Naya-Nazgani asked, puzzled. "Who's the Eternal Savior, and who are the Thunder Dancers?"

"You are the savior, most venerated one," Brother M'Dessun answered, his eyes lowered to the ground. "We live to serve, and we serve to live."

Confused, Naya-Nazgani glanced over at Pinga, who merely shrugged. The Goddess was equally clueless. The perplexed Naya-Nazgani didn't like the idea of people kneeling to him or calling him a savior. "Stand up!"

"As you wish, Eternal One," said M'Dessun, signaling the other Thunder Dancers to rise.

Naya-Nazgani was starting to lose his patience. He was not in the proper humor for this cryptic nonsense. "Who precisely are you people?"

"I am unworthy to converse with the Eternal One," answered M'Dessun. "If you desire answers, please honor us by visiting the Cave of Seven Thunders and speaking to the illustrious Grandfather. All your questions will be answered there."

Naya-Nazgani had a hunch this was something he should definitely look into. Whoever these men were, they may or may not be fanatics. In his experience, fanatics could be dangerous.

"Very well. I'll come," the Monster Hunter said. "I am intrigued."

"Are you quite certain this is wise?" Pinga asked. "This One finds them dubious."

Naya-Nazgani couldn't argue with that. "True, but I need to find out more about this. When someone calls me a savior, my curiosity must be satisfied. Don't worry. I won't let them harm you."

"This One knows you won't," she said, reluctant to go with these people. Still, she had learned how determined and forceful Naya-Nazgani could be. Naya-Nazgani was a man of action who lived for the challenge. She understood that this stubbornness was a character trait of someone who lived for centuries.

"Let's go see this illustrious Grandfather of yours," Naya-Nazgani ordered.

M'Dessun bowed and gestured to the rest of the group, indicating they should lead the way on the long walk back to the Cave of the Seven Thunders. Naya-Nazgani and Pinga followed along, cautious but too curious to refuse the invitation.

CHAPTER TWENTY-EIGHT

M'Dessun and the other Thunder Dancers walked in silence during the trek back to their base of operations. The trip took quite some time, and Pinga was starting to wonder if these strangers weren't leading them into a trap. She didn't trust these men. What was their agenda? She was relieved when they finally reached their destination.

The Cave of Seven Thunders was on the shore of the Blue Patowa'Kacha, near the Little River and Pygmy Forest. The ingress was a watery cave-mouth that required a raft to make the journey inside. Seals sat basking in the sun on the shore. As the Thunder Dancers stepped onto the raft, Pinga hesitated, looking nervously at her brawny companion. He gave her a reassuring look, letting her know he was in control. He boldly stepped onto the flatboat, offering his hand to Pinga, helping her onboard.

M'Dessun and the other Thunder Dancers paddled the conveyance, taking the two, ageless travelers to a secret lair deep in the ground. Naya-Nazgani kept his ax at the ready, prepared for a trap. However, when they floated to their hidden destination, their reception was quite the opposite of what either of them had anticipated.

The secret site of the Thunder Dancers was a single mast sailing ship from across the Blue Patowa'Kacha, that they would later learn was called a Breman Cog. Pinga hadn't seen such a vessel since the days when she was forcefully taken overseas by the Red Lord. The cog had somehow been sealed in the cave, either intentionally or by happenstance.

Stepping onto the ship, the two looked around the torch-lit grotto known as the Cave of the Seven Thunders. The most disturbing thing Pinga saw aboard the vessel was the skeletal remains of a small whale. It upset her that such a magnificent creature was now nothing but a decoration.

What was particularly disturbing to Naya-Nazgani was the statue. He observed that the 10-meter-high clay sculpture strongly resembled himself. *Did they build a statue to me? I don't want people erecting statues of me.*

The duo was taken below to a small chamber called a 'captain's cabin.' Pinga took hold of her companion's well-muscled arm, pressing closer to him because it comforted her to be as near as possible. Inside the cabin was a very old man. This was the leader of the Thunder Dancers. The elderly, bearded man wore a long coat and an eye-patch. He sat with an outward façade of extreme serenity, but there was an uncharacteristic look of excitement in his eyes, which he was trying to hide.

"Welcome, exalted savior," he said with a coarse voice. "You do us honor beyond words with your presence. I am Ney-Ney-May-Kiva, the Thunder Grandfather."

Naya-Nazgani stood before the old man, while Pinga watched the Thunder Grandfather suspiciously. "You'd be the leader of this group, I assume."

"I have that privilege," he answered. "I would stand to greet you, great savior, if my old bones didn't creak and crackle."

"You needn't stand," Naya-Nazgani said. "However, I'd like some answers."

"Of course," the Thunder Grandfather replied. "It's our honor to assist you in any way at all. We live to serve, and we serve to live."

Naya-Nazgani was already getting tired of that phrase. "I want to know who you people are."

"We are the ones who worship you," the old man explained. "We are the allies you never knew you had. We are the Adherents of the Undying One."

"The Undying One?" Naya-Nazgani asked but immediately deduced the answer, even before the bearded old man told him. The pieces fell into place. "You mean me, don't you?"

"Of course, great savior," the old man said, a slight smile slipping onto his stoic face. "We serve you, as we always have."

Naya-Nazgani was left speechless. He didn't know what to say. What was this all about? This made no sense. How long had this been going on? And why? "Explain this. Why do you have a statue of me?"

The Thunder Grandfather leaned forward, hiding his pleasure at being the first of the Thunder Dancers since the beginning to speak to the immortal one. "Do you think the deeds you've done would go unnoticed? Did you think a man who lives for centuries and kills the most dangerous monsters in the world could be forever anonymous? We've known about you and watched you since our first leader, Evening Star, began spreading the tales about you. He wasn't believed at first, but as the legends of the great eternal hero started to spread, people knew the esteemed Evening Star was telling the truth."

"Evening Star?" Pinga asked. "Brother of Morning Star, the descendant of This One's lost husband?"

The name struck a chord in Naya-Nazgani's mind. A long time ago, he'd met someone by that name. "Evening Star? Who was... Oh yes, I recall now! The sailing man! He and I fought Anglabemu, the giant frog, together. He claimed to have been sent by the Spider-Mother. I didn't quite believe him."

"Indeed so," answered the Thunder Grandfather, leaning back in the seat. "He left her service because he knew that he'd found his true siren calling as a man of the sea, devoted to the Thunder beings. He took those lost people who were once called Pirates and taught them to respect the Thunder Beings. He gave them real purpose."

"This One had never heard that story from Tawa, the descendant of Morning and Evening Star," Pinga said.

"It's all true," Grandfather Thunder said. "He knew that the true savior walked among us. He knew there was an immortal protecting us, and so he spread the word. Evening Star created the Thunder Dancers for your sake. For centuries, the duty of the Thunder Dancers has been handed from parent to child. We've trained to be there when you needed us. We've helped you without your knowledge. We defended innocents against unholy, demonic beasts as best we could. We do whatever we're able, in your name. We dedicate our lives to your never-ending purpose. We live to serve, and we serve to live."

Naya-Nazgani couldn't believe that this had been going on so long and he hadn't known about it. The meeting with Evening Star and the frog was 250 years ago. How did he not know about this sooner? And was it just a mere coincidence that he was finding out about this group the same time he encountered the False Faces, who also treated him like some deity? Naya-Nazgani didn't believe in that level of coincidence. This meant something, but he decided he would figure that out later. For the moment, he had to address this issue with the Thunder Dancers.

"You shouldn't be doing this!" Naya-Nazgani snapped. "I don't want you doing this! I don't want to be worshipped!"

The Thunder Grandfather waved his withered hand, indicating that the suggestion was not going to be complied with so easily. "Do not fear for our safety. Our warrior Thunder Dancers are well trained. We do not fear death. You give us a purpose. We'd rather live with purpose than die with none. We live to serve..."

"Don't say it again!" Naya-Nazgani cried out, not wanting to hear that slogan again. "Listen to me! What I do is very dangerous. Far too dangerous for you. I don't want anyone dying in my name. I demand you stop this ludicrous worship of me."

The Thunder Grandfather looked dismayed. "Please, great savior. We..."

"Enough!" roared Naya-Nazgani.

Naya-Nazgani marched to the statue and, with a forceful heave, pushed it over. The thud of its impact echoed around the cavern. However, other than a long crack, the statue didn't break. The Thunder Grandfather and the dancers gasped at his actions. Pinga was surprised as well.

Naya-Nazgani glared accusingly at the Thunder Dancers but addressed the Thunder Grandfather. "I'm saying this once more, and it will be the last time! I do not want your help, and I don't want statues in my honor. And most of all, I do not want to be worshipped! I've outlived too many people. I've seen too many slain. I don't want to hear about you strange people dying next. What I do isn't to be taken lightly, and it isn't something a group of former pirates can do. I'm telling you now to stop this idiocy! I don't want to hear any more about your little assemblage. Disassemble this society of yours and go back to sailing and treasure hunts. Leave the dangerous part to the real warriors. Now if you'll excuse me, I must go back to Shipapa-Lina. I have things to do there. Remember what I said. Come along, Pinga."

Naya-Nazgani stomped out angrily, leading Pinga by the hand. He took their raft without asking. As he drifted away, out of the cave, he was still having a hard time accepting that there was a religion devoted to him. The whole idea of someone worshipping him was insane. He was happy to have put a stop to this lunacy before anyone else got killed.

After Naya-Nazgani and Pinga had departed, the Thunder Grandfather sat silently. M'Dessun and the other Thunder Dancers looked at the Thunder Grandfather with expressions he'd never seen on their faces before. He registered that they seemed disconsolate, as if they'd lost a friend. Worse, they'd lost a purpose.

M'Dessun approached the Thunder Grandfather and kneeled respectfully. "What shall we do now, illustrious Grandfather?"

The Thunder Grandfather thought for a moment, reverting to his state of outward calm. "We do what we have always done. We live to serve the Undying One."

M'Dessun was obviously confused. "But he just said..."

The Thunder Grandfather held up a finger to silence him. "Don't you know why he said that? He's just trying to protect us. He is very noble. He'd rather fight this fight alone than to see us hurt."

"Ah! Of course!" M'Dessun said, seeming very relieved. "How honorable."

"Indeed," said the Thunder Grandfather. "And that is why we can't abandon him. Despite himself, he needs our loyalty. We will continue on the course set by our founder, Evening Star, so long ago. We will keep our society a secret, and we'll work covertly to stop the inhuman, eldritch threats that the eternal Naya-Nazgani has dedicated himself to fighting. We will be the secret assistants to the savior. Now and always, we live to serve, and we serve to live!"

As the Thunder Grandfather planned, the Thunder Dancers would long continue steadfastly in their devoted undertakings. They would persist in their crusade.

CHAPTER TWENTY-NINE

She's here! Hayoka thought.

The wily Hayoka sat atop Moozoonsi the moose, looking into the distance. He was lurking just beyond the periphery of the Land of Everlasting Summer. His demeanor was more intense and glummer than was usual for him. Two of his children were being held prisoner by the people he hated most. He was relieved to see that his third and most powerful offspring had finally arrived.

He watched Skadega-Muth's distant form get larger as she neared, followed by the army of the Desert of Death. It seemed that the sky got slightly darker as she approached. Animals raced panicked from her putrid presence. The air seemed to fill with a smell of death.

She's terrifying, Hayoka thought. *And I love her for it.*

Hayoka had to calm Moozoonsi, who recoiled from Skadega-Muth. "Behave yourself. That's my daughter!"

Skadega-Muth, surrounded by her swarm of insect flies, gave a respectful nod to her father. "I am ready, Father. My brothers await our coming. It would be intolerable if we should think to hesitate."

"No hesitation," Hayoka said. "And no mercy!"

"I promise you that!" she said. "There will be death today!"

Kia witnessed the arrival of Skadega-Muth in her dreams. A dream that was like a nightmare to her. Opening her eyes with a gasp of apprehension, she knew what she had just envisioned was the truth. The foul, skeletal entity was near the village of her birth. She knew that Pahana, Calian, and Naya-Nazgani were all absent, leaving Shipapa-Lina vulnerable.

She sprang out of her feathery bed and quickly dressed in her robes made of rabbit pelts, turkey feathers, and yucca fibers, with a snake-skin belt. She walked quickly through the huge, adobe Sun Dagger House, heading to the ceremonial Kiva where the Curing Sisterhood were meditating. The Curing Sisterhood was Kiva's equivalent of the Shakowin. They were her closest advisors, and she planned to leave them in command of Kolhu while she rushed to assist Shipapa-Lina.

She was intercepted by young Wuti, who seemed highly distressed. "Cacique! You're needed!"

"Not now, Wuti," Kia said. "I'm needed somewhere else."

"It's Molowia!" Wuti said. "The end is here. The medicine woman says that holy Molowia is about to meet her ancestors. It may happen at any moment now. The holy one has asked for you to be there when she passes."

Kia stopped, distressed by this news. "Is the medicine woman certain?"

"She is," Wuti replied. "Molowia will not live out the day. You must come now. Molowia is asking for you."

Kia wavered, torn by the decision she was faced with. How could she refuse Molowia's request to be at her bedside when the end came? Molowia was more than a teacher; she was like a second mother. However, her real mother and the people of Shipapa-Lina were facing a danger none of them had the power to defeat. Could she ignore their peril?

"Why do you delay, Cacique?" Wuti asked. "Holy Molowia is dying and entreats you to come to her."

After vacillating, the conflicted Kia made her decision.

"The enemy is coming!" Yoki shouted, riding rapidly on his bison mount.

Acting chieftain Aholi was dealing with a minor issue between two tribesmen over a turkey when he heard the sentry charging in with his warning. He rushed to converse with Yoki. At the same time, the temporary War Chiefs O'Yewa and Masewa were also incited into action. O'Yewa had been sleeping while Masewa was scolding one of his Two-Horn Riders for not properly filing and trimming the hooves of the rider's bison. Both brothers responded to the alarm cry.

"It's Hayoka!" Yoki shouted. "And he has an army of those damned Tunerak Destroyers with him!"

"Set up defensive positions!" Aholi ordered the brothers. "You two get your Two-Horn Riders situated immediately! And you, Yoki. See to it that the children and the non-warriors are safely hidden at the Sun Temple on top of the mesa. Have Faw-Faw guard them. They'll be hard tasked to get passed him."

Atira came as quickly as she could. She couldn't move the way she once did. "What's happened?"

"Another attack by our traitorous friend," Aholi said. "See that the Bow Sisterhood is assembled and prepared to fight."

"Consider it already accomplished," Atira said and shuffled off as fast as she could to see that the women archers were set for action.

Despite the absence of Pahana and Calian, they had trained their people well. The Itiwana smoothly and efficiently arranged themselves in the proper positions. The women were perched upon the cliff housing, while the men were lined up protectively in front of the village, astride an intimidating troop of trained bison. Aholi was in front, flanked by his sons, O'Yewa and Masewa.

Hayoka and Skadega-Muth led the army of the Desert of Death until they reached the defensive line of Itiwana. The presence of Skadega-Muth was disconcerting to the Itiwana and their mounts. Her look, her unearthly presence, the insects surrounding her, and her smell made everyone leery.

Hayoka shook his head disapprovingly when he saw who was at the head of the force opposing him. He was an expert at playing mental games, as well as a master of wordplay.

"Disheartening," Hayoka said. "I had hoped we'd be able to kill haughty Pahana and that insolent Calian, but instead, I find this inadequate ancillary assemblage. I see that my wife's killers are not here, either. No Kia or Naya-Nazgani. Frustrating. Still, I suppose I should be satisfied that rescuing my children will be much easier than I anticipated."

"You continue to underestimate the Itiwana," Aholi said. "Turn around and walk away before we humiliate you again."

"Did that constitute a joke?" Hayoka asked. "You, Aholi? And these two buffoons? If I were in a better humor, I would laugh. But I am not in a laughing mood. You have my children, and I intend to get them back. Give them to me now!"

"If you surrender yourself, we'll release them!" Aholi said. "That's the offer."

"Is that a fact?" Hayoka asked. "Well, hear my offer. Release my children and die quickly, or you can all die slowly and I'll rescue them anyway."

"Surrender, Hayoka, or your children will suffer for it!" Aholi said.

Hayoka sneered. "Do you know that it's not an easy thing to be utterly and unflinchingly ruthless? It takes more force of will than someone like you could understand. It can't be explained in words. Only the example of deeds can show what true mercilessness is. Let us show you what it looks like. Daughter ... proceed!"

Skadega-Muth stepped forward. She spit out that horrid cloud of green, toxic breath. It covered Aholi, and he began to spasm and cough. Even his mount jerked and trembled. The ground turned scorched black beneath them as they both fell gasping to the earth. The rest of the Itiwana stared, unable to comprehend what they had just seen.

"Father!" Masewa screamed, and he rushed to see if he could aid his sire. The acidic feel and deathly smell of that green cloud caused him to pause, but he was determined to pull his father out of that poison death. O'Yewa, on the other hand, realized it was too late.

"Don't go any closer!" O'Yewa shouted, pulling his brother away. "He's gone. Father is gone!"

"You were warned!" Hayoka said. "That's one death. Shall she continue, or will you free my sons?"

O'Yewa and Masewa were too emotionally shattered to answer. Still reeling from their father's death, they had no idea how to combat a creature such as this. How could they defend against such a power? The Two-Horn Riders waited for commands from their leaders, but none came.

From atop the Cliff Palace, Atira watched in shock. Unlike O'Yewa and Masewa, she recovered her wits and shouted to her archers. "Arrows at the ready! Take aim!"

The Bow Sisterhood, although shaken by the power of Skadega-Muth and the death of Aholi, regained their focus when they heard Atira's commanding voice. The all targeted Skadega-Muth.

"Kill her!" Atira ordered.

Before a volley of arrows could fly toward Skadega-Muth, thousands of biting flies swarmed over the women. Startled and disoriented by the attack, it was impossible for the women to accurately aim their weapons. The few that did fire missed the mark by yards.

As Skadega-Muth stalked forward, the Itiwana backed away. One of the warriors lobbed a spear at the putrid enemy. To everyone's surprise, she quickly snatched it out of the air with one hand and broke the spear over her knee. The two chieftains tried to regain control, although they were rattled by the situation.

"Stay away from her!" O'Yewa yelled. "Give her ample space!"

Masewa pointed to the Tunerak Destroyers. "Go after the others! Destroy the Destroyers! Kill everyone!"

Relieved at not having to battle the strange woman, the Two-Horned Riders rushed at the 1,000 men who followed Hayoka.

The Two-Horn Riders sprang into action. The Tunerak Destroyers scattered in alarm because they didn't want to get run down by those large bison. The Two-Horn Riders made their presence felt very quickly!

The twins targeted Hayoka, but he retreated, hiding behind dozens of his soldiers. The brothers fought to get to him, but he was well protected. Hayoka continued to shout for his warriors to advance, while the twins did the same.

Masewa raced forward in a madness of rage, striking some Destroyers with his long spear. He underestimated the sturdy wooden shields of the Destroyers. They were damaged but survived the spear attacks. The army of the Desert of Death struck back with wooden swords. O'Yewa rushed to his brother's side, joining him at the forefront of the battle, not wanting to lose a brother, as well.

The rest of the Two-Horn Riders followed the War Chief siblings into the fray. While the Tunerak Destroyers' well-made shields were useful against the Itiwana spears and arrows, the protective weapons were less effective against the massive bison and their horns. The Tunerak Destroyers lashed out desperately at the big, wild animals with their wooden swords and clubs, but such meager attempts were useless against the savage power of an angry bison.

Skadega-Muth moved through the village with little resistance, other than an occasional arrow that missed. Whenever one of the Two-Horned Riders came close, she spit out her venom cloud and the rider retreated immediately.

She reached the pit house where her two brothers were being held prisoner. Skadega-Muth looked down at them, seeing their dismembered condition. The two sons of Hayoka reacted excitedly when they saw her. She reached down and felt the invisible wall of magic that Kia had formed over the pit.

"Don't despair, brothers," Skadega-Muth said. "This will not deter me."

Keeping her hand on the unseen barrier, her deathly pestilence flooded into it. Countering Kia's shamanic energies, she disrupted the field until it collapsed. She almost seemed to smile at her success.

"Come out, brothers," Skadega-Muth said. "You're free."

The Wampus Cat and Stikini scampered out of the pit. In their own wordless way, they thanked their sister, who examined their physical injuries. She was furious. "Go to our father. You are in no condition to fight. Leave it to me. I will destroy these despicable swine!"

While her brothers fled, Skadega-Muth didn't notice that the Yehasuri was still alive and scampered away, losing himself in the chaos.

Skadega-Muth looked around for the nearest target. She intended to create a large body count before she was finished. She was confident no one here could harm her.

Unnoticed at first, some new arrivals were riding into Shipapa-Lina. War Runner stormed into the chaotic village, carrying Naya-Nazgani and Pinga. Lady Pinga was appalled to see battle raging and the sons of Hayoka again on the loose. Skadega-Muth scared her.

"This is madness!" Pinga cried. "This One never imagined we'd return to such anarchy."

"Go find somewhere to hide!" Naya-Nazgani said. "I need to know you're safe before I can act."

"This One will conceal herself!" Pinga said, kissing him. "Go save her people!"

As Pinga snuck away, Naya-Nazgani unlatched his ax and rushed into the combat. He hit Shipapa-Lina like a storm. He hacked away at Hayoka's men with unrestrained bloodlust. They tried to avoid his ax but couldn't. He plowed through wave after wave of attackers. Even the shields they had developed were no match for the power of mighty Naya-Nazgani.

Every Itiwana's spirit was lifted by the arrival of fierce Naya-Nazgani. He rallied the besieged Two-Horn Riders, who fell in behind him rather than the brothers O'Yewa and Masewa. Even they were glad to let him take the lead.

"Now, brother!" O'Yewa shouted to his twin. "Let us go after Hayoka!"

Agreeing, they searched the battlefield and spotted the big moose. They fought their way to Hayoka.

Meanwhile, Skadega-Muth had detected a new threat. This one was not like the rest. He had to be dealt with. She approached the legendary monster hunter like a spider moving with deadly intent toward an insect in the web. She didn't allow his bloodied ax to deter her.

Naya-Nazgani had cleared a large area of the battlefield. The Tunerak Destroyers who hadn't fled from him lay in sections on the ground. He spotted the cadaver-like female walking toward him. Her odor of death mixed with what was in the air around them. He had seen and killed too many monsters to be intimidated by this one.

"You assisted in the murder of my mother Dagwona," Skadega-Muth declared.

"And did so gladly," he replied without remorse. "As I will do with you!"

"You deserve death!" the hideous woman said.

"Perhaps I do," he responded. "But it won't be you who gives me what I deserve."

"Die now!" Skadega-Muth cried.

From somewhere nearby, Yoki shouted, "Be careful of her deadly poison breath!" but the warning came too late.

Skadega-Muth hatefully spit her green breath at the monster slayer. He staggered back for several moments and teetered as if he would collapse. The watching warriors gasped, thinking the unbeatable Naya-Nazgani was about to fall.

To everyone's shock—particularly that of Skadega-Muth—he shook it off as if it were an annoyance.

"I am not impressed!" he stated.

Skadega-Muth and the distantly watching Hayoka were both flabbergasted. "Impossible!" she exclaimed.

"Tell your father not to send children to do his fighting for him," Naya-Nazgani said. "You're an overconfident stripling. Do you think I never encountered a carrion, life-sucking creature before? They all make the same mistake. You can suck 100 seasons of life out of my body, but there will always be more. I am ageless. You can feed on me, but I am a bottomless well of time, and you can never drain me dry!"

He lunged forward with his ax ready to strike. Skadega-Muth backpedaled, never having encountered someone she could not easily kill.

The Wampus Cat, who was still nearby, dived in front of his sister to defend her. This sacrifice cost him his life. It took only a few swift and strong chops of the ax to end the Wampus Cat forever. Entrails and blood were splattered across the field as a brother gave his life for his sister.

Watching from a distance, Hayoka screamed, "NO!" as his son died violently before his eyes. Just as his wife had.

Skadega-Muth unleashed a banshee wail of grief. Standing sadly over the remains of her sibling, she glowered with loathing at Naya-Nazgani.

"You have earned my hate!" she said. "You have not seen the limits of my power yet. Look now, to see what forces you dared challenge!"

Waving her hand over the dismembered Wampus Cat, she drew a clear, transparent energy from the remains. She used a technique that her mother had taught the Salt Witch, who later used it to attack the Itiwana, albeit unsuccessfully. She used the energy gathered in her hand as if she were making a snowball.

She tossed the glowing ball at the stationary old stone form of the fearsome rock entity, Stone Coat. The energy ball seemed to seep into the stony body of the large warrior. Moments later, Stone Coat moved for the first time in many years.

Even Naya-Nazgani took a few steps back, realizing the magnitude of the threat he now faced. He had heard about the power of Stone Coat from the tales the Itiwana liked to tell. The creature felt no pain and struck with murderous impact.

"And now you understand the unfathomable depth of the power I possess!" Skadega-Muth boasted.

"Coward!" Naya-Nazgani shouted. "Don't hide behind your beast! I will let nothing stand between us! I will destroy both it and you."

"You'll do nothing but become another tribute to Taxet the death God," she said. "And my mother will be avenged."

Naya-Nazgani knew an ax wouldn't be a useful weapon against a stone. He used his superior speed to avoid the monster's hands, avoiding blows from those large appendages. Naya-Nazgani grabbed a wooden post used for protective netting and swung it as a club to pummel Stone Coat. The desperate tactic failed. Stone Coat shook off the impact, shattering the post. They locked up and battled with feverish, primal savagery.

Pinga watched from hiding, on the edge of the village. Since she had long been stripped of her Goddess natural powers and without any combat training, she could only watch and hope. The enemy was beyond her power to hurt, and she would only get in Naya-Nazgani's way if she tried to interfere.

"May the Gods be with you," she whispered, so softly.

Minutes later, there was a pause in the battle. The monster hunter took a few steps back. "Your strength is truly formidable," Naya-Nazgani said. "I am impressed. But it will take more than physical power to defeat me. I have slain too many monsters to fall now."

Naya-Nazgani resumed battling the creature, although it surprised him with its strength and durability. But it was nearly mindless, only obeying its master and lashing out in blind, primal savagery. Naya-Nazgani managed to deftly leap upon the shoulders of the creature to snap its neck, but he was quickly thrown off.

Regaining his footing, he glanced up to the top of the mesa and saw his friend Faw-Faw standing atop the cliff, guarding the non-combatants in the Sun Temple. The monster hunter got an idea. *Sometimes one must be smart instead of strong!*

Naya-Nazgani moved backward in a strategic pattern as he battled Stone Coat in the heat. Stone Coat didn't get tired, but the cumulative effect of exhaustion, heat, and the blows he took were starting to weaken the monster slayer. Still, he had more skill and experience than the Wampus Cat spirit controlling the monster. That was more important than mere brute strength, he convinced himself. *I can win this!*

The monster slayer grabbed one of Stone Coat's arms in a tight grip and flipped him to the ground. The path was now clear to the cliff palace. The monster slayer ran toward it. Stone Coat stumbled back to his feet and pursued him. Naya-Nazgani began to climb the ladders of the Cliff Palace and then to skillfully scale the cliff-side itself.

Stone Coat, slower and clumsier, managed to follow by grabbing parts of the adobe structure in his rocky hands. He did the same when it came to climbing the cliff. The slow chase proceeded up the side of the mesa.

Below, Skadega-Muth watched, hoping that Naya-Nazgani wouldn't escape. In the meantime, she chose to inflict more punishment and death upon the Itiwana. She decided to vent her hate on Masewa and O'Yewa, who were in the mists of the battle, clearly moving toward her father.

She approached the battling warriors, and people on both sides of the conflict moved out of her way. Another spear was thrown toward her. Once again, she caught it and tossed it aside dismissively.

Before she could reach her quarry, she was surprised to see her swarm of insects dropping down over her, like little black raindrops. She looked down at the bugs, whose wings were moving, but for some reason, they couldn't seem to fly any longer. She was unable to imagine what could have immobilized them.

Looking up, she spotted a small silhouette hovering in the air. It seemed to be levitating. Everyone else on the battlefield spotted the figure and stared upwards, speculating on who or what it was. The aerial figure began to descend, allowing everyone to get a clear view of the identity of the flying newcomer. As she touched down lightly on the dirt, the assembled Itiwana let out a relieved cheer, while Hayoka hissed with anger.

Kia had arrived!

CHAPTER THIRTY

The two powerful women stared combatively at each other, neither saying a word. The fierce battle between armies abruptly paused because everyone present realized that something dangerously astonishing was about to occur.

The two female foes stood cautiously, sizing each other up. Both sensed the awe-inspiring power of the other. Skadega-Muth trembled with endless rage. She had waited many years for this moment.

"It's you!" the withered woman said. "At last, I meet my mother's killer! I thought you would hide from me forever!"

"I've never hidden from you," Kia said. "I don't have any fear of an odorous, odious hag who prowls the desert killing innocent wanderers.

You've gone unrestrained for too long. I'm here to stop you!"

"If you believe you can do so, then come ahead!" Skadega-Muth replied. "I've dreamed of your death all my life."

"The only time you'll ever see that is in your dreams," Kia said. "No more talk! Let's have at it!"

Kia lobbed a fireball at Skadega-Muth, but the withered desert queen spit out her misty venom, which extinguished the fireball. Before Skadega-Muth could reorient from the first attack and react, Kia pelted her with large ice crystals. Skadega-Muth was staggered by the barrage. The strength of the shamanic Cacique Kia was nearly equal to that of a Goddess.

Skadega-Muth spit her lethal cloud of death at Kia, but the Itiwana evaded the attack by waving her arms and creating a strong wind to disperse the cloud. Skadega-Muth let loose a deafening shriek that installed fear in Kia's brain, but the shaman resisted the urge to flee. Kia responded by summoning moving weeds and plants from the ground, which was the same way she killed Dagwona years ago. She enwrapped Skadega-Muth in flora, which proceeded to drag Skadega-Muth into the ground.

Skadega-Muth would not let the same thing happen to her. She fought back by using her deathly power to drain the life force of anything. The plants suddenly shriveled, turning brown and gray, finally crumbling to flecks of debris.

Next, Skadega-Muth connected with a physical open-handed slap which stunned Kia. She tried to finish off the Itiwana shaman with a lethal burst of venom, but Kia recovered in time to levitate to safety, touching down yards away. This gave her a few precious seconds to recover.

As the cadaverous woman came after her again, Kia summoned another snakelike root to grab Skadega-Muth by the ankle and trip the daughter of Hayoka. Skadega-Muth easily broke free of it. Kia was back on her feet once again, and there was a pause as they glared with intense abhorrence at each other, plotting their next strategy.

Above them, Naya-Nazgani had skillfully climbed the rock wall to the top of the cliff. Reaching the mesa, a hand unexpectedly reached down to help him up. It was Faw-Faw. Naya-Nazgani took the Wood Man's hand, allowing Faw-Faw to yank him up.

"Thank you, my good friend," he said. "Do me one more courtesy, will you?"

As the menacing Stone Coat grasped the edge of the cliff, pulling his massive body to the top of the mesa, the rock creature was greeted by the sight of Faw-Faw standing over him, holding a huge, iron hammer over his hirsute head. The Wood Man soundly slammed his hammer down on Stone Coat's head, cracking the monster's granite skull. The impact caused the handholds which Stone Coat was tenuously grasping for support to break apart. The handholds crumbled and the creature fell.

Stone Coat plummeted down, bouncing off the Cliff Palace and then continuing his freefall until he smashed onto a cluster of rocks below. The monster shattered to pieces upon impact. Naya-Nazgani patted Faw-Faw on the back.

"Well done, friend," he said. "Now I must go help Kia."

The battle between the Two-Horn Riders and the Tunerak Destroyers resumed, although Hayoka had taken the opportunity to flee the battlefield and remove himself from the village limits of Shipapa-Lina. He watched from safety, still distraught and enraged at the death of the Wampus Cat. He had sent Stikini away, escorted to safety by a few of his Tunerak Destroyers.

How do I salvage this situation? he thought. *I saved one son, but I lost another, and now my daughter is fighting for her life. What should I do?*

Circling the village, he spotted the bright skin of the Lady Pinga, mother of Pahana. She appeared to be hiding behind a large rock, watching the conflict from safety, just as he himself was. Hayoka brightened, suddenly possessed by a new, cunning idea. Dismounting his moose, he used the stealthy skills he had learned years ago from Pahana himself to sneak up on the chieftain's mother.

Springing out from behind her, he roughly spun her around. "Hello, dear lady."

"Hayoka!" she yelled in alarm, trying to back away, but she was pressed against the big rock, so she had nowhere to retreat to. "Keep away from This One!"

"Ah, you're retaining some unkind feelings, are you?" Hayoka asked. "Well, I'm in an unpleasant mood myself. Your people have just killed my son and I am in a foul mood."

"Are you going to hurt This One?" she asked with a tremulous voice.

"I thought about it," he said. "That would certainly make your daughter, Kia, feel some of the pain I felt when she killed my loved one. But I've rethought that."

"What do you plan to do with This One?" she asked, nervously.

Hayoka jerked his thumb toward the battle. "My daughter is in danger, and you are going to help me get her out of it."

"This One does not understand what you're suggesting," Pinga said.

"You don't need to understand," he said menacingly as he grabbed her by the wrist. "You'll know soon enough! Come along with me."

"Unhand This One!" she yelled.

"Stop your whining," Hayoka said condescendingly. "Behave or I will kill you. To help my children, I will kill anyone, even a former winter Goddess of the North."

"This One has never harmed you or your family!" she yelled in fearful frustration. "She supported you when Pahana wished to allow you to stay in Shipapa-Lina. Please release her."

"If my plan goes well, you may get out of this alive," Hayoka said. "For the present, just cooperate and come with me."

Without her lost Goddess powers, she couldn't free herself from his grip. "Villain! This One's children and Naya-Nazgani will make you suffer if you harm her."

"Perhaps," he said. "But that doesn't help you now."

She continued her attempts to convince him to release her, but Hayoka ignored her pleas. He dragged Pinga to Moozoonsi. Hayoka placed her on the animal's back and then mounted the big moose himself. She tried to jump off, but he clamped a hand around her wrist, preventing her.

"Don't make me angry!" he said. "Just cooperate."

As he rode back toward the battle, a very small figure leaped out of the bushes, waving his arms. Hayoka had forgotten all about the Yehasuri.

"Give me transport away from here!" the Yehasuri cried. "I've been a prisoner for days because of your flawed plan!"

"Ah, it's my diminutive friend," Hayoka said. "Certainly, I'll give you a ride back to the Bitter Root Valley. However, I need you to do me a small service. Keep a watchful eye on this woman while I talk to these Itiwana fools."

The Yehasuri looked over the ageless Pinga. "This mission is far superior to your last one. I'll be happy to look after this beauteous female."

"Good," Hayoka said. "Take the reins of Moozoonsi. I'll meet you on the goat path at the other side of the valley."

Back in the village, the Itiwana were winning the battle with the army of the Desert of Death, while Kia was fighting Skadega-Muth to a draw. Both women were unleashing a variety of devastating attacks, but neither one could get a distinct advantage.

The return of Naya-Nazgani changed the balance of the fight. When Skadega-Muth saw that the monster hunter had come back down from his clash on the mesa, she cursed. The withered crone had seen Stone Coat fall and crumble. She'd been expecting him to reenter the fray. The desert queen had hoped she would have defeated Kia before then, but that hope was gone. She knew she was in danger, flanked by two such powerful foes.

Hayoka tried to sneak his way into the village, avoiding the Itiwana warriors. He hoped he could keep from getting killed long enough to save his daughter. He remembered the terrain well enough to avoid detection while so much violence was occurring. *I've got to get close enough to get their attention.*

The Yehasuri was happy to be away from Shipapa-Lina after being locked away with those two beasts for days. He was thankful they didn't eat him alive. Now he was astride a massive moose that made him look smaller than ever.

Pinga was an unwilling passenger on Moozoonsi. She debated fighting the Yehasuri, but the Puk-Wudjie were ferocious little warriors with razor-like fangs. The Yehasuri caste were the most formidable of all. Without her powers, she chose a show of passive compliance.

"Where are you taking This One?" Pinga asked, sitting behind him.

"We're merely going to wait for Hayoka at the goat path," the Yehasuri said. "He's plotting again. He should be here presently. Beyond that, I have ideas for what I'd like to do with you."

Pinga winced at the thought. "If you violate This One, you'll end up back in that dark prison again. Her children and Naya-Nazgani will make you regret it."

"Such lovely lips shouldn't say such vile things," the Yehasuri stated. "Aside from that, they'll never catch me again."

Reaching the goat path, the Yehasuri climbed down to the grass. "We'll wait here. Come down, pretty one. I can think of a pleasant way to pass the time."

Lady Pinga saw an opportunity. She tried to urge Moozoonsi to move, hoping to ride the moose back home. But the animal wouldn't move an inch. She kicked it harder and only suc-ceeded in causing the big mount to buck her off its back angrily.

Pinga was sent hurtling through the air, tumbling to the ground. Yehasuri laughed at her failed escape attempt. "Such a delightful morsel that falls from the sky. Moozoonsi doesn't like being kicked. And he only moves for Hayoka and those who trained it. I was one of those trainers. Now stop your foolish behavior. I like your fire, but it can be better used entertaining me. Come lay with me."

Looking out at the broad expanse of the wilds of the valley she knew so well, she considered losing herself therein until Yehasuri got tired of looking for her. He didn't know the Land of Everlasting Summer as well as she did. She felt sure that, after losing him, she could slip back safely to Shipapa-Lina. *It seems like the wisest plan,* she thought.

Once the Yehasuri was laying down, seemingly off his guard, she made a dash for the woods. She was far ahead before the Yehasuri noticed her attempted escape. She hoped that he would not use the moose to chase her, because she could not outrun Moozoonsi.

The Yehasuri leaped up and pursued her. She reached the woods and hoped to conceal herself. Looking over her shoulder for the Yehasuri, she didn't see the lurking menace until she stepped on it. She awakened a sleeping monster.

It sprang up instantly, looking for a meal. It was a very long snakelike beast, which had been brought to the Land of Everlasting Summer by the Enemy Way and left to prey on the Itiwana. It reared up, studying its prey. Lady Pinga backed away, knowing that she couldn't fight this creature in her present powerless condition. The beast, sensing its prey was no threat, toyed with the woman. It slithered in a loop, surrounding her. She attempted to vault over it, but its tail whipped out and wrapped up her legs. She fell to the ground.

The snake began to wrap itself more tightly over her legs, constricting her. It slid its way up her body, encircling Pinga around the waist and torso. One of her arms was pinned. She stretched out with the other, hoping to reach a rock or some other possible weapon. But nothing was within her grasp. Even at such a moment, she thought only of her people. She feared dying alone in the woods.

Defeat seemed certain for Skadega-Muth. Between Naya-Nazgani and Kia, she was overmatched. As powerful as she was, Skadega-Muth knew her limitations. Kia could deflect her best attack, and Naya-Nazgani was immune, and both could hurt her if she let her guard down.

Before they could deliver a finishing blow, Hayoka got close enough to make his presence known. "Stop!" he yelled.

"Ah, the worm has crawled back," Naya-Nazgani said. "Stand there and be patient. We'll kill you in a few moments."

"Just as you did my wife, eh?" he said. "Well, you won't be killing me or my daughter today. Not if you want to see the lovely Lady Pinga again." He opened his hand to show a palm full of the white hairs from the rabbit furs that she wore.

"Mother?" Kia asked.

Naya-Nazgani sneered, grabbing Hayoka in his strong hands. "What have you done with her?"

Hayoka would not show that he was intimidated. He wanted to control the situation. "Nothing as yet. And if you want her returned to you, you'll let my daughter and myself leave here unharmed."

"Vile, craven coward!" Naya-Nazgani roared, throttling Hayoka. "I should kill you."

"No!" Kia shouted. "We can't risk my mother's life. Very well, Hayoka. You and your disgusting offspring can leave here. But if anything happens to my mother..."

Naya-Nazgani reluctantly released Hayoka. "If you put so much as a single bruise on that woman, there will be no place in the land or skies or beyond that you can hide from me!"

"I don't intend to hide," he said. "I'll be back, and my next visit will be the last. I'll have no further need to come again. My purpose here will be completed. That's my promise. Come along, sweet daughter. Say goodbye. We'll be seeing these fools again very soon."

Skadega-Muth sneered hatefully at Kia. "Next time!"

"Next time," Kia replied.

At Hayoka's signal, the warriors of the Desert of Death stopped fighting and the battle ended. Hayoka and Skadega-Muth led their army out of the city. While they departed, the Two-Horned Riders turned their attention to the wounded and dead. O'Yewa, Masewa, and a large group of warriors surrounded the body of Aholi. Atira came down from the cliffs and hugged the brothers in sympathy.

"I grieve for your family," she said.

"We'll have to tell our mother," O'Yewa whispered in misery.

"Everyone loved him," she said. "This is a sad day for all the Itiwana."

Naya-Nazgani looked at the departing enemies. "It will be sadder still if something happened to Pinga!"

"Help!" Pinga screamed, fearing no one was near enough to rescue her.

But someone was. She heard something that sounded like bison hooves. Two bison, in fact. Pinga's feeling of doom turned to delight when Gluskap appeared. He was carrying the mystic tomahawk.

"Don't fear, Grandmother!" Gluskap shouted, chopping the head off the snake with the weapon. As he uncoiled the snake from Pinga's body, the sound of a scuffle was heard just beyond the bushes.

"Are you hurt?" Gluskap asked.

"This One is undamaged," she said. "Your arrival was timely. Thank you."

Calian stepped out of the woods, holding the battered Yehasuri up by the scruff of the neck. "See what I've found," he quipped.

"We must get back to the village," Pinga said. "There is danger!"

EPILOGUE

Pinga, Calian, and Gluskap returned to Shipapa-Lina. Naya-Nazgani and Kia were relieved to see her safely home. Gluskap and Calian found the village in mourning for the dead. They were disconsolate to hear of the tragic death of Aholi. The bodies of the fallen were moved, and Atira announced that a ceremony would be held in honor of Aholi.

His longtime mate Evaki wept for hours, comforted by her twin sons.

"This isn't over," Kia said. "But it soon will be, one way or another!"

Pahana had abandoned his costume as the Husk Face Man and reclaimed World Giant. It was time to leave the Red Sky Forest. He had managed to secure an alliance with the False Faces, despite the interference of his mother and Naya-Nazgani. He made some promises, although keeping them might be problematic. He had hopes that this alliance would draw Katche-Monedo to his cause.

He planned to visit Eithinoa before returning home. But before he headed back to Shipapa-Lina, he had another stop to make. His machinations were deep, and he hoped that this next phase of his plan would be vital to the final battle, which he knew was coming soon.

Hayoka glumly led Skadega-Muth and Stikini back to the Valley of the Blue Mists. He was more motivated than ever to get his revenge on the Itiwana. During their trip, the scorpion reappeared unexpectedly. Hayoka told him it wasn't a good time for conversation because he had just lost a son. The insect respectfully allowed him a day to grieve but insisted that Malsumis had been waiting too long for information. He asked Hayoka to live up to his deal.

"Come see me on the morrow and I'll tell you," Hayoka said.

The scorpion slipped away. Hayoka addressed his two children.

"I don't actually have the information he wishes," Hayoka said. "But I now have an idea how to learn it. I believe I know how to find Kokopelli, and when we do, he will be the key to freeing Malsumis from the volcano. And in exchange for my help, I will insist the Itiwana finally be crushed and eliminated as they so deserve. Soon, this war will be over, and I'll have my revenge! The end of the Itiwana is nearly here!"

END OF BOOK FOUR

COMING SOON TEASER

Book 5 blurb: The Winter of War

The Winter God, Malsumis, is finally free and the cold war of the Gods heats up. The Sky Elders battle, giant monsters walk the earth, and the Itiwana must desperately fight to protect the Tree of Life.

Pahana's complex plans come together but at a sacrifice to his well-being. He is weak and dying. Knowing he can no longer be the leader his people need at such a vital time, he announces that his son, Gluskap, will fight in his place. His sister, Kia, is unhappy with this decision, and the tribe is unsure about the young Gluskap having such responsibility at age 18. Many of them turn to the powerful Naya-Nazgani to lead the warriors of the Two-Horn Riders.

The servants for both factions of the Elder Gods converge in combat as the Elder Gods themselves go to war, with devastating results. Can the Itiwana survive being caught in a war of Gods, or will this be the end of the people of Shipapa-Lina? Will the long winter return?

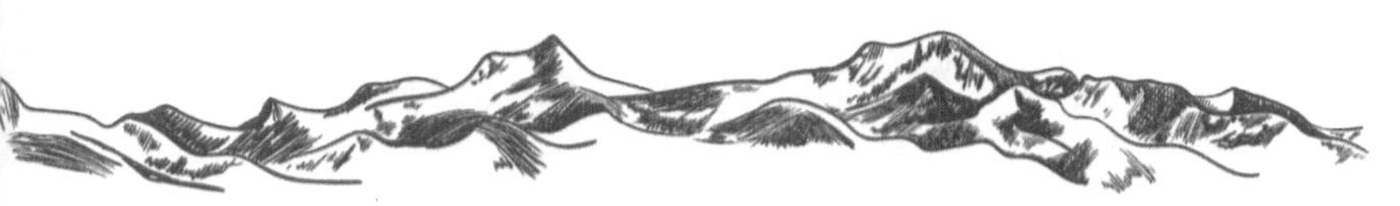

AUTHOR BIO

R.J. Young has been everything from a dog groomer to a custodian to a hospital worker, but his one true love has always been writing. The son of an immigrant, he's had a lifelong fascination with fantasy and sci-fi stories depicting exotic and astonishing locations. The first time he saw *The Wizard of Oz* at seven years old was like a magical experience. A journalism major in college, he enjoys writing online reviews and articles. R.J. loves discussing fiction with anyone who will listen.

BOOK CLUB QUESTIONS

1. Although he plays the role of a villain, was Hayoka justified in his feelings and actions regarding the Itiwana, considering that they killed his wife, father, and later, his son?

2. Was Pahana wrong in telling Kia that she should not lead the Itiwana in battle because she isn't a trained warrior, despite her vast power, while appointing his inexperienced son Gluskap to the role?

3. If you had been Kia, would you have left Kolhu to defend Shipapa-Lina while Molowia was dying, or would you have stayed with her on her deathbed?

4. Was Pahana wrong to so frequently leave Shipapa-Lina during a time of war? Would Aholi still be alive if Pahana had been present to lead the Itiwana during the attack?

5. Should the Thunder Dancers be trusted, or will they one day become a danger to Naya-Nazgani and the Itiwana?

6. Should Pahana have killed the non-aggressive Sanopi just to honor an old promise by his father?

Discover more at
4HorsemenPublications.com

10% off using HORSEMEN10